Prais

MUSIC AN

'A sublime work of literature, filled with fierce intelligence, gentle humour and, above all, enormous heart' Alice Pung

'Morrison's fiction never falters. Her style sings and the structure revolves like a spiral staircase . . . [She] opens up access not just to the way Alice's mind works but how language can evoke classical music' *The Age*

'An ambitious and considered debut novel. Morrison's characters are vividly drawn, and their relationships portrayed with exquisite sensitivity . . . Morrison writes about sound and music with a joy and poetry even the unmusical can appreciate – providing a stunning and heartfelt counter to the dark relationship that forms between the two main characters. *Music and Freedom* is challenging, stylistically sure, accomplished, and consistent. Above all, though, it is simply a good story, beautifully written' Maxine Beneba Clark, author of *The Hate Race* and *Foreign Soil*

'*Music and Freedom* urges us toward "balance . . . Rhythm versus rubato. Tightness versus looseness. Head versus heart." In tracing Alice's journey of discovery and recovery, Morrison reveals how this harmony can be achieved – in music, life, and the written word' *Australian Book Review*

'A rich, fierce and satisfying book, animated by a deep love of music' Anna Goldsworthy, author of *Piano Lessons*

MUSIC
AND
FREEDOM

ZOË MORRISON

VINTAGE BOOKS
Australia

A Vintage book
Published by Penguin Random House Australia Pty Ltd
Level 3, 100 Pacific Highway, North Sydney NSW 2060
www.penguin.com.au

Penguin
Random House
Australia

First published by Vintage in 2016
This edition published in 2017

Addresses for the Penguin Random House group of companies can be found at
global.penguinrandomhouse.com/offices.

National Library of Australia
Cataloguing-in-Publication entry

Morrison, Zoë, author
Music and freedom/Zoë Morrison

ISBN 978 1 92532 422 8 (paperback)

Women pianists – Fiction
Psychologically abused women – Fiction
Music, Influence of – Fiction
Man–woman relationships – Fiction

A823.4
Cover image courtesy of Arcangel
Cover design by Sandy Cull, gogoGingko
Typeset by Midland Typesetters, Australia
Printed in Australia by Griffin Press, an accredited ISO AS/NZS 14001:2004 Environmental
Management System printer

Penguin Random House Australia uses papers that are natural, renewable and recyclable
products and made from wood grown in sustainable forests. The logging and manufacturing
processes are expected to conform to the environmental regulations of the country of origin.

For C. J. James
and Doreen Oldfield

I knew what the sound was when I heard it, but I didn't believe it. It could have been anything, I told myself, a bell tolling in the distance, someone else's alarm clock.

I'd descended the stairs that morning wearing nightclothes and layers of old bedding; they dragged behind me. I was already very cold. At that time of day the house was grey and all shadows; then again, when was it not. I might have been confused for part of the house itself – the layers, the shape of them, even the colour of the materials, which blended in so uncannily; I could have been a walking piece of furniture. Except for my face, that is, glimpsed within this odd shroud, my hand coming out to touch the wall. No, you would be mistaken in thinking I was anything but a person.

My aim was to die slowly so that I could organise the house. I had developed a structure for those dying days, a sequence of four actions I repeated. So far they had not been interrupted.

Down the hall, still close to the wall, into the study, and all of this done slowly. I was already slight, my white hair uncombed. By the fireplace I struck a match, held the small flame downwards, it crept onto a page, appeared to pause for a second as if looking around, checking, then started upwards. I put some books onto the fire, lowering them carefully: *A New Theory of Capitalism*; *The Significance of Monetary Policy*; *Capitalism and Freedom*.

On the desk by the window were stacks of sheet music, albums, catalogue labels and file boxes; there were also piles on the floor. I was only up to B. I picked up an album of Bach partitas, heard the first one begin in my head as I made a label, tucked it away. I reached Beethoven that morning, a book of his Bagatelles, then went out to the hall. The phone was a relic, old, black and heavy. I dialled the number; this time he answered quickly. *He-llo?* he said, relaxed. *Hello?* Sharp. I hung up, hastily.

So far everything had progressed normally. I went to the piano.

Usually, at this point, I would play a single note over and over for some time. Then I'd go back into the study to burn more books and papers, and file music. This was the habit circle I had developed. Burn, file, call, play. Repeat.

The note I played happened to be concert A, which is like a starting gun musically speaking. It tunes a child's violin (see her frowning down the fingerboard of her little instrument, bringing the bow onto the string); it tunes a symphony orchestra (and there she is again, a young woman now, in the leader's seat, playing the note for the rest of the orchestra). Sometimes when I played it I'd hear an orchestra tuning up in my head: first the strings, then the woodwind, the brass, the timpani. Everything playing that note until it all faded and the silence began, that anticipatory silence between tuning and performance, although now there was no music because I had not played for many years.

I got onto the stool. The slump of my spine mirrored the shape of my index finger, which started tapping the note in a way that did not expect to be heard. It was expressing something, I suppose, that I was not yet able to put into words.

A, A, A.

I was feeling eerily light, as if part of me had separated from my body, one of the physiological effects of starvation, I was thinking; it was several days since I had eaten.

A, A, A.

My eyes shifted from the wood of the instrument to the street outside, Chardwell Road, where I had lived since I was nineteen. The houses opposite were identical multi-storeyed terraces; they looked empty, although people lived in them. A boy sped past on a bicycle and turned the corner, a student probably, it was nearly term-time again.

A, A, A.

(Whoever thought beginnings and endings could co-exist so closely?)

A, A, A.

And then I heard it, I heard it, bell-like at first, a bell hit repeatedly. It was another concert A, also played on a piano.

I took my finger from the key immediately and sat upright. I listened closely; there was nothing. I started playing the note again, quietly. There it was, the other concert A, keeping up. More than this, it was played exactly between my concert As, turning crotchets into quavers, walking into running.

It was an echo, I thought. Something had shifted in the structure of the house overnight, all that rain; a freakish phenomenon, ephemeral. I played the note once, loudly, and it came back three times (A! A! A!). Happy toots.

The instrument must be malfunctioning, I thought next, the hammer rebounding. I got up and played the note, watching the mechanism hit the string; it struck only once. I sat back on the stool.

It sounded as if the note was coming from behind the wall to my left, a common wall with a rental property similar to my own. An American family had moved out at the beginning of summer and I hadn't seen anyone move in, but perhaps someone had done so without me noticing. It seemed unlikely; surely I would have seen them coming and going.

I went over to the wall and felt it with my hands. The plaster, painted grey, was cold and smooth. I leant into it, pressing my ear flat.

I moved to the window and looked at the neighbouring porch. Junk mail, wrinkled from the rain, was plastered on the tiles around the door: desiccated supermarket catalogues, faded menus for Indian takeaway. I watched the place for the rest of the day, then into the night. No one came in and no one went out.

The next day I dismissed the other concert A. I assumed I had been hearing things, and that my ears were now broken as well as my hands. I went nowhere near the piano. It was erased from the habit circle. I burnt papers and books about economics, filed music, made calls – and that was it.

I felt, at times, upset about the conclusion I had drawn about the other concert A, and uncertain. At one point I got down on the floor beside the piano, felt the carpet around me and thought: floor. Then I held my arm out in front of me and shook it: arm, fist. I patted myself on the head, hard, harder, so I could feel it, know it, see it. This did nothing to solve the mystery of the other concert A either.

If this were where the story finished there would be nothing more to tell, except for someone else to describe the sight of an old woman's emaciated corpse on the carpet beside a Steinway grand piano (strange place to rest, poor thing, or maybe she fell), a study with empty shelves (now what happened here, do you think? Is it all at the Bodleian Library already?) and some neatly catalogued boxes of sheet music and albums that completely and precisely covered the surface of the big desk.

I think forgiveness is an overvalued concept. It is the sort of idea perpetrators and their associates suggest to victims for their own purposes, after all those victims have done for them already, sponging up the hatred as it was poured upon them. I have no use for forgiveness, not yet. But other ideas like that, kindness, for example, I think that is fundamental. Resurrection; I like that too. And love, of course, love, love, love.

Currabin, New South Wales, Australia, December 16th, 2006

Here is the view from where I sit. The remains of the lawn, brown at this time of year, stretch from the edge of the veranda to the orange trees, which ring the house and extend acres beyond it. The garden (violets, wisteria, magnolia) is gone, except for the solitary date palm that stands bent in one corner and now looks comical to me. The owners sold the water rights last year and when I saw what they had done to the oranges, as I rounded the bend in the drive in the hire car, I stalled it. Total disorientation. I was under the sea looking at a forest of bleached and broken coral. I was on the moon. Then I saw the house, still flat, weatherboard and splayed like a foot. I restarted the vehicle, drove it up the small incline into the car port.

All the orange trees have been cut to stumps or short, amputated branches, and have been painted white. Apparently this preserves them with little requirement for water, and the paint protects them from the sun. I'm sure the owners have done this in the hope someone will want to resurrect them and it will add to the value of the property, which is on the market. I have faith in none of it. This was never a good place to grow oranges. The soil may be alluvial and rich but the rainfall is equal to that of a desert.

I flew in ten months ago from Heathrow and have the place on lease, the rent rolling over until they sell it or I leave. At first I did nothing; I just sat here, thawing. Then I got on with a few other things: for example, I'm on the visiting roster at a local nursing home; my neighbour Shirley helped with that. Mostly, though, I've been sitting here thinking about writing this.

Perhaps I could blame Romantic music for what happened. Those clear and simple melodies, the harmonies that dip then lift, the grand, over-arching themes. I learnt many years ago at music college that the Romantic movement was about individual striving, and the triumph of fantasy over reality.

In a week, three house guests are supposed to be arriving. If they don't come it will break my heart. I have readied their room: it has a big window, excellent blinds and an air-conditioner so modern and enormous it chills the space in no time. I paid Shirley's niece to dust it thoroughly, wash the windows, the mesh, the sills, even the walls. Last week I got her over again and she moved furniture, covered the space with sheets and painted it a sort of warm custard-yellow; it has been airing ever since. I have made and frozen several meals; tonight I shall make a cake that slices well and improves with age; and today, finally, I sit to write this. It needs to be finished by the time they come. If they come, that is. I've allocated one day, today, to write of the first seventy-three years of my life, and the next six to write about what has happened since. I think I can do it. I've started early; the dawn has just passed. The place still whirs with birds at this moment, despite the drought. The light is yellow, faint, no need to assert itself yet, the full force will come. When it gets very hot I'll go inside, eat a quick lunch, fill another jug of water, make more coffee. I don't intend to be deterred.

One of the reasons I like writing so much these days is because I can see it – there, on the page. These blue biro words cover the paper, they indent it; I can feel them when I touch the page with my fingers. When I write I am better at telling the difference between what is something and what is nothing. And when I do this, I am not dead anymore, or dying. I am here, I have arrived, I am defined in clear lines: I am myself.

6

I

1.

My first concert consisted of a piece by Schumann called 'The Happy Farmer'.

The audience was my parents and two of their friends visiting from the city. I was three years old, it was summer, the curtains were drawn; because of its aspect and the thickness of the walls the parlour was the one room in the house that stayed moderately cool. It also had all the good furniture in it from the English relatives. The four adults sat in a line; the lady from the city had a parasol leaning against the side of her chair, which I coveted, desperately.

I pumped out the oom-pah-pah bass, the cheery tune; sometimes the accompaniment had little off-beat rejoinders that made everyone smile. When I finished they clapped loudly, I looked up at my mother, climbed onto my father's knee; he kissed me on the cheek, wetly. Four big faces smiling down on me, they were suns, stars, moons; I orbited around them.

The visitors left and I began working on a piece called 'Andante'. My mother was sitting beside me. Again, she said, again, and I played it until I got it right. Wrists up, she said, touching them with a flat fingertip. Fingers bent. Then I played it all the way through and my mother stayed silent, there was nothing more to correct. I realised she wasn't sitting beside me anymore, she had got up and was looking out the window at the rows of orange trees. I kept my hands on the keys until only the tiniest sound was left, then nothing.

I lifted my hands, she turned her head. That was very good, she said.

It was a sad piece, and I'm not sure how I knew such sadness then. Was I sad about practising so much instead of playing with other children? Or was it sadness by proxy? Sadness for Mother, preparing to send her only child to the place she herself longed for? Or for Father, who was out on the block, going mad again?

He was up in a tree, feet and hands on branches, counting oranges. Then he was down on the ground, stalking fruit that had already fallen. He was muttering the number of the oranges he had counted in the tree, he was counting the fruit in the pile on the ground; when he added both numbers together he got ninety-three. It was a number so low in relation to what he had hoped for, and expected, that he refused to believe it.

He leapt back into the tree, poked his head in and out of the spiky branches to find more oranges; he scrabbled around in the dirt at its base. He added the two numbers again; ninety-two. He was staggered. He was enraged. A bastard, sneaky orange had disappeared right in front of him. He started to shake, his legs, his arms, he pulled out his shirt, ripped off his hat.

I was lying on the scratchy couch lawn watching all this, covering my mouth with my hands to hide the giggles. In this mood, Father was scary close up but funny from far away.

I saw him eye the fruit on the next tree, consider adding some of those, but then his body countered – that just wouldn't do. He was Walter Murray, most bountiful orange producer in the district, he was a magician, and he bent over suddenly and stared at the ground. I put my hands over my ears, expecting him to shout, but he just walked further into the block, stumbling a little on the crusty edges of the furrows he and Mother had dug that morning for the irrigation.

He came back later in the truck with sacks of fertiliser. He hauled one out, fast, and ripped into it. With huge shakes he sprayed the stuff all over himself, the trees and the ground beneath them.

My mother was furious. The fertiliser was expensive, the money was from her family, and the money had nearly run out. She scolded him when he came inside, hands on her hips, her voice rising then falling dangerously low.

I was under the table in the playroom and I saw my father rush at her as if he were about to do something terrible. My mother flinched, her shoulders tensed, she turned away. He spun around and banged out the back door.

My mother put her hands in the kitchen sink and stood there without moving for a long time. When the light dropped I went into the kitchen, put a hand to her skirt, pulled at the waistband, squirmed between her and the edge of the sink, and she took her hands out of the water with the wet still on them and held my back, and we didn't say a word.

~

My father became interested in manure. He told me its effectiveness had been scientifically proven, and that chicken manure was best of all. Every day he shovelled the shit out of the chook house into a bucket and sprinkled it around some trees. There were only a few chooks and not nearly enough shit for acres of recalcitrant, under-performing sneaky bastard orange trees. He watched the chooks pecking about, threw them weeds he had pulled, even crusts of bread spread with lard. Once, a cake my mother had baked.

He decided he would accept any sort of shit. Shit from cows, dogs, horses, pigs. He went around the district, sloping up people's drives, asking for shit, which might have become a running joke except that I think people were a bit scared of my father and the madness that streaked his yellow-white eyes. He didn't tell them why he needed the shit, but they usually bagged some up and delivered it, because everyone remembered, or said they remembered, what he was like before the war.

He shovelled the shit around the trees and stood watching them like a dog watches a ball someone threw for it weeks ago.

~

Urine, he decided. It was very fertile-making; there was a chemical in it that made it liquid gold. Every time he needed to pee he strode onto the block, undid his pants and aimed at the base of a tree. When he asked my mother and me to do this she just looked at him. As he peed further down a row his purposeful walk turned into a hurried wiggle. He stood in front of trees trying to squeeze out more; there might have been a dribble. So many trees, so little urine. He went quiet for a while.

Then he started to look sly and walk with a swagger. He kissed my mother on the cheek with great smacks of his lips. He had a secret in his chest that he was proud of. One night I heard the rumble of an unfamiliar truck in the drive. Kneeling at the window I watched my father help a man guide a hose from its side to the irrigation furrows. Something dark chugged out and slopped onto the soil. The trees were still and silent as if reflecting philosophically on what they had been given to drink.

In the morning he didn't tell my mother that the truck was from the abattoir, carrying blood from the animals they killed and cut up. He only told me. But when she saw the blood on his boots her lips zipped up and she turned away when he tried the smacky-lip kisses again. I went near the trees tentatively, but nothing seemed to change about them, nothing at all.

Not long after this, when he thought no one was looking, my father got the axe out of the shed, walked purposefully past the woodpile and stood at the top of a row of oranges. He considered the tree in front of him. With the blade of the axe he chipped off some of the small twigs and thin branches near the bottom,

12

exposing the trunk. Then he gripped the axe with both hands, made his legs into two sides of a triangle, his mouth into one flat line, drew the axe back and threw the blade hard into the trunk. He wrenched it out, swung it back, plunged it in again. With even, lethal blows he chopped the tree to the ground.

2.

After hearing the concert A, I heard scales. I was upstairs in bed. I thought I was dreaming and I rolled over, looked at the window, and the scales pealed on. They were played in every key, up the keyboard chromatically, and they were played perfectly; they were like water poured from a spout.

I shoved back the covers, staggered down the stairs feeling furious for some reason, and stood in front of the piano, staring at it. The keys were still, the strings unstruck; no, this instrument was not playing itself. And the scales were even louder.

I started searching the room, marching around picking up cushions, pushing back the couch, jerking my head up to inspect the cornices of the ceiling; all the while the scales ran on and on, up and up. What was I looking for anyway?

When the scales finished I sat on the couch panting, dizzy, nauseated. The silence extended.

I went to the phone. 'Hello?' he said, in a normal voice, then, '*Hello!*' cross. 'You again! You, the silent —' but before he finished I hung up.

3.

Currabin, 1936

My mother planned to send me to boarding school in England. Her great-aunt had offered to pay the fees. My father disagreed; he thought Australia was best, that England was the enemy (among many) and that his daughter should remain at home. They fought about it when they thought I was asleep. They fought about other things, too. Living at Currabin, for example, growing oranges (my mother had never wanted this, she wanted to be in the city; my father detested city work). When my father drank, the fighting was louder. Sometimes I heard crashes and I shut my eyes tight.

In the days afterwards I would watch them stay as far as they could from one another: my mother in the house, my father in the far reaches of the block fixing a fence. Then my mother was out on the block and my father in the truck. It was as if there were a string pulled tight between them, making a straight line, as if they were at either end of the same axis. When she moved left, he moved right, and so on.

My mother thought education was important and that I wouldn't get it in the back blocks of New South Wales. The local primary school was bad, the options afterwards worse. The people who lived here were ignorant, uncultured ruffians. I could go to the city, of course, but why board there, she reasoned, when England was far superior? I had answers to this question but said none of them.

Like all the women in the district Mother worked non-stop; it was rare to see her sitting down. She was tired, her hands were cracked. She should have been a musician, but instead her life was this, and she was angry as well as lonely; she wanted better for her only child, her daughter, and she believed better was as far as possible from the citrus block.

She always made time for my piano lessons and was a fierce but excellent teacher. This was the thing she was able to give me to take to England, it was my ticket. Sometimes she taught me from the kitchen when she was cooking the tea. Wrong, she would shout, her hands wet in the colander, rinsing beans. Start again.

My father had not yet worked out the link between piano playing and going to England.

He was sensitive to noise. If I walked down the hall with too much of a thud he shouted; when my mother sneezed he yelled; a door slammed had him airborne; certain foods were banned – those that made too much noise in the mouth, like apples, celery. But he always loved music. Even if my mother had Beethoven's Sixth Symphony, 'The Pastoral', playing as loudly as it would go when he came in from the block, he didn't complain at all.

He cried when he heard decent singing; a good rhythm had him twitching, moving limbs as if it was involuntary. If my mother was about, he would catch her at her waist, put her arm up; they'd face each other and then they were off, circling round the room. Once they did this to Ravel's 'Boléro' and they circled out the door, across the lawn, tango-charged down a row of orange trees, disappeared and came back later brushing dirt from their clothes and leaves and twigs from their hair.

~

When I turned six my mother got out the big trunk and took it onto the veranda to dust and wash it. Now, Alice, she said, it won't take a year to pack, but I'm getting it out so one can get used to the idea. I wasn't sure who she was talking about, but it made me nervous. I started kicking the edge of the veranda, hard. She told me to stop that kicking and brush my hair, which she'd just washed. I did it out by the strawberry patch, watching carefully in case a snake slithered out; they liked it in there. Once, a red-bellied black snake had got into the house and lay motionless under the dining table. My mother fetched the broom and stared at it for a moment, wiping her hands on her skirt. Then she made some strange puffing noises out of her nose, charged at the snake, and it reared and started to slither towards her, and with huge movements up, down, curving motions with her arms, she swept it out the back door. I remember that snake flipping and writhing and swelling, flashing its bright underside, mouth opening, its tongue on fire, as if it were roaring at us, although it made hardly a sound.

By this point I was advanced at the piano. I was learning Bach's 'Preludes and Fugues' and a Beethoven sonata.

When the trunk came out my father started listening to my practice. I heard him casting about outside the parlour door, saw his shape flick across it and smelt him — alcohol, sweat, cigarettes, petrol — and that scent of the block: tree, soil, wind, water, sky.

One day I was playing a waltz by Strauss and he erupted into the room and tried to pull me off the stool. My body went rigid; I pulled away, he pulled me back, the stool fell with a bang, I dropped, urine leaked out warm around me on the floor. My mother rushed in. What are you doing? she said loudly, what are you doing? And he looked at her for a second, looked back at me and skulked out.

4.

Arpeggios the next day, arpeggios supreme; two hands arched effortlessly over phantom keys, hands like gymnasts, like Olympians. The B flat minor played as easily as the E major, the F sharp major as smoothly as the C; nothing fazed that music, it seemed.

I crept down the stairs hoping to catch them, it, unawares, but when I got down the notes continued even louder, untrammelled.

When the music finished I stood at the window, staring at the place next door. I heard the creak and bang of the pipes of the old house, the tap dripping in the sink. I went down the hall to the kitchen, palming the walls, put my finger beneath the drip, felt the cold water tap my skin.

I filed Clementi. I burnt an enormous volume, extremely heavy (*Economics Explained, Volumes 1–11*), which smouldered for several hours. Then I went to the phone again. 'Hello?' Pause. 'All right, now you're starting to piss me off. You're actually going to have to say —'

I hung up.

5.

Currabin, 1938

I was seven, my leaving day was close. My father had started to drink more, and openly, shamelessly, as if showing us how. No longer were bottles hidden in the crook of the lilly pilly tree, or that place in the chook shed, or that hole in the lawn. He held them himself, slouched against the side door, moaning.

My mother ignored this at first, ignored the fact of him. She just started to get very thin. She still cooked the same meals but she didn't finish what was on her plate; she fed it to the chooks instead.

I refused to believe I was going anywhere. I could see Father drinking and moaning and plotting. I could see Mother turning to sinew and bone. I could watch them dig the furrows beside the orange trees in the mornings so that the water from the channel from the river could flow in. I could feel the heat and contraction of the land. But I didn't think I was going anywhere. I didn't know anywhere else. I just kept playing the piano.

A fortnight or so before I was due to leave, I was sitting at the piano and for the first time in my seven years I did not want to play. Come on, my mother said, hurry up. She had been digging for the irrigation since dawn. I put my hands on the keys but did not press them down. What's the matter? she said sharply. Stop wasting time. I started a slow scale but I did not finish. Instead, I swivelled around on the stool, looked out of the window beyond the curtains and mesh to the garden, the scratchy lawn, the lone palm tree bent in the corner, the rows of orange trees, the saltbush scrub, the white blue sky, and everything so still, so still, and I saw my mother looking at these things too.

Play, Alice, she said, drawing her eyes from the vista, it's time to do your practice now, and I turned and faced the instrument, but I didn't know what to play; it was as if I couldn't remember any music. Play the 'Andante', she said, reading my thoughts. Skip the scales today. Remember that 'andante' means at an easy walking pace and that it is graceful and accepting. Remember that when you play one note there will be one after that, and then another, and that you needn't rush any of them, they will be there, they will come.

I started the 'Andante', and for a while I found it difficult to breathe, my stomach was tight, I felt cold and shaky. But I continued to play, and she was right that day; after one note there was indeed another, until the music was done.

That night my father went to the hotel and came back very drunk. I could hear him outside, shouting. He slammed the door, locked it behind him and yelled, Where's my girls?

I froze in bed. I could hear him blundering around in the dark, trying to work out how to get down the hall to the bedrooms. Then I saw a figure of white: my mother had flown from her bedroom without using her feet, she had me in her arms, her hand close to my mouth. Now, just be silent, she whispered. It seems your father has had a bit too much to drink. Her breath smelt of bad milk or something worse. She took my hand, gestured under the bed. Get under there, she said; I looked at her, we'd never done this before. Get under the bed, she hissed, staccato.

Where are you? he shouted, and in her flimsy nightdress, I could see my mother's breasts, the hardness of the nipples against the white cotton, the hesitation in her step; one hand was scrunching her nightdress, she was thinking about what to do. I quickly obeyed, sliding on my stomach across the floor.

20

I hid my face, I couldn't bear it; I started playing a fugue in my head. In the end she got under the bed with me, scrabbling across so that I was between her and the wall. She didn't look at me when we were lying under there together.

By now he had found his way down the hall. Come here at once, he was shouting. He reached my bedroom door, paused, swayed. Alice, he said, won't you play me a tune? He came towards the bed, stood above it breathing fire, then staggered at the sight of the empty sheets. He ripped at the linen, threw the pillow to the floor, the blanket, got tangled up in it and fell, bang! He was level with us now, my mother was pressing me hard into the wall. He groaned, rubbing his head. Then he got up and raged out of the room, up the hall, and Mother and I uncoiled our bodies.

He broke most of the good furniture in the parlour that night. I could hear the strings of the piano humming in fright. Mother, I said, amid the noise of the cracking, splintering wood, I do hope he won't touch the piano. Mmm, she said, as if her mind were somewhere else entirely, wondering why a couple of the chooks had stopped laying eggs or pondering what to do about the rampant wisteria escaping the trellis. We ended up falling asleep under there.

At dawn we woke, stiff. My mother listened for a moment, got out from under the bed, straightened her nightdress. She went out the back door, returned holding the axe and walked up the hall into the parlour.

He was asleep on the floor, shattered furniture all around him. She tapped his leg with her foot. He woke with a snort, then a yelp at the sight of my mother with the axe. Je-SUS! he shouted, and he started crawling towards the door. Don't move, she said, lifting the axe, and he stopped, extended a hand. Don't you move, she said, and the hand stayed mid-air, shaking. Don't you ever try that again, she said, do you hear me?

And he stared at her, said nothing, eyes saying it all. Did you hear what I said? she said, slowly raising the axe higher, I know what you were going to try. Did you hear me? And he nodded then, finally. She looked at him for a bit longer, turned around, took the axe back outside to the shed, locked the shed door, put the key on a chain around her neck beside the crucifix and started another day.

I left not long after, with my Bach, my Beethoven, my 'Happy Farmer' and my 'Andante'. With a trunk that had taken a year to pack. With an orange, slightly squishy, in my hand. Keep playing, my mother said, standing on the quay. Keep playing, won't you, dear, won't you? My father blew his nose in long honks that rivalled those of the ships, my mother seemed to sway with their force, the seagulls' screams reached a higher pitch and I sailed away.

6.

After the scales and arpeggios there was music. Bach, the first prelude of Book I of the Preludes and Fugues. It almost made sense, a baroque beginning; I could see myself dreaming this up in my depleted state. A grand recital, it would be, to march me to my death. I was momentarily lulled, standing by the fire, moving my fingers in the air, listening. One can embellish that prelude, try to make it into something it is not, but this was played simply, beautifully, each note perfectly weighted and connected to the next. It was an even meditation in the key of C, which had always suggested morning sunshine, orange juice and wholesome beginnings to me.

I jerked back, realising where I was. I stared wildly at the old gramophone, the dusty knobs, then over at his fancy sound system, all those steel buttons – was it turned on? But it wasn't even plugged in.

The Bach stopped for a second, a minute correction was made, then it wended its way to its close.

I felt wetness on my face, looked up at the ceiling, searching for the leak, the beading drip. But the roof was intact, the walls stood tall.

When I rang that day there was a long pause, then: 'If you have something to say,' and the voice was icy, 'I think it might be about time, don't you?' At which point I started swallowing convulsively, my hand shook on the receiver; he hung up.

23

I burnt some books, many books (*Against the Welfare State*; *Capitalism and Humanity*; *The Road to Serfdom*; *Studies on the Abuse and Decline of Reason*; *The Fatal Conceit*). I picked up an album by Debussy, the first book of his Preludes, found number two ('Voiles') and then I was away, away, on thoughts of ships and waves and harbours.

eyes from those sleeping girls. The one nearest to us had her mouth open and was snoring softly. The white sheets against the black night made the beds look legless – white boats floating into the dark. Wordlessly she showed me where to place my shoes, the section of cupboard where I was to hang my clothes, and the single drawer where everything else was to go. An immediate sense of constriction when I saw all of this, as if I had stepped into a box.

The sheets had a coarse, hard texture. I squeezed myself between them, moved my legs around to loosen their tuck into the mattress. I had a sensation of falling, falling down a long way into darkness.

~

When the girls woke in the morning they looked at me without expression, eyes pausing and sliding on. They started to dress. It was presumed that I would know what to do. So I watched, copied. We went into a bathroom, took turns to splash cold water onto our faces, rub them with soap.

Later a girl was chosen to show me around. She was older than the ones in the dormitory. Outside, that wind was still there, and it whisked her long fringe into her eyes or out of them, depending in which direction she stood. She showed me around several buildings, then took me to the hockey field, which we stood beside for some moments. It seemed to be the climax of our tour, this desolate oblong of shorn grass with nets at both ends and white chalked lines. I glanced at her. Her eyes were squinting hard into the wind, her lips pursed. She had started to look like the woman from the night before, and I wondered if this expression on these people's faces meant I was expected to say I was impressed, or grateful.

I looked past her to the town of Whitby below. In the harbour dozens of fishing boats were tethered, they rocked and reared

27

in the choppy water. On the opposite side of the bay from the school, up on the grassy cliffs, stood the ruins of Saint Hilda's Abbey, white, skeletal, half there, half not. You're shivering, the girl said. We'd better go back in.

8.

Whitby, North Yorkshire, 1938

On my second day I was introduced to Miss May, the piano teacher.

'Alice Murray,' she said, and she stood when I walked into that room at the top of the stairs of the Victorian building. The room was warm, which seemed extraordinary. I looked around, saw a bar heater in the corner. She kept it on all day, I heard later, against regulations. There were potted ferns, a brass watering can; the place smelt like a greenhouse.

Miss May wasn't old or young; her hair was piled on top of her head, escaped wisps stood up all around it.

'Play something,' she said, smiling, beckoning to the piano, a large upright.

I took off my coat, climbed onto the stool. I felt energised for the first time since I had arrived, as if warm water were flowing fast through my body. I played Beethoven, the 'Appassionata' Sonata. What noise it made, what shout. Such confidence music has, even when transplanted. And just the same in that room as it had been at home, which seemed miraculous.

She leant forward, 'Who taught you that?'

'My mother.'

And there she was in a flash, standing in the kitchen, slitting apricots in half, flipping out the stones. Make it more staccato, she shouted, as if the keys are too hot. Ouch! Ouch! Afterwards those apricots drying on racks in the sun, shrivelling, getting smaller and smaller, sweeter and sweeter.

'This place must be quite a change,' said Miss May, examining me. Her grey eyes were slightly hooded.

'I beg your pardon?'

She got up, went to the music cabinet in the corner and started pulling things out, looking at them, pushing them back in.

'It must feel cold.'

'A bit.'

When I'd been told I was going to meet my piano teacher I'd gone to the bathroom, breathed hot air onto my hands then stuck them beneath my armpits, and it was only October.

'Try that,' setting a piece down before me.

It was by Béla Bartók, the nationalist composer who collected folk tunes from his native Hungary and Bulgaria. The tune was weird, nasal, the bass pounding, atonal, repetitive. I pecked then bashed at it, finding its rhythms surprisingly satisfying.

'Oh, well done. That was excellent. Didn't you take to that well? Now, what about this?'

A piece called 'Dance of the Wild Horses' by another nationalist composer, this time from South America. (Miss May had musical friends, she told me later, who travelled.)

I played it for my first performance at school. Up I walked past the rows of silent, watching girls and teachers, Miss May sitting with her head slightly tilted, looking demurely downwards. I sat at the piano, inched up the seat.

I started the piece very fast, at a kamikaze speed, or was the music playing me? And riding me hard, soon I was rolling behind it, I was flying in the air, the whole instrument started to shake and I galloped on, hands flying, hitting, body rocking, dancing, fingertips just clinging on, a tearaway. I ripped the last glissando up and down the keyboard, crashed the final triplet of hooves and pulled my hands away. Silence. Then an eruption of applause. It was thunder, lightning, rain on the roof.

It was a great, sweet-scented downpour, and it drowned out everything else.

~

It was easy in the end to assume a different accent, a different way to be. When you learn to play an instrument from an early age you are also learning to mimic, as well as to perform, and that is what I did. I made friends easily, although those hockey girls were not really my sort; I was able to garner enough respect and affection to save me from the worst of it. And I always had the music practice room to retreat to. Sometimes I felt as if I were in a very long concert, and when it finished I would go home and turn back into me.

9.

Whitby, North Yorkshire, 1940

Miss May took me to many concerts in the years that followed. We often caught the train to York. Even when the war started we kept going. Once during a concert in York the air-raid siren started. She pointed to a note printed in the middle of the program: 'If the alarm sounds, the concert will continue. Patrons may leave if they wish, but please do so as quietly as possible, avoiding any disturbance.' We remained in our seats.

My great-aunt had died by then. She had left money in an account at the department store in town to pay for basics like shoes and soap and underwear, but there wasn't much, and I was always frightened it would run out. No cash, either, so no treats, and no tuckbox from home at the end of holidays, which were mostly spent at school unless a friend invited me to her house.

When I stayed at the school I could practise for as long as I wanted. With the other girls who were left I would lie in the sun on the hockey field, which had been allowed to return to seed, then take myself off to the practice room. It was tiny, a cell, just the instrument, a stool, a door that closed and a tall narrow window looking out onto the roof. I'd climb sideways out of that window in summer, sit on the roof and watch the gardener and his young assistant below. In winter I'd sit with my hands in my lap and watch the rain clouds roll in over the cliffs and wish that rain home. Back then I still prayed to a god in that sky, a large, benevolent man with a languidly pointing finger.

I did not write to Mother asking to return. I knew there was no point. But I wrote to her often and told her about everything. I worried about her, about both of them, and the block. I longed to be back there, always. My yearning for home was like a song that never left my head.

She replied about once a term. Some girls got a letter once a week. My mother was busy, I told myself, that was it. When I got older I decided it was because she had little left to give. She'd had to sever so many parts of herself by then that all that was left were soldered bits and blunted ends. In her letters she always asked for more information about what I was playing. When and what are you performing? Have you learnt a concerto yet?

My father wrote once the entire time I was at school, a postcard, it looked like he had used a number of different pens. The writing sloped haphazardly downwards and contained a quote from Job, unfinished, reference missing.

~

After the 'Dance of the Wild Horses' Miss May gave me the Prokofiev Toccata in D minor, a study in virtuosic anger, beating discord after discord, crashing crescendo after crescendo, that relentless pounding bass. My god, I loved playing that sort of music, I should have played it more. Why didn't I? Why did I ever play anything else?

But Miss May said it was time to advance. She pulled out of her cabinet the first of the Romantics she taught me, a Liszt Consolation.

'This requires an entirely different technique,' she said, smoothing the pages open in front of me. 'Less bash, more squeeze and knead. A touch that lingers at the keyboard, approaches it with ease, lifts up slowly from it, gently. "Sticky fingers" said Liszt.'

I started to play, but the melody, so beautiful, so yearning . . . I stopped, pretended to be squinting at the music.

'Are you all right?'

'Yes, just the D flat major, it's unusual.'

'Oh yes, isn't it cryptic, and so soft and tender, all those black notes taking your hands forever inwards. Here, let me show you.'

As she played I started to invent a secret technique. When those beautiful, terrible melodies threatened to undo me, I pictured a set of glass vials lined up in rows along my ribs and poured my tears into them.

'Here. You try.'

I sat down, lifted my hands, began again.

'Wring the emotion out of it,' Miss May interrupted, demonstrating with two hands, which looked like they were strangling something. 'Press your fingers into the keys deeply, join each of the notes together, each one, link them, do not allow any space between them.'

I took a breath, continued.

'Not that much. Hold back a bit. You need a balance.'

I stopped again. No, I had not yet mastered the Romantics.

10.

Oxford, October 7th, 2005

Beethoven, the 'Appassionata' Sonata, first theme of the first movement, was hammering itself into the house.

This time I was determined. I got down the stairs as fast as I could, knuckling the banisters with both my hands, seeing stars, seeing nothing, seeing white, then stood staring at the piano, reeling. It did not move, it did not sound, why did I persist in trying to see that sound?

The music built again, the even quavers pounded, the rippling broken chords, soon they were wrapping themselves around me and I was caught. I started playing it in the air, arms jerking up and down, hands jerking back and forth, not caring for a moment what was real and what was not. Mid-phrase the music stopped.

I felt cold after that, even colder. It was the hunger, which had almost taken me over, it had a grip on me now and restricted movements of my head, my eyes; I could see less and less. I was going to have to do things faster. I made a cup of tea, spooned in a little sugar.

Into the study. I packed texts into the grate (*The Market, Unfettered*; *Market Supremacy*). I lit a match with a shaking hand, a flash of light, of warmth. I held it there.

I filed all of the works I possessed by John Field, every pretty nocturne. With one looping gesture I swept it all up, dumped it into F.

I'd originally thought I would give all the scores to Richard, my son, who lives in London and is a composer, and quite famous for it. Premieres at the Proms, at Carnegie Hall, recording contracts, soundtracks for movies, international tours, profiles in the arts pages of the dailies (his genre is described as 'post-minimalism'). But I knew he wouldn't want them, he had told me how much he detested such music, especially the Romantics – Rachmaninoff (a cliché, Mother, pure Hollywood), Chopin (over-dressed fop, says it all) and Liszt (show pony, basically) – which meant the scores would end up at the Oxfam Shop on St Giles, if not in the rubbish, although I hoped the filing would prevent that, would make them look more valuable, or valued.

(My fantasy: someone would take them to an auction house. I liked to picture an auctioneer with a gavel the size of a giant hammer in his hands, and as the bidding went up and up he would start to hit the scores again and again, demanding a better price. But no, the scores would be taken to the Oxfam shop, if I was lucky, and priced for next to nothing.)

And then night fell, at least I thought it had. I could hardly tell the difference between day and night in that study, and when I went out to the hall and dialled the number he said, each word carefully articulated, 'You need to identify yourself and state what your issue is or stop this right now, and if you don't I will call the police.' For a moment I appreciated this idea – me *not* talking being reason to call the police. He hadn't hung up and I sat there frozen. I heard breathing and suddenly I wanted to cup his breath in my hands and inhale it. Then the line went dead.

Later that night I heard the Beethoven again, but with less punch to it, as if it were reflecting on the man who, near his end, had heard strange music in his head too.

11.

Whitby, April, 1949

In my final year of school Miss May asked me to play for a man visiting from the Royal College of Music in London.

'They have some scholarships available for their one-year Diploma of Performance. It would be an audition.'

I must have looked as surprised as I felt.

'I've told them about you. He is visiting especially. You're brilliant, you know. You must take this further. It's a gift.'

I fiddled with my books. I had not heard my playing described that way often and for just a moment the sun rose inside me, its rays rippling out. But I was not going to music college in London. I had done my time; I was going home.

'Why don't you just do the audition? It's unlikely you'll get it. He's travelling all over England listening to people.' She paused. 'Well, I've gone and invited him now, I don't think we can disappoint.'

I had a polished performance repertoire, it was easily done. I could play whatever he wanted.

When Miss May received the letter two weeks later, she read it in front of me, sitting at the piano, eyes travelling fast.

'You've got it. Oh Alice, they want you!' and she leapt up and embraced me.

I blanched, gave her a quick hug back. 'Do I have to say yes?'

'*What?* Alice! It's a *full* scholarship to the Royal College of Music. You cannot pass it up. Few have even been considered, let alone offered such a thing.'

'Oh, I'm very grateful,' I murmured.

How weary I was by then of such expressions of gratitude, of saying thank you for things I had not even asked for, of saying thank you because I had nothing in the first place. In my head I started to walk to the little harbour at the bottom of the town, where I went on weekends to watch the sea, the birds, and the boats, sitting on an old wooden bench, the texture of the damp wood crumbly beneath my hands.

'It's only for a year,' she was saying. 'Can't Australia wait?'

I put my book bag down on the floor. I had a sudden impulse to grapple the piano into my arms and throw it out the window.

'Tell me more about it,' I said.

She told me that the most talented young musicians in the land went there to learn and play together, become friends, and discover the cultural attractions of the capital. It sounded good, the way she put it.

'When do they need to know?'

'Soon. There'll be a second round of offers depending on who takes up the first. As I said, it's only for a —'

'I'll write to Mother.'

'You'd better telegram.'

'She won't telegram back. It's too expensive.'

'I'll let the College know,' Miss May said, 'that due to geography, our response will suffer a mild delay.'

Dear Alice, my mother wrote back, air-mail. *Of course you take the scholarship. Is it a full scholarship? We can't afford to help. There is no money left here, the block is in ruins and your father is very unwell. I send you our congratulations. You have worked hard and done well.* And this last bit is the only time she ever said it: *I miss you. I have been counting the days for some time. For years. Ever since you left. I will be there with you in spirit. You and your playing. Your music.*

I wanted to sprint towards her then, across all the oceans, towards those words, that rare love. I hatched a plan. I would visit Australia before I went to London. The trip there and back would take more than two months (the notion was ridiculous, no one did that). I wrote to her in a rush, suggesting it. The response was swift.

The notion is absurd, she wrote. *You find the money for such a folly. You lift it from the land with your hands.* She said I was to go to the Royal College and work as hard as I could.

I cried and cried. It was only another year, but I remembered what I always did: the delight on my parents' faces when I played well; the feeling of my mother's arms around me; the beauty of the wide open land, the big, hot, white sky, the birdsong of a butcher bird, a pallid cuckoo, a grey shrike-thrush.

'I have nowhere to be,' I told Miss May at my next lesson, 'over the summer.'

'But won't you stay on here?'

The thought of finishing school then hanging around for months with the little girls, the usual humiliations compounded tenfold.

'Actually,' she said, glancing away. 'I think I might write to the Royal College. There will be scholars and students there over the summer, visiting and so forth. You can go there early, get a head start.'

I frowned, it sounded unlikely.

There was no room available at the hall of residence I would be living in when term started, but there was a room available in another, where I could take all my meals. I could use the College facilities. What's more, Miss May must have mentioned my lack of finances, because an advance on my first stipend cheque was enclosed.

~

Before I left I spent a week with a friend, Esther, a day-girl who lived in Whitby in a big cottage on a hill with a garden full of flowers. When I arrived, her mother, Rachel, was standing at the door, her arm extended, Esther's little sister peeking out behind her. I walked down the hall with my carpet bag. Most of the windows were open and the place smelt of the sea, the flowers, and something baking. We ate scones in the back garden that afternoon with blackberry jam. The next day Rachel offered to do some washing for me. I refused, of course, not wanting to impose, but she insisted. From where Esther and I were sitting I could see into the little laundry house, Rachel's back bent over the basket, her arms working fast, sorting the wash. I can still see the way she started to move in slow motion when she reached my clothes. Most of them, and there weren't many, she ended up throwing out; a couple of things she mended. Then she must have asked discreetly around the parish. She assembled a good-as-new wardrobe for me to take to London, including several concert gowns, and even a smart suitcase.

Oh Alice, she said on our way to the station, almost weepy, this is a special occasion, it really is. Alice Murray, she said, off to the Royal College of Music.

Oh Mama, sighed Esther, don't be such a sap. But she rubbed her shoulder anyway and gave her a kiss.

They stood close to each other on the platform. They did their hair in the same way; they started waving in the same way. I turned from the window back to the empty carriage. The train snaked its way to London on the same line that had taken me north. The carriage was peaceful after the bustle of the school and Esther's house, and as the evening slipped into night the gentle rock of the train sent me to sleep. During the night the carriage grew cold and I covered myself with my coat and slept on.

Esther's father had drawn me a map of the route from the station to the College the night before, sitting at the old kitchen table. Rachel was in the rocking chair, sipping the tea he made her every night after dinner; I remember the scraping sound of the chair as it rocked back and forth on the floor. When he'd finished he handed me the map and said, Not a chance you'll get lost now, not a chance in the world.

The train slowed, stopped. I stepped off, into London.

12.

London, June, 1949

'Alice Murray. Yes, we've been expecting you,' the porter said at the entrance of the hall of residence, and he took me to my room. He stood by the door, telling me when meals were served. Then he put down the case and left. I sat on the bed, bent over to take off my shoes.

I crept around the place in my socks. All the doors were open; the rooms were empty, just stripped beds and bare cupboards. I was the only one there. I nearly laughed, just to hear the sound of it bouncing off the white walls. There were a couple of months before College began and I had no one to answer to, no one at all.

I started practising for several hours a day. And then not as much; I lay on my bed instead and read. I'd found a well-stocked bookshelf in a lounge on the ground floor. Some other students had arrived and I saw them at meals, and on the walk to and from my practice, but I avoided them. I wasn't lonely; I was an only child from a land that lay flat, still and quiet.

I soon discovered Hyde Park and walked all over it, inspecting flowerbeds, trees. I'd lie on the grass and read stories for hours, I even wrote some poetry. Then I started walking around the city. In Whitby, all the shopkeepers knew my uniform and often my name; in Currabin everyone knew everything. Here, I was anonymous. I walked around shops; I stepped into churches and famous buildings. I visited all the galleries and saw paintings by artists I had never heard of; I picked out favourites. Then I'd feel guilty about doing these things, I'd think of my parents working hard on the block, or in the house, and the next day I'd practise for longer than ever.

I was still playing the repertoire I had learnt from my mother and Miss May. One day I walked down the empty aisles of the College music library pulling out scores. I didn't know what I was looking for, perhaps something that reflected the huge city I was getting to know, those sights, the art, all that I was feeling and thinking. Perhaps I wanted to hear great cathedrals of sound, music that came from my hands like an architect's grand buildings. But I did not know where to look for that sort of music. Sometimes I played whatever came into my head, lines of music and harmony that became more and more complex, but I didn't remember it the day after and I never wrote it down.

In September, everyone began to arrive. I moved into a bright, modern hall of residence that filled with the sounds of voices, running feet, banging doors. And in the College I heard the sounds of all sorts of musical instruments.

My piano teacher, Arthur Joiner, specialised in Beethoven. He liked the late works best, which form the edge between the Classical and Romantic eras. The first time I played for him he sat listening behind his desk. The room was big, neat, tasteful, a few framed watercolours of vague landscapes on the walls. Out the window I caught a glimpse of the glazed iron roof of the Royal Albert Hall. When I finished he got up very quickly. 'Oh, ho, ho,' he said, and then he leant sideways on the desk, awkwardly. I had surprised him.

In the lessons that followed he adjusted my technique to create more control and depth to my touch. I took note of everything he said and worked hard at it. I felt that what he was teaching me was improving my sound and allowing me to achieve more at the piano, expanding my repertoire. But then he did something that surprised me. He hardly said a thing. During my lessons I would play and afterwards he would make a couple of brief comments, which I wrote down and used as my guide for the following week. I had expected his teaching to be driven, demanding, formidable. What was the matter? I could tell he was holding something back.

I checked with him that I was progressing as he wanted. He nodded, his face impassive. Yet there was nothing further, and certainly no encouragement. He never spoke of my future.

I worked even harder. I entered competitions. I won some, including the prestigious College Concerto Competition for my year level, and after that Joiner said, Well, I suppose you work quite hard, don't you?

I felt enraged by this, and also bewildered. I looked around his neat room, all the pens and papers in precisely the correct spot, my hands and wrists positioned exactly as he wanted, the Beethoven played just right, too, every note and rest and dynamic in place: he was fastidious about everything. Perhaps he was one of those people who thought that a woman of my station should aim to be nothing more than Miss May's successor.

I remembered something that had happened when I was at boarding school. I was at the house of a relative, the daughter of the great-aunt. I stayed with her rarely: as soon as I met her I could tell she didn't like me. She probably resented the dent my fees and upkeep had made to her inheritance, the potential obligation I represented. Or perhaps it was something else.

She knew I was musical. I hadn't spoken of it, but she received everything the school wrote about me. And she had a piano in the parlour. One weekend I asked if I could do some practice. Oh, she said, trailing off, all right then. I was working on a Mozart concerto and that day I mastered a particularly tricky section and was pleased by the music and by what I had accomplished. I went down the hall and into the kitchen where she was sitting with her husband.

He was reading the paper and raised his eyes. She slowly, finally, acknowledged me, then looked over my shoulder and said, So what are you up to now, then?

It was as if, with just a few words and gestures, they had made that music I had been playing disappear.

At the Royal College the fact of my playing was unassailable, but its quality, my ability, my talent, my future: all this was subjective, definable.

I withdrew during my lessons, I hardly spoke. I found my feelings about it coloured what I felt about the Beethoven I was studying; those long, involved sonatas with their technical demands. I came to dislike them.

At the end of the year I performed in front of the piano professors, almost all of them applauded enthusiastically and they gave me top marks. Yet my eyes found their way to Joiner, his slow clap, that way he touched his moustache.

~

Pianists were not only assigned a piano teacher, but also to accompanying work, or an ensemble. I had been put into a piano trio with Hetty on the violin and George on the cello. When Joiner began to frustrate me, I gravitated towards the trio and organised our frequent rehearsals.

Hetty was from Edinburgh and on a partial scholarship (a rich infirm relative was paying the remainder; Hetty had to nurse her for a spell once she'd finished at the College). The sound she made on the violin tore at me. I yearned for it at strange times – like when I was in the bath or out walking. Hetty was tall, had buck teeth, and when she finished playing she would lift her bow and hold it for a second, mid-air, then lower everything and wriggle her shoulders, not even bothering to look at you.

George was tall and thin, had messy orange hair, knobbly elbows and knees and when he played he pulled weird expressions on his face. The sound he made crawled right up into me and wrapped itself around me. There was a depth to it, layers of velvet in it, one note contained many. It was as if I could finally relax, I could just close my eyes and smile and be warm. He was from the slums of Liverpool and an older gentleman had paid for all his lessons, encouraged him, even got him elocution classes.

We played together well from the outset and improved quickly. It was the first time I had played with others in that way and I enjoyed it immeasurably. Interweaving my music with theirs, accompanying them when it was asked for, playing above them when the music said. Rushing and dropping and stopping together, tossing the notes high, lifting off at exactly the same time. When we performed, it felt to me as though we were holding each other's hand, had closed our eyes and were rushing together across a dark field.

One of the professors took a particular interest in us (a Marxist; he used to hold readings of *Das Kapital* in his rooms with various music playing in the background). He gave us pieces by new composers from England and Europe, and got us free tickets to London concerts, sometimes more than one in a night. We would run from theatre to theatre, Bruch's Violin Concerto, Beethoven's Ninth, then wander home afterwards, walking on air, piggy-backing one another, screaming with laughter. The city dogs would yap, windows slam, curses would be hurled from doors, and we didn't care, we were night vandals.

We spent most of our free time together, and by second term a loose group of other students had formed around us. We sat and talked in the common room or in Hyde Park, went to dances and the cinema. I met my first boyfriend, Lucas, in the common room, where from the windows you could see right into the labs of Imperial College next door. He took me to a dance, turned out to be a terrible dancer, yet insisted I remain with him all evening. So I broke up with him after that and went with Clarence, another pianist: he didn't last long, either. I wasn't serious about any of those boys I went with at the College, I was too busy for courting, and, besides, soon I would be going home.

At the Saturday cinema there was an advertisement that made all my friends smile and nudge me. It was for the Assisted Migration Scheme or Ten Pound Poms, and was silly, amusing. People in various states of undress or unpreparedness rushed aboard a boat to Australia, desperate to reach their fantastic new home. They all stood on deck smiling and waving. I really liked that ad, it lit me up, and I liked my friends noticing it, too. I hadn't looked or sounded Australian for years, but they all knew where I was from, and where I was going.

14.

Oxford, June, 1950

Towards the end of the academic year the three of us were
selected to take part in a prestigious series of master classes and
concerts to be held in Oxford over the summer. George and
I were invited as soloists as well as ensemble artists, Hetty as
part of the trio. To accept meant delaying my return to Australia
until the end of September and my impulse was to say no, but
if I didn't go Hetty couldn't either, because there would be no
trio. Then I heard what an honour it was to be selected (I liked
the thought of telling Joiner). My mother wrote to say that if the
Royal College was paying, of course I should go. So I accepted
on the proviso that I'd sail as soon as it finished; by then I had
saved enough from my stipend for a cheap ticket.

The Summer School was held every Wednesday. That first
day, we caught the train from Paddington to Oxford, then took
a taxi to New College. The streets were almost empty, just a few
men on bicycles, almost as if there had been some sort of evac-
uation. What a contrast it was to central London; the scene was
almost pastoral. Except for the buildings, that is, those grand,
spired buildings with their studded gates and thick walls; some
even had a sort of guardhouse at the entrance. The taxi drove
slowly past them. We were silent, taking it all in. Then George
started to whistle softly and Hetty tapped her knee; I smiled.

The porter at New College escorted us down a drive, through
an arch in a wall, a quadrangle, a gate in another wall, another
gate and quadrangle, to a door. We stepped into a room with

a faded silk carpet and a high ceiling. Young musicians stood around holding their instruments.

During the day there were master classes and rehearsals, then late in the afternoon the room we'd met in that morning was set up for the first concert.

I got there early, and with a couple of the other pianists watched two men and a woman, college staff, push a grand piano into the centre of the room, at the front, which was to be the stage, carry in music stands, lift chairs into rows. By this point people were streaming in and I turned to look for George and Hetty.

This was when I saw Edward. He was standing at the back of the room, leaning against the wood-panelled wall with his arms crossed. I would have noticed him anyway, because he was beautiful. He was tall, broad shouldered, and had dark, slightly wavy hair, which looked recently clipped and was perfectly combed. He was classically handsome: high cheekbones, an aquiline nose, also crinkly bits around his eyes – perhaps because he was older than us musicians – which suggested to me a face that had been in the sun, laughing, smiling. He wasn't doing that now, though, he was staring straight ahead at the empty stage.

I'd been asked to play part of a Mozart sonata, which I took too fast (I still did that sometimes, as if the music wasn't enough in itself), and then a Beethoven sonata, the Opus 109 in E major. When I played the Beethoven, for the first time I felt at one with that music. What I heard in my head finally came out of my hands, the two were one. I was the vessel; the music ran through me. The last movement especially, with its hymn-like refrain and variations, it felt elemental to me, the first melody. When I finished the room breathed in, then out, then someone stirred and the applause started. I bowed. He was still standing in the same place, clapping in a small way, private, but he was smiling now, it seemed at me.

Trestle tables were set up, covered with white cloths; tea and crockery were brought out. There was still rationing then, and some of the food that was served we hadn't seen for years. Rich cakes and slices, a leg of ham, a block of butter, a huge cob of fresh bread, a few slices already cut, even a dish of sweets; the table was crammed. People pushed out of the rows and crowded around to look, then formed a queue. The room was packed and raucous, people were elated, post-performance. I was being jostled and felt disorientated. I was looking for him, I wanted to put my eyes on him again, but I couldn't see him anywhere. I made it into the queue, and when I turned around to look once more, he was standing behind me. I nearly jumped. It was as if he'd followed me. I turned my back to him and stood still, silent, staring in front. People were elbowing past, shouting at one another to be heard. I had started to sweat. I felt a tap on my shoulder.

'You played the Beethoven, the 109.' His eyes were large, brown and looked at me intently.

'Yes.'

'It was very good. It was intelligent.'

'Thank you.'

'I have several recordings of that sonata, of all the sonatas. The way you played that tonight was better than any of them.'

And the way he said it, too, as a statement of fact. I was pink, suffuse.

'Thank you very much.'

'You played the Mozart too.'

'I did, yes.'

'That second movement . . .' and now he looked away, over my head, and squinted at the windows at the back of the room. 'Well, do you like that music?' Swinging back to look at me.

'Oh yes. I mean, it's beautiful.'

'Tricky, though, isn't it?'

Not really, I thought, not at all, a child could play that. But a man had appeared at his side, they started to speak, heads bent together. Then Edward glanced back, murmured, Excuse me, put his empty plate down on the corner of the table and walked out.

~

On the train on the way back to London I took the Mozart album out of my bag and reconsidered it. That week I practised it a lot. The next week, once the applause had died down after my performance, I sat back at the piano and played the second movement without repeats as an encore. When I got up I bowed and smiled, deliberately not looking at him at the back of the room.

The concert finished; the noise surged once more. I thought he would come over to me straight away and talk about the Mozart, commend me, even thank me – but I couldn't see him. I felt bereft. I also felt foolish. To think I had spent so much time that week practising that little schoolchild's piece for him.

I found Hetty and George, who were talking to an oboe player everyone had noticed (he'd played part of the Oboe Concerto in D minor by Albinoni; he looked like an angel Gabriel: curly hair, soft lips), and I made to join the conversation – the gentle words, the funny rejoinders – but I found I couldn't concentrate. I was thinking I mustn't have played the Mozart well, that something was wrong with it, although I didn't know what, and that he had left so he wouldn't have to talk to me about it. Or else I had misjudged the interaction between us completely; made it into something much bigger than it was, and that thought was even more embarrassing. I found myself suddenly annoyed with the conversation around me – it seemed flippant, silly – and I felt the oboe player looking at me, and I was self-conscious, not wanting him to, not like that.

I decided to leave. I got my things together at the edge of the room, went back into the crowd, struggling between people with my arms full to tell Hetty and George I was off to catch the early train, and just as I was walking towards the door, there he was, right in front of me, from out of nowhere, his eyes flashing, his lovely hair – a strand had fallen forward and almost touched his forehead, and he was breathing as if he'd been running. When he saw me he smiled, and it was a beautiful smile, like being enveloped in warmth.

'Not leaving already, are you?' he said.

'Oh, well . . .' not meeting his eye, as if distracted, uninterested.

'That Mozart.'

'Oh yes,' frowning now, looking at the door.

'It was extremely good.'

'Thank you,' touching my ear, glancing at the door again; of course I had expected more. And how loud the room was, irritatingly so, as if people around us were actually roaring.

'It was almost perfect. When I listen to you play, just you, I am transported.'

The noise fell away, the jostling people; everything went.

'Let me take those for you,' he said, pointing to my bags. And then I was lighter, and we floated out through the door.

Back we went through all the gates and arches of the college into the street, where the lamps were lit, even though it wasn't yet dark. I remember the feeling of his arm beneath my hand, and light upon light guiding us on our way.

As we were waiting on the platform, the steam of the train billowing and hissing around us, he told me that his name was Edward Haywood, he was an economics don at the college and involved with the organisation of the Summer School. My name is Alice Murray, I said, but I think you know that already. Yes, he said, of course.

15.

Oxford, June, 1950

The following week, straight after the concert, he invited me on a tour of the college. We left the concert room and stepped into silence. Just our footsteps on the flagstones, no rhythm to it, his legs much longer than mine. I was nervous, I could barely look at him.

'What a hush,' I said, just to say something.

'It's always like this in summer. Come October the place is transformed.'

'Do you enjoy the peace?'

'I liked the music tonight. Yours most of all.'

'So where are we starting this tour?'

'Right here,' and he stopped.

Another quadrangle, smaller than the last, with a shaded cloister, also a pond in the middle with a fountain and a statue.

He strode over to the pond and started to talk about the fountain and the statue: facts, names, dates. Then he peered at the cloister, which was quickly getting murkier as the sun set, and started on it. I was still at the entrance, listening. His anecdotes about these architectural features could have been entertaining, they had that promise, and he used at times a jocular tone – perhaps someone had told them to him in a way that had been amusing – but there was something wrong with his version; his stories had no point, they were square-shaped like the quadrangle we stood in.

'So there you have it,' he said, satisfied. 'That's your tour for today.'

I couldn't believe it. It was as if someone had taken a hammer to that statue in the middle of the pond and with a few big blows destroyed it. He was *boring*.

'Well,' I said, glancing away, shifting my feet; they made a crunching sound on the stone. 'It's certainly an ancient place. Do you think we ought to be getting back? It's rather late, isn't it?'

He looked at me then, hard, for just a second, and with a few strides he was at my side.

'I've been a bore.'

'No, no . . .' I laughed.

'Ah, you see,' pointing, 'I know now that was very boring for you.'

'Well, not quite that bad, I mean —'

'I reverted. To tutor. Nervous.'

'Nervous?' But he wasn't looking at me: topic closed.

'Well, what do you like about this place? It can't just be the history and so on. Why bring me here?'

He turned to the quadrangle, as if he were thinking about it.

'I like the way the moss grows up this gutter,' he stepped over to it, 'and all over the head of that gargoyle up there.'

'The moss?'

'Without asking permission. And what I really like about that statue is the shape of it, the curve of that shoulder. When it catches the afternoon light at this time of year, because of the way it's positioned, the very sinews of it are highlighted, exaggerated, and I feel quite sure the artist did this on purpose, that they knew, absolutely, the effect they were creating. Sometimes when I see things like this I want to tell someone about it, what I know to be true.'

'Yes, I understand,' and I was staring at him now, and he turned so that he was facing me.

'I like the way you look when you play the piano. The hair that escapes from behind your ear and falls across your face when your head dips . . . it happens a lot.'

He reached out, picked up the strand of hair in thumb and finger, hooked it behind my ear, his thumb brushing the edge of my ear, and then behind it, and I had that feeling again of losing my feet, of the earth disappearing beneath me, and just as I was about to go up on tiptoe to kiss him, he said, 'Come on then,' and turned away.

A piano student I'd done a master class with that morning was standing just inside the door and I stopped to talk with her. I could see him close by, he was talking with a couple of men but he had his body angled towards me. He caught my eye, smiled; I excused myself, went over to him – it seemed the only thing to do.

I can't remember everything we discussed that night. He must have asked about Australia because I know I found myself telling him things I hadn't told anyone since I had been in England. I told him how much Australia was still a part of me. How much I missed it, yearned for it, and wanted to see my parents. That I was going back there to be a concert pianist. I remember the way he listened to me, absorbed, those brown eyes focused on me. When we talked about music and litera-ture and paintings it turned out we had similar tastes. When he talked about his work, his field of economics, the passion he exuded, his energy took me with him, and made clear that he was brilliant, inspired, and that his work was his engine, his lifeblood. He had achieved his professorship at a very young age, and had served as an economist in London during the war.

We stopped only when we noticed the silence around us. We looked up; there was no one else left in the room except a young woman in a uniform quietly clearing the table. We rushed from the college. He found a cab, and when we realised that I had indeed missed the last train to London, he found me another cab at the station, handed over a wad of money to the driver (refusing to even countenance the notion of repayment). As the vehicle started down the concourse he kept pace at my window. I asked the driver to stop, rolled down the glass. Edward stuck his hand forward, over the glass; I put mine out too. We held on.

'Don't go,' he said, then smiled. 'You'll be here next week, won't you?' and those brown eyes had grown even larger.

'Of course,' I said, smiling. I couldn't help it. 'Of course I will.'

I remember the long empty road home, the dark countryside, the loudness of the engine, and a small round moon, very high, flickering in and out of the thick streaks of cloud. I was hearing it all again: the conversation, the music. I looked down at my right hand, the one he had held, turned it over, felt it with my lips. It was not a hand that had been held very much.

I didn't tell anyone what had happened to me. I spent most of that week in a practice room at the Royal College or in my room. I practised with a feverish, nerve-filled intensity. I felt hot, took off my sweater, but then my skin felt cold to touch. I felt pangs of hunger and thirst, yet to eat or drink sickened me. I looked for him in the streets of London, expecting to see him every time I went out, except that he was in Oxford, and the thought of bumping into him terrified me, yet it was all I could think about, all I longed for. At one point when I was practising I wrote his name on the side of a score, drew a box around it and then arrows pointing into it; it made no difference, he was in my head all the time.

I was still playing Beethoven, all the works I had studied with Joiner, but what I was playing that week was so far from his big neat room with the watercolours on the walls it could have been an entirely different genre. This was Beethoven that soared, that walked on clouds and possessed the moon; I saw a little crescent moon that week from my college window and I thought: you are mine.

I found myself fascinated with the process of playing. This object of wood, string and ivory creating sound – an entirely different dimension – from seemingly nothing, just a few actions of my body and all that was inside me. It was like an experiment, two substances mixed together then changing colour, spitting, fizzing, creating a third, except that to think of science at such a time seemed absurd to me, and entirely missing the point.

I missed everything that week, except my practice. Meals, appointments, trio rehearsals, sleep. I just kept playing.

And then the excitement of being on the train again, early on a Wednesday morning, leaning forward in my seat, heart pounding, stomach leaping, train rushing, rushing, chuffing, tooting, that pounding rhythm, the overwhelming noise. I had the window open, I could hear nothing else, travelling towards Oxford.

16.

Oxford, October 8th, 2005

Liszt, *Années de Pèlerinage*, 'Sonetto 104 del Petrarca'. I heard
the beginning boom and rush of chords, the beaming cadential
melody. It was played easily, expansively, the left hand opening
itself out, stretching itself over the accompaniment, the right
hand singing the melody into space. The ornamentation was
played lightly, the dynamics were not overdone, it was played so
well it could have been a recording.

A recording, I thought, lurching to the window, scouring
the street for speakers, megaphones, machines making music.
Someone was out there playing this music to deliberately
torment me. They had seen me lurking, a thing possessed. But
there was no speaker hovering in the air, no gramophone at
the gate, just that black and white cat of the neighbours on the
bitumen, twitching the tip of its tail.

The Liszt carried on and on, pressing, pressing. I could bear
it no longer. I had to escape it. I started up the stairs, heaving
myself up with a swinging motion, but the music came after
me, it was chasing me, it was whispering in my ear, Go, go!
Up, up! I reached the top, let the banister go, ricocheted in slow
motion across the bedroom to the window, heaved the heavy
pane up, and the music stopped.

Cold air fingered my face. I looked at the pavement where
the cat had been sitting, at the line of houses (forever that line
of houses), the gutter of the roof. Liszt, the virtuoso pianist
and composer, the rock star of his age: women in his audience

fainted when he played, those repressed and censored Berliners. They wore strands of his hair in clasps around their necks, made his broken piano strings into bracelets, fought over his discarded cigar butts. Liszt, the heart-throb who became a monk and spurned them all.

I started thinking about the possibilities again. The Americans moving out four months before; I had really seen that, hadn't I? I turned from the window, back to the silent house.

I burnt; I filed; I called. When he picked up he didn't say anything, it was as if he was waiting for something, waiting for me to speak, although I could have been imagining this. We held on like that for some moments. My hand with the receiver started to shake, my mouth went dry. I hung up, shaking my head, I nearly cried, it nearly broke me then. I sat listening to the silence, listening and starving, and glad of it, glad it would be all over soon.

17.

Oxford, June, 1950

'Will you come with me?' he said, touching my wrist after the concert. 'I want to show you something.'

Out of the music room again, towards the college gate, and this time walking fast.

'Where are we going?' I said, panting already.

'It's a surprise.'

'So fast!'

'Sorry,' taking my hand, 'I don't want you to miss it.'

'Miss what?'

Up the street, veering sharply left.

'You'll soon see, if we make it.'

Past the Bodleian Library, past St Mary's Church, down to Christ Church College where I stopped at the entrance, I couldn't help it. It was the grandest of colleges, the big decorative gate, the huge quadrangle at the front with the great hall behind it, the sheer magnitude of it all. He was unmoved by this, of course, used to it. He nodded briefly at the porter, strode in.

We went into what looked like the chapel (it was a cathedral, he told me) and at the front were some stained-glass windows by Burne-Jones depicting a medieval scene in brilliant colour. With the evening light coming in, the stained glass made a pattern on the floor; different coloured shapes outlined in black.

'Isn't that lovely,' I said, breathing heavily.

Without saying anything he put his hands on my shoulders and guided me into it. I was softly coloured: a little red, faintly yellow, tinged green, purple, blue.

'Turns out we're early,' smiling.

'Really?'

'Stay there, though. That's good. Don't move.'

I stood still for a few seconds, staring straight ahead, then looked up at the window. It wasn't to my taste, but I could see it would be beautiful to others. The chapel was very quiet, it was just the two of us in there, breathing six feet or so apart.

'Nearly there,' he said presently, looking at his watch, lifting a finger, *'Now!'*

And at that moment the sun shifted and the light that had been coming in through the stained glass was suddenly concentrated and so sharply delineated it was like a solid block coming out of the window towards me. I was in it, I was covered by it, and I gasped and reached out, but there was nothing to touch, of course, just air. My arms were sapphire, emerald, mauve, ruby, my body was burning orange, my feet were gold. I had tears in my eyes, my heart was thudding, and I looked around and saw with surprise that he was standing to one side, entirely unmoved. He was observing the effect, my reactions, quite carefully, and then he smiled.

We walked out of Christ Church back to New College. Oxford was unfolding itself around me. Not just the buildings, which had gathered shadows, but the silvery sky, the scent of the air, the calls of the evening birds. He was telling me how stained glass, along with flowers and the liturgy, all those things spurned during the Reformation, had been aesthetic reflections of a theological point: that there was too much focus in the world on commerce and industry rather than beauty, compassion and nature. The idea seemed to articulate so much of what I thought was important, what I valued. Then, after a short silence, he said, 'You are music to me. You are light. You are a whole new world,' and he turned to me, lifted my chin with a finger, tucked my hair behind my ear again, and kissed me softly, with such tenderness, and it was exactly what I desired.

And perhaps I could have said then: But I am flesh, you see, I am also a soul, I am not those things you say, not at all, I am me. But it was wonderful to be thought of like that, even if it were hyperbole, and in any case I wasn't thinking like that; who would be?

18.
Oxford, July, 1950

Every week, when the concert ended, we left and walked out into Oxford. He showed me the Sheldonian Theatre; I stood on the stage looking out at the hundreds of empty, tiered seats; he pointed out the baroque, painted ceiling. We went into the Holywell Music Room, the oldest concert hall in continuous use in Europe, he told me. He always had the key to these places, I don't know how, and on a summer night we had them to ourselves. We went up Carfax Tower, into the Bodleian Library, and into many colleges and private galleries. I saw ceilings so ornate I could hardly take my eyes from them; more walls of stained glass and pictures, walls bejewelled; flagstones beneath our feet with letters carved into them long ago; relics in glass cases covered with dark velvet.

One night he took me into Hertford College, up a spiral staircase and into an octagonal-shaped room at the top, which contained a gold-lacquered harpsichord. (He told me later he'd had a man clear the room and carry it up there in pieces and put it back together.) I played a Bach partita. The fast, plentiful notes clattered up to the ceiling and back down, they ricocheted off the walls. The place filled with the music and I could hear what I had just played, what I was playing and, in my head, what I was about to play, all at the same time. I started to laugh, and he clapped and said bravo, and started laughing too, and all those sounds, the laughing, the clapping, the bravos, the music, which was still ringing, were all mixed up and magnified in that odd-shaped room.

The oldest part of the city had narrow laneways with tall stone walls on either side, and because there had been no rain (this was a drought by English standards) they were often coated with dust. I was mid-sentence the first time he pressed me up against one of those walls, the stones grating my back, and kissed me. The week after, he lifted me over the fence of the South Park, which shut in the evening, and we lay in a patch of long, green grass. He was nothing like the boys I'd been with at the Royal College. He was focused on me, and slow, artful; his own desires came second. I was drunk on it. We would walk from historic building to historic building (he still liked to lecture and I listened now and asked questions), and all the time, for me, our destination was the South Park, its darkened benches, stretches of cool grass, and over-hanging plants.

We didn't have sex – I believed you only did that when you were married (all this made sense to me then). He didn't mention it. After we'd kissed we'd lie on the grass on our backs, then hop back over the fence.

He started hiding a picnic basket in the park before it closed, all those delicious foods he'd somehow got hold of, and we'd eat there together before going back to New College. A choir was singing in the chapel one night as we walked back in. I don't know what choir it was, the New College choir rested over the summer, but it sounded like them, the boy sopranos with the men's deep voices. They were singing Fauré's 'Cantique de Jean Racine', the voices entered one after the other, the lowest first, the melody smooth, calm, building, the inner part of flowing, ceaseless triplets. Everything in the college was still and listening, buildings, trees, even the wind. He translated some of the French for me: 'We break the silence of the peaceful night; Saviour Divine, cast your eyes upon us!'

Everyone had spilt out of the music room onto the college lawns and people were sitting in big circles beneath the drifting clouds of midges, talking and laughing. I beckoned to Edward, we sat in one of the circles and I joined in one of the conversations. While I was talking I looked over at Edward and he was staring out into the college grounds instead, as if suddenly fascinated with landscaping, paving, botany. After a while I found myself drifting off and looking out at the gardens, too, and it was as if I could still hear the choir singing, that beautiful music.

19.

London, July, 1950

Back in London, I played through the Beethoven I was meant to be working on that week, but I already knew it. I leafed through some of my other music. I put on the stand an album from my days with Miss May, something by Brahms, I think, and played it. The yearning melody, the tug and release of the rubato, the way the theme was repeated and built on, the final, gentle resolution; all of this was just right. I got out some other books, reintroducing myself to the Romantic repertoire. They were usually short, spectacular concert pieces portraying one or two intense emotions.

In Oxford that week I performed the Beethoven, but when I'd finished I rose in the silence, closed the album, put it to one side of the piano, and played Rachmaninoff's Prelude in C sharp minor. There was a brief, stunned pause (it hadn't been on the program) then long, heavy applause. From the keyboard, before I even got up, I looked at him. He was clapping hard and smiling, and when I bowed someone else, not him, called, Encore. Afterwards people wanted to talk to me and he stood beside me the whole time. Then he squeezed my hand and we travelled slowly through the room, through all the people, out the door.

After this I continued to practise what was required, but also this Romantic repertoire. So I was very distracted; in fact, I'd been distracted ever since meeting Edward, and missing trio rehearsals. Hetty and George were understanding; they thought I had a crush. They hadn't known me long and they respected that sort of thing and didn't want to meddle. But I knew I had veered close to offending them. The Summer School wasn't just about solo work; we also rehearsed and performed as an ensemble. It wasn't right, either, to keep rushing off like that at the end of the concerts, we were supposed to stay and talk with the other musicians and tutors.

Hetty and George didn't like Edward. When I'd introduced them to him he wasn't polite. It was after a concert and I knew he was in a rush to go, he had another big tour planned for me, and he cut the conversation short and didn't even smile at them. I told him he should have been more friendly.

'We shouldn't have left so soon, they'll think you're rude.'

'But I've been waiting all week.'

'They're my friends. I wanted you to meet them.'

'I did,' he said. 'Hetty and George.'

'There are others, too.'

'Oh, I'm sure.'

It was our first disagreement, and as usual we were rushing from the college, by now we were down one of those narrow alleys with tall walls on either side.

'If you want to know the truth of it,' he said.

'I do.'

'You shouldn't bother with that trio, you're wasting your time. You're a brilliant soloist, absolutely brilliant. You should concentrate on that.'

I should have been angered, but part of me felt complimented and I spent even more time after that on my solo work.

When we said goodbye at the station I often wanted to cry. It sometimes felt as if I were revisiting all my goodbyes, all those tears never shed. He held my hands, he kissed me, but he never said much at those times of departure, and when I looked up at his face it was expressionless, as if wiped across by a hand.

'You could come up to London,' I ventured once, 'for a visit.'

'I have to work here,' he said. 'You have to practise.'

20.
Oxford, July, 1950

He started to meet me at the train station when we arrived in the morning. He'd be standing there on the platform with his hands behind his back, that little frown on his face, his hair still wet and flattened, just combed. When we saw him I could sense Hetty and George bristle behind me. He always ignored them.

He had a gift for me behind his back the first time he met me like this. It was an old silk shawl wrapped in soft tissue. I'd never received such a beautiful present. As I stood admiring it Hetty and George walked past us and up to the college.

After this he always had a present when I arrived: an antique book about Beethoven with a rose tucked inside the cover; some sweets in a twist of paper. A card with a pressed flower glued to the front, a snakeshead fritillary, bell-shaped with spots resembling scales. It was a native wildflower, he said, and used to grow in many parts of England. You can plant it, he said, but it only grew wild in a few places now. He had picked it in Magdalen Meadow, which they didn't mow so it would continue to seed. I showed it to Hetty and she said they only bloomed in spring, those wild flowers, she'd read about them in the paper, so who did he pick it for then? Taken aback, I said that Clarence was giving me flowers back in April, and also flowers took a long time to press, so maybe Edward had picked it on a whim then decided to give it to me. Maybe, she said.

Edward said Hetty was a troublemaker. He said she was jealous of me. He said that George's expressions when he played were so dreadful they detracted from our performance, and something drastic should be done about them.

'Stop, Alice, stop!' Hetty said at our next trio rehearsal.

'What's the matter?' I asked, turning from the keyboard.

'You're getting faster and faster.'

'Yes, I like that, I like getting faster there. It's exciting.'

'Great. We can't keep up.'

'Oh.'

'You're losing us.'

'Sorry. I'll make a note on the score.'

'Don't you agree, George?'

'Ah, well . . .' staring at the music, not wanting to be drawn. 'I suppose we weren't really playing together.'

'You see?' she said.

'All right, I said I wouldn't do it anymore, I've made a note. Look. Here.'

'Humph!' Hetty flounced in her seat. Then George let out a hoot and the three of us started laughing.

Perhaps it would have all changed anyway. We knew we were about to part. Hetty was off back up to Edinburgh to do her internment, as she put it, with the rich relative; George was off to Wales, where he'd got a job with an orchestra. And I was leaving for Australia.

21.
Oxford, August, 1950

Around this time I performed the Rachmaninoff Prelude Op. 23 in D major. While practising it, I noticed its tendency to return to the tonic, the D. It was as if the piece were an ode to the note. Even when complicated swirls and eddies took it elsewhere there was still a little reminder of the D, up high or down low, played every bar or two. Each and every climax and crescendo built to it; all the time, every time, that piece returned home. A lot of music is like this. It begins like this, it ends like this; this is the basis of classical music theory.

After the concert I told Edward what I had observed, which led me to talk of home again. I told him that night about the smell of the place, the scent of orange blossom that you could detect even when you were far away; you could smell it even when the trees weren't in bloom. And when you smelt it you knew that you were nearly home. He listened, nodding, smiling. Maybe you will visit one day, I said, and he smiled at that too.

Later, when we were in the South Park, he sat up and said, 'Where will you perform when you are back in Australia?'

'Where?'

'Yes, which concert halls?'

'I don't know. I haven't thought.'

'Are there many good concert halls in Australia? Is there a culture that fosters excellence in pianists?'

'Well, there are concert halls in the cities, of course – Sydney, Melbourne, Adelaide . . . I expect I'll perform in them once I've got myself, you know, settled.'

'But you don't know any of this. You don't know of any concert pianists who have done this and succeeded.'

Of course I didn't. I hadn't even been to any of those cities, except to Melbourne when I left. It was the concert halls of London, Oxford and Yorkshire with which I was familiar. But I thought my mother would know what to do, and we would contact her old friends who were in the classical musical circles of the city; this is how I would start.

'Just as long as you're sure,' he was saying. 'You seem quite . . .'

'What?'

'Fixed on this notion of returning to rural Australia. I'm simply trying to reconcile this with your development as a musician.'

'I'm going back,' I said.

'So you say. And becoming a concert pianist.'

'Edward . . . this is what has always been planned. I haven't seen my family or home for twelve years. I must go there.'

'Of course. Everyone must do what they want; that is very important. Everyone must find their way home. That is the most important thing of all.'

22.
Oxford, September, 1950

On the second to last Wednesday in Oxford, after the concert, we walked straight out of the music room, out of the college and kept walking. We went up one of the roads that led out of the city. As we talked it started to feel like that first night again – we didn't notice the time or how far we'd gone. When we saw where we were and how late it was we started running, cutting through smaller streets and lanes, once even a field. By now the light had fallen, the birds had gone quiet, and although we were going fast it was clear we weren't going to make the last train.

We saw a car, a brown sedan, coming slowly down the street towards us. Edward stepped into the road, flagged it down and bent to the driver's window. We both got in, clambered into the back seat. The driver wore a hat that cast a shadow over his face, but I could tell he'd been drinking – I could smell it. Just before he put the car into gear he cleared his throat loudly and spat out of the window. We sat in the back not saying anything, holding hands. The man seemed to exude disapproval despite agreeing to give us the lift. Perhaps he thought we were doing something clandestine; and there was of course the age difference between us. Anyway, that night we made it to the station on time.

~

On the last night of the Summer School, I played the Prelude in C sharp minor again. Huge applause, the final concert was over; time for the last supper.

Instead of taking me out through the college gate that night, Edward led me deeper into the grounds. We passed through an arch in an old wall, crumbling at the top; it was part of the wall of the medieval city. There was a small hill or mound in front of us covered in grass, wooden steps cut into its side; and at the top a bench made of two slabs of wood. Bushes grew around the bench so that when we sat down on it, all we could see were the stairs going down and a sliver of moon in the sky, white, tilted.

He took a ring out of his pocket. No box, just the ring. It had a cluster of diamonds on it. I remember looking at it and starting to feel very cold, and thinking how quickly it had all happened – the light dropping, the summer ending, the sun disappearing to the other side of the earth. I knew there had been an enormous misunderstanding, and that I had to immediately set it right, but I was shocked to find myself in such a situation. I prevaricated.

'Where do people live,' I heard myself say, 'when they marry in Oxford? Do they live in the college?'

He looked at me sideways. 'Most wives want a house of their own in North Oxford.'

'North Oxford . . .'

'Up there,' pointing north, smiling, the ring still in his fingers.

'And these houses in North Oxford . . .' I said, all the time thinking: how could such a mistake have been made? 'Do these houses have pianos in them?'

'Oh, *absolutely*. Lots of pianos. A piano in every room.'

Which I started to imagine for just a second – streets of houses with a piano in every room, the space the instruments would take up, having to walk around a piano when you wanted to get to the sink or lavatory or a chest of drawers, and the noise, the ruinous din when they were all played at once.

'And other rooms, I suppose,' I said. 'Studies, and so on ...' (I had actually started to think about composing, of putting some of that imagined music onto paper.)

'I would have a study, of course,' frowning. 'Alice, the question is a rather larger one. Should I do this?' and he went to kneel in the dirt before me.

'No! Don't! Please. Oh no, get up, get up,' and I started to cry. And into the terrible silence that followed I said, 'You'll get your trousers dirty, they're always so clean.'

He got up silently, sat down, and that look on his face, it was awful. I put my hands over my face. It felt horrible to disappoint him. Everything was falling, steel, ladders, scaffold, plank after plank, all the things that had felt so tall and solid, they had turned out to be nothing, nothing more than words and touches and a few outings in a university town over a dry English summer.

'Edward, I have spoken to you so much about it, you know that I am going back to —'

'Oh yes,' jaw clenched, *'Australia,'* as if he hated the entire continent, as if he were spitting at it.

Then everything changed. His face relaxed, he became calm, his voice was silken. 'I have taken you by surprise. Look,' he said, pointing to my hands, 'you're shaking. I had no idea this would be a shock to you. I thought this was what you wanted.'

But why would he say that? Had he not heard what I'd said? Any of it?

'We've spoken so much of me going home,' I said again.

'I think you need some more time to think it through.'

'All right.' I just wanted to leave that place.

He put the ring back in his pocket, took my limp hand, raised it to his mouth. He seemed happier now.

'You're freezing,' rubbing my hand. 'Here,' taking off his jacket, putting it around my shoulders on top of the shawl he'd given me. 'All right?' He smiled at me.

'All right,' I nodded, staring at the steps.

'You can let me know in a couple of days. Write me a letter. Or send a telegram. You have the address?'

'Of course. Edward, look —'

'Why don't we go and find the others,' he said, standing up. 'We'll go and find your friends.'

By the time we got back only the stragglers were left: the double bass player who criticised everyone's playing, and a pianist who played nothing but Strauss. The bass player told us that a group had gone to swim in the river, and I remembered Hetty talking about it on the train. I could just imagine it, the clothes discarded on the bank, the naked drop into the cool, deep water, limbs paddling furiously, mud squelched between toes, the shrieks, the laughter. I was so sorry to have missed it.

At the station, when he handed me onto the train, Edward kissed me, and I felt embarrassed by that, doing those sorts of things in public. As the train pulled away, I waved.

~

A few days later I still felt as though I'd been hit by something. I was nauseated and having trouble sleeping. And there was nothing that could fix it– no Wednesdays left, no talking to him, embracing him. Several times I took out a sheet of my best writing paper and began a letter to him, but I didn't know what to write. I had said it all already, yet it was as if I had said nothing; as if he had heard nothing.

I didn't want to talk about it with anyone else, not even to George or Hetty, when they disliked him anyway. Finally I took out a sheet of airmail paper, fluttered it onto my desk, flattened it with my hand and wrote to my mother. I told her of the Summer School, and Edward, including his proposal. Then I asked if she knew of the places in Australia where concert pianists could perform and whether there was a culture that fostered excellence in performance musicians. I sealed it quickly and sent it airmail.

23.

Oxford, October 9th, 2005

I heard the Liszt again. It was night-time, I was in bed. The music was very soft, the notes sneaked into the room and crouched on the carpet beside where I lay. I reached down, touched the carpet, imagined touching the notes too, shaping them myself. When it came to the part where the singing melody begins, that grand old theme, only the right hand continued. A skeleton of notes glued together, notes like long, curved bones. Then that stopped too and the silent night eased back in.

24.

London, August, 1950

A telegram from Australia arrived for me at the Royal College. The porter was on his annual holiday in Blackpool and Frank, the temporary replacement, did not know me. I never checked the telegram box because I never received telegrams, so it remained uncollected.

A couple of weeks later another telegram arrived from Australia. When it wasn't collected Frank looked at it with consternation; these telegrams from Australia were starting to clutter up the box, which was, strictly speaking, for newly arrived telegrams. They would need to be put somewhere else.

When a third telegram arrived he let a morning pass, an afternoon. Then he found another box, scrawled 'Uncollected Telegrams' on the side, put mine in it and placed it in a dark corner of the foyer beyond the student pigeonholes, where it wouldn't get in the way. And that, for a while, is where my telegrams stayed.

25.

London, September, 1950

A week after the Summer School finished I was on the grass in Hyde Park with those of my friends who were still in London, talking about such serious matters as whether George should shave off his beard.

My plan was to sail to Australia once Hetty and George had left. I'd been told I'd get a cheaper ticket and the chance of a better berth if I went down to the wharf and bought it at the last minute. I was adamant all my goodbyes would take place in London; I did not want anyone waving from a pier in Tilbury.

Around lunchtime we got up to go back to the college. The foyer, as we entered, was dark after the bright sunshine of the park. So I did not see the figure rising from the long bench that looked like a pew, I was not looking in that direction, I was laughing with my friends. Only when the dark shape walked towards me did I recognise who it was.

'Edward.'

'Alice,' he said. 'Hetty,' nodding, 'George. Mary.' He went on, 'Hilary, Solomon, Edmund.' I hadn't realised he knew their names.

I had on an old dress (I'd always worn my good clothes to Oxford); I hadn't done my hair. And I had still not written to him.

'Would you like to walk?' he said, gesturing to the gate, and he smiled at me.

He looked different in London; he looked even better: taller, broader, more expansive. A coloured hanky was folded in his pocket, it could have been a bloom.

We walked about aimlessly, not saying much. Perhaps he had chosen to forget about that last night in Oxford — that would be ideal; we could say goodbye properly. From time to time my stomach rumbled audibly, which I found embarrassing. I soon realised that the silence between us meant he hadn't forgotten about that night, and it started to feel, bizarrely, like a form of punishment.

'I should have written,' I said eventually.

'Oh no,' he said at once, 'never mind about all that,' and he smiled at me again.

Ah, the relief. It was behind us. He was going to save face this way, by ignoring it. We kept walking.

'I have something to show you,' he said.

'What is it?'

'A surprise.'

'A surprise . . .'

We were back in Hyde Park, down one of those narrow paths closely planted with shade-loving plants on both sides, camellias, azaleas. He took my hand, swung it.

'I think you'll like it.'

'Well, where is it then? Is it here, in the park?'

'No. It's in Oxford.'

'*Oxford?*'

'I thought you might like to come and see it.'

'Go with you to Oxford?'

'Unless you have other plans,' glancing at me. 'I wouldn't want to interrupt something.'

My feet kept up an even pace. 'I was going to practise this afternoon.'

'You'd be back by dinner. There's a train in twenty minutes. If we head in that direction,' pointing straight down the path, 'we'll make it easily.'

Not so aimless our walking, then.

'I have intruded,' he went on. 'You have other plans. I should have let you know I was going to be in London today.'

'No, no, it's just . . .' And then I started to think that perhaps this was the opportunity to have a proper conversation, clear things up, depart on good terms; it was what I wanted. And it really was good to see him again, smiling like that.

'I haven't brought a cardigan,' I said. 'I don't have my purse.'

He took off his jacket, put it on me. He bent down, picked a pink azalea, tucked it behind my ear: 'As lovely as ever.' He reached into his shirt pocket and drew out slowly, like a conjurer, two first-class train tickets. 'No purse needed.' Then he reached forward, took out of the pocket of the jacket a paper bag, opened it: a banana. (No one saw bananas in England much in those years after the war.) 'In case you get hungry.'

Into the great shade of Paddington Station, stepping up into the carriage. At Reading the train started to sway, our bodies braced against the motion; by then he was holding my hand; he kissed me on the cheek.

We got into a taxi at the station and he gave an address in North Oxford; the car veered left, away from most of the colleges and university buildings. Past grocers and news-agents; past children on the pavements (I had never seen a child before in Oxford). What was he going to show me? An obscure gallery? A painting of two lovers parting? (Funny how you can retain a redundant idea in your head when it's of comfort.)

We pulled up in a suburban street lined with large houses. He hadn't said anything for a while. I thought he seemed nervous.

'Well, what a mystery!' I said, to lighten things, to be kind.

'Up here,' he said, serious, and he opened a squat iron gate in front of one of the houses. It was a grand terrace with a flight of steps, recently washed, up to the front door, and a big bay window at the front to the right. It rose two or three storeys.

I walked up the path, up the steps; he opened the door. It was cold inside, goose bumps pricked on my arms. The hall was dark, empty. There was a smell of dust, wood smoke and a sharp sourness.

'In here,' reaching in front of me, opening a door into the front room with that big window. The light was brilliant, such a contrast to the hall, and then I saw it, the grand piano by the window.

'Try it,' he said, gesturing to the instrument.

I was a bit reluctant. What were we doing here? Besides, there was no seat. The place was unfurnished, except for the piano. I stepped over to it, saw it was a Steinway, raised the lid. I played a few chords with my right hand.

'Lovely tone.'

'You told me you like Steinways.'

'Did I?'

'Yes, you did.'

'All right,' looking away.

'I haven't got around to buying any other furniture yet.'

And that was when the panic started to rise, an insistent flutter ascending from my stomach into my throat.

'When did you buy it?' I said, looking around.

'Last week.'

'Last week. So ... recently.'

'Come and have a look,' impatiently. 'It's quite sizeable.'

We tramped around each floor of that empty place. I dutifully examined the rooms as he opened and closed each door, and I commended them, politely. It was a large house and it might be lovely, I thought at one point, if it were repainted in light colours to offset the terrible heaviness that came with so little natural light. The right furnishings would help too. Plus the footsteps of happy people, of course. I peeked out of a window into the garden. Hip-high weeds, a shed set against the back fence. Yes, you could make something of this place, I thought, but it would take work, and after it was finished it would still be a huge, dark old terrace with too many stairs. We climbed all the way down then stood in the hall near the door.

'You've done so well,' I said. 'What a big house, and so much potential. I'm sure you'll be very happy here.'

He didn't reply. There was no more delaying it, denying it.

'Edward,' reaching out to touch the plaster, 'you know how much I care for you, and how much I've enjoyed the time we've had together. It was a magical summer. It's just that I haven't been back to Australia since I left, I haven't seen my parents, and I've always known that —'

'You're not still on about that, are you?'

I looked at his face, his gaze trained on me, so rigid. How tired I felt then, how fed up with it all. Why could he not listen? Why did this man not hear what I had to say?

'Well yes, I am, actually.'

'I wanted to show this place to you straight away,' he said slowly, articulating each word carefully, 'because you seemed unusually interested in houses and their floorplans and contents.' And I think it was only then that I realised how angry he was.

'And what an impressive place it is —'

But he was on me, he had lunged forward and was kissing me, his hands were on my arms, and I kissed him back for a moment, but then he pressed me hard into the wall with his chest and his hands moved down to my skirt, and I didn't want this, not at all, and I was so scared that I found myself suddenly unable to speak, my throat had closed. I finally got out a hoarse no, no, launched myself towards the door, threw it open, I was down the steps, out of the gate, into the street, looking around wildly, trying to work out which way to go.

Part of the horror was the sheer awkwardness of it, standing there looking around while he locked up, because my train ticket was in his pocket, and I hadn't brought any money. Standing in the street trying to regain some semblance of dignity, smoothing down my old dress, still grubby from the morning in the park, and wishing, most of all, to be out of there, to be out of Oxford.

'I'll get a taxi,' he said, coming towards me.

'I can easily walk,' edging a little down the street. 'Why don't you just point me in the direction of —'

'There's one coming.'

And there was indeed, trundling up the street as if on cue.

At the station I handed him his jacket, he gave me the ticket, looking hard at me.

'Goodbye, Edward.'

'I shall call in at the College.'

'Well,' I said, looking at the tracks. 'I sail soon.'

~

I went straight to my room, washed my face, neck and hands, where he had touched me, kissed me. I put on a clean top, trousers, a sweater, did my hair, put on some lipstick and went down to dinner.

'Where have you been all afternoon?' Hetty said.

I waited a minute before I spoke.

'Oxford.'

'*Oxford?*'

I was very hungry, I realised, my hands had started to shake. There was some bread on the table, I reached out, took a slice. Yesterday's bread, dry, I ate it quickly, drank some water, reached for another slice. Hetty, watching, started to laugh.

85

'I missed lunch,' I said. 'I had a banana.'

'A *banana*. He gave you a *banana*? What was it like?'

'I don't remember.'

'You don't *remember*?'

'It was like a banana, Hetty. A banana is just a banana, as it turns out.'

She didn't say anything.

'He's bought a house,' I said after a bit.

She looked at me, still didn't say anything. Then she reached out, picked up a piece of the dry bread and pinched it tight between her fingers.

26.

London, September, 1950

George was leaving in a week to begin his position with the orchestra in Wales. Hetty was also about to leave – the relative in Edinburgh was waiting for her. She hadn't a job yet but was going to keep looking. Work for musicians was never easy to find. In my head my career back home was settled, though sometimes I felt flickers of doubt; natural nerves, I thought, when one was about to embark on a new stage of life – I pushed them down.

We played a few times as a trio that week, just for ourselves, slowly for a change, savouring it. Afterwards I found myself walking around the parts of the city that were now familiar, thinking about the areas I still didn't know. I went to the National Gallery and the Portrait Gallery, looked at all my favourites, found some new ones too. I lay in Hyde Park, watched the clouds pass. Every time I returned to my room I half-expected to see Edward in the foyer, rising from that pew-like seat, but I never did.

One day I came in from the park and saw a package in my pigeonhole. Finally, I thought, a reply from Mother. Without looking at it properly I opened it right there. There were two small parcels inside, and a folded letter in unfamiliar writing. It was from Dulcie Abbotsford, who lived around the corner from us; I'd been friends with her daughter.

I am writing to confirm you received the three telegrams informing you . . .

I looked in my pigeonhole, put my hand inside the empty space, touched the wall behind it.

. . . of the death of your parents. The rabbits were very bad, ring-barking the trees. He was cleaning his gun. We think that when your mother found him she must have thought there was still a chance. Somehow she got him into the truck. You know she could never drive that thing. She got it onto the road, took it over the bridge, there was a truck coming the other way, she must have put her foot down, pressed the wrong pedal, accelerated through the barrier . . . An orphan now, all our thoughts and prayers are with you, dear.

I might have been reading these words but I didn't believe them. It was a hoax. I looked at the letter again.

. . . sneaked these things out of the house without them bank people seeing . . .

I pulled out the brown packages, about the size of two fists, tore them open. My mother's rings, including her wedding ring. The crimson scarf she wore on special occasions, still smelling of lavender eau de toilette. Her pearl-drop earrings.

I staggered out of the foyer into the sun. I had been shot and drowned myself. I could not walk, I could not breathe. I looked at the words again, tearing at them with my eyes, willing them to say something else.

'Coming for lunch?' someone said to me, passing.

Turning the pages over, looking, looking, but the words did not change, the words were still there, my parents were dead, the block had gone back to the bank, and I was about to scream. I clapped both hands over my mouth, the letter fluttered to the ground.

'All right, Alice? Lunchtime?'

I bent down, picked the letter up to read it again, but I was going to be late, late for lunch, so I pushed it all back in – the letter, the jewellery, the scarf, the wrapping – held the packet by my side and walked in.

~

The meal started with watercress soup, which tasted like nothing, but watercress was bland, I thought, and sitting there, shot and drowned, I tried to eat it.

Henry, a violinist, not someone I knew well, about to take up a position in London, leant across the table.

'I say, Alice.'

Henry had gone to excellent schools, had a well-positioned family, he was a young man for whom life might go exactly as he wanted it, and I looked at him and hated him, but then he faded from view.

'You're very pale,' I heard him say softly. 'Are you all right?'

I said nothing. I was shot and drowned and drinking soup, but now he had spied the package.

'I say, Alice,' he began again. Not because he was a bad person, just someone who had not learnt the arts of restraint, empathy, kindness, love. He had seen a creature without its shell and was rushing towards it, eyes glittering, ten fingers extended. 'Have you had some bad news?'

I felt the soup rise from my stomach to the back of my mouth. I must have started retching because there was George taking off his brand new hat, the felt one with the feather, putting it under my mouth, then Hetty swooped in and I was lifted up, up, away from the table, back out into the sun, and I had my hands over my ears because someone was screaming. I watched from the college roof as I curled into a ball on the grass below, Hetty and George crouching beside me, trying to reach me, trying to get me to move.

27.

London, September, 1950

'Alice? Alice!'

People at the door, I did not hear them.

'Alice, Alice.'

Someone shaking my shoulder, I did not feel it.

'Alice, Alice,' right in my ear.

'What?' I mumbled. 'What?'

'You need to get up. You need to eat something. You need to drink something. Here.'

A man's voice next. Who was it? George? No, not George.

'Miss Murray, there's a gentleman here to see you.'

I opened an eye. Edward was standing by my bed. My God, what was he doing here? I looked around in confusion for Hetty and George. Where were they? But there was someone else. That new porter, Frank, he was in the room too. He had keys in his hand. He had telegrams in his other hand. He had let Edward into my room. Was I dreaming this? I closed my eyes.

'Miss Murray, try to get up, come on now. People are worried about you.'

So? I thought. What is worry?

'Do you know, Alice, the sunset this evening is quite beautiful.'

What nonsense was he speaking?

'It has turned Hyde Park entirely pink. I wish you could see it before it finishes. If you just get up for a minute and look out the window —'

Other voices. Hetty, George.

'What are you doing here? She's had a terrible shock. You shouldn't be here.'

'She shouldn't be left alone. She isn't well. People should be looking after her.'

I was so embarrassed I kept my eyes closed.

'Just give us a minute,' Hetty said, her voice carrying through. 'Let her get her clothes on, for goodness sake.'

I sat up. I was still wearing the clothes I'd had on three days earlier when I'd come in from the park. But I put another cardigan on, for form's sake, ran a brush through my hair. Hetty pulled up the covers on the bed; I sat on the edge.

'All right,' she called, 'she's ready now.'

In they came – Edward, Frank, George – in a row, as if they were about to perform a stage number, and I stood up and said, 'I'm terribly sorry,' and for some reason my voice now sounded exactly like Henry's (*I say, I say, I say*). 'I've received some very bad news from Australia.'

'Some very bad news,' Hetty repeated.

'There is absolutely no need for you to apologise,' George said, and he looked distressed, then looked away; and this I could not bear, this I could not see. I looked down at the bed.

'I've been told,' Edward said gravely, po-faced.

I looked at Frank and saw that he was still holding three telegrams in his hand. His face was pale, there were hollows beneath his eyes, the skin sagged from his cheeks. All of us in that room knew that death often arrived by telegram, or letter, and that it must be borne, it must be borne. And I could see that my reaction was alarming them, that it was foreign. I rubbed my face for a second, then looked at them and said, 'So where's this sunset then?'

And they looked as if the strings that drew them up so taut had been dropped. They drooped, someone pressed a hand to a forehead, another twisted a mouth into a smile, and all in a muddle they turned around to look out of the window, to see this spectacle of fading light, this last great blast of bright, bright colour. And I tried to forgive them for not seeing the blood pouring out of my ears, the water pouring from my mouth, for not realising that the pain this was causing me was so extreme it had stopped me thinking or seeing anything else; for not knowing the significance of two people dying in a faraway land, the magnitude of the bankruptcy of a small citrus block. For how could they know that an entire continent, an enormous jigsaw piece of the world, with all its crags and lakes and fault-lines, had just cracked from the earth's crust, slipped from its platform and sunk deep into the dark, dark ocean.

28.

London, September, 1950

I was standing in my room looking at its four walls, thinking they must have moved. They seemed to be at strange angles. I got onto the floor, slid under the bed. Lying there, I counted my money.

I had saved all year, enough for the trip home, but that was all.

I stayed under the bed for a long time; it was calm under there, in that dark space. I did not have to look at those walls and their alarming angles, or anything else.

Eventually I got up and looked at the calendar on the desk, counted the days I still had in the room. Death and bankruptcy notwithstanding, the college needed the room for a new student at the beginning of term.

I sat on the bed. I got back into it.

I was lying on my side. I was watching a grey sun rise sideways over London then sink back down.

~

When I got up I felt that I must walk, I must move, and that I must do this immediately.

I stood at the front door of the hall of residence, watching cars speed by. I had never noticed before how loud they were, how harsh the noise, how close they came to where I stood.

I walked along the pavement keeping as far from the road as I could, right next to the fence. My feet were not feeling the path in front of me. I turned and went back.

～

Bach, Bach, Bach. My fingers even, steady. The C minor Prelude, the running semi-quavers that went on and on, pummelling, pummelling. I played it without dynamics. Clean playing, immaculate. My fingers were moving, but I was not.

～

Hetty wanted to stay on until I'd got myself sorted out, as she put it, but she was expected in Edinburgh. I told her she must go.

When George left for Cardiff, he pressed a fiver into my hand just before leaping into the carriage, which in all likelihood was his entire savings; he was as poor as me. I ran after the train with the money in my fist, trying to give it back to him; he leant the top half of his body out of the window of the third-class carriage, blew me a kiss.

Stay over there, Dulcie's letter had said. *There is nothing left for you here. Go to your mother's relatives.*

Time and again I thought of that thin, critical woman in the house in York, her indifferent husband, that piano of theirs in the front room that could only be played on Sunday afternoons, and nicely, quietly, and I could not bear the thought. These were no real relatives of my mother.

～

He was there in the foyer a few days later. I knew he would be. I stood before him, not saying anything, and he looked down at me. Then, with two fingers, he reached out, raised my chin.

29.
London, October, 1950

He wanted me to stay in Oxford; there was a visitor's suite in his college, but I didn't think that was right (and my mother would have been appalled by the idea). Fiona, a flautist, had a cousin with a room in a boarding house in Shepherd's Bush; she'd just left for a couple of months in Spain. It had a single bed with a worn blanket, a nightstand that rocked whenever you put anything on it and a huge wardrobe still filled with her clothes. Most seemed to be made of tatty lace and other fancy fabrics. They looked second-hand but stitched cleverly into something else; they intimidated me. I kept my things in my suitcase. There was a kitchen along the corridor that was filthy, downstairs a bathroom with slimy tiles.

The Royal College allowed me to use a piano. I took the bus there every day to begin with, then walked to save the fare. I practised mechanically, automatically.

At night I couldn't sleep. I walked around the streets instead, tracing a geometric shape of the path I trod in my head so that I wouldn't get lost. I was so frightened of getting lost, this fear was like a force pulsing in my veins, but I persisted with that dark walk because being in the room was worse. In that room the air had been sucked from the world and I was trying to learn how to breathe something else.

~

He caught the train to Paddington on Saturday to collect me after my morning practice and took me back to Oxford. He said the change of scenery would be good for me. He was quiet in the train, serious; it was term time, I remember thinking he must have a lot of responsibilities.

In the summer Oxford had been green, gold, soft, dappled. Now it looked grey: the buildings were grey, the streets were grey, even the clothing people wore was grey and many held up umbrellas against a fine drizzle. At intersections bicycles piled up in groups then took off fast. Walking from the station I stepped into the street, not looking properly, and a man whizzing past on a bicycle yelled at me, not even a word, just a shout, very loud, and I jumped back, clutched Edward's arm.

He took me to a teashop down one of those narrow streets around the Radcliffe Camera. He ordered a pot, some bread and butter, then a plate of bun. I remember finding myself in that warm shop very hungry. I started to eat the bread and butter and then I couldn't stop; I started to laugh and I couldn't stop that either.

'You haven't been eating at all, have you?' he said. 'Or sleeping. I can tell. You'd better finish those,' pushing the plate of sliced bun towards me.

It was floury, that bun. I couldn't help but remember the groaning supper table after the summer concerts, that bounty of luxuries. What I would have given to have put a slice of chocolate cream cake into my mouth, or a luscious fruit salad. I ate the whole bun, drank a pot of tea, then almost fell asleep.

He got up; I got up too. He tucked my arm into his.

We went for a walk in Christ Church Meadow, my limbs still felt heavy, I was woozy. When it started to rain properly he held his umbrella over me and his left side was drenched. We weren't talking like we used to, he seemed to be thrumming with something that kept his lips tight. We went back to the college so he could change.

'Why don't you sit there?' he said, pointing to a brocade armchair in the sitting room.

I must have fallen asleep. I woke in a strange bed wearing all my clothes, except my shoes. I sat up, looked around; it was dark and I got up in a panic, threw back the heavy covers; I had to push them hard to free my legs, then I started searching frantically for my shoes.

'You're awake,' he said, coming into the room.

'I have to go,' I said. I had found my shoes tucked neatly beneath the bed. 'I can't believe I fell asleep. I'm very sorry.'

'You were exhausted.'

'What time is it?'

'It's eight o'clock. Not late.'

'I must go,' I said. 'I'm very sorry, Edward, I can't stay here. Please. Take me to the station.'

~

In London autumn had arrived too. Leaves lay in mounds on the pavement, in Hyde Park the trees were brown. A cold wind whipped across the lawns, whisked up the leaves, churned them around. The boarding house was very cold, the heating intermittent, tepid when it was there at all, and the system exuded a fetid odour, like rancid gravy. I slept in several layers of clothes.

I walked briskly to the College in the mornings to practise, hands in my pockets, head down. John, the porter, beckoned to me one morning. He'd heard what had happened, why I was still there. How are you? he said, concerned. Oh, I'm fine, John, as good as can be expected, and he looked pleased with that; I remember thinking that I'd said the right thing. He told me that if I ever had trouble finding a room to practise in I should just ask him.

I'd linger in the room after I finished playing. I'd take a book with me and sit on the floor, propped against the wall, then lie down and sleep. I spent whole days in that room, beside the piano, sustained by a bit of cheese and bread, some water from the washroom, drunk from cupped hands.

Edward took me to a teashop again and ordered more this time. He pushed plates of bland pastries in front of me without saying anything. I was embarrassed by my appetite. He ate little, if anything. When I spoke he barely answered, and he often looked out of the window.

We went punting, Edward standing at the end of the narrow boat, plunging the pole into the water, wrenching it out again. He manoeuvred the thing down the river in a straight, determined course, and all around us were boats of happy, excited students, laughing and talking, trailing their hands in the water. When we returned to the boat ramp he helped me out, wiped his hands on his handkerchief and said, 'That is how punting is done.'

On Broad Street we passed the Sheldonian Theatre and he pointed to it, I nodded. We stepped into a second-hand bookshop and he walked straight through it to a room at the back that was filled with shelves of old sheet music. There were no labels, just stack upon stack of browning, curling scores. He began pulling things off the shelves indiscriminately.

'You'll need to start your own library,' he said, giving the scores to me. I had my arms outstretched like a tray for him to place them on, 'now you've left the Royal College.'

I had nowhere to keep them; he had them delivered to his college.

The train was late that night and I could tell he was very annoyed by this, hands gripped behind his back, not saying anything, jerking his head now and again to look down the line. You go, I said finally. You don't need to wait. He stayed until it came, but he was obviously put out. I knew he thought I should stay in Oxford.

The next time we planned a visit he said on the phone that I would need to meet him at the college, he couldn't collect me from the station; and I said, of course, that was fine. When I asked for him at the college lodge it was a while before he came down.

The week after that he sent a message to the lodge to ask me to wait for him at the teashop. I sat in a window seat, spinning out a pot of tea. Finally I spotted him walking down the road. I felt limp with relief; I'd started to think he wasn't going to come at all. Everyone had left me, it seemed, except him.

Sometimes I felt like I was not entirely present during this time. Another person, not I, was the one down there operating within the world – catching trains, talking. The following week we sat in a tavern and he bought me an ale, and as I sipped it I was hardly in that seat, I had gone somewhere else, perhaps to those high clouds above the building I had glimpsed before we stepped in, or maybe I'd kept walking down the road outside the tavern, my figure slowly receding.

Edward talked about leaving home very young for boarding school, and not feeling a thing when it had happened, just watching one of the dogs, an old brown and white spaniel, bow its head, then slowly walk back into the big house. He had spoken only a little of his childhood before. He told me about never really knowing his parents except as two tall, handsome figures in a grand drawing room; being paraded in front of them by different nannies when he was young, and being asked questions by them. He did not seem to remember a single act of kindness from these people. He liked school, he said; he was very good at it. He liked university too; he was even better at that. He won a lot of prizes. Discovering economics was like a calling, being able to explain all those complicated, important things with just a few grand theories, lines and numbers. He told me about an older brother he had not seen since adolescence, who was somewhere in America. 'Left as soon as he could.'

'You didn't want to leave?' I said.

And he said, 'I didn't feel the need.'

I thought of my figure walking down the street, disappearing, and thought: because he already had. He told me about an old aunt in Surrey whom he disliked intensely; she sounded like his mother, now dead. He said that when his parents died he'd felt nothing, that the funerals were tiresome, a burden to attend, and that his older brother hadn't even bothered. And when he told me all this I knew there must be more along these lines, and that what he was not saying was worse.

I remember that he did not look at me much, but rather stared straight ahead, or at his ale; he didn't ask me any questions. He reached across the table, took my hand.

After this he took me to a shop and bought me clothing; it was the most new clothing I'd ever owned. I walked out wearing a new dress, a new coat, a new hat, new stockings, a new pair of shoes, an entirely new outfit, and with more of everything in the parcels he and I were carrying. As we were walking back up the High Street two colleagues of his stopped us, separately, and greeted us, and both times he introduced me as Miss Alice Murray, and their faces remained expressionless while their eyes travelled all over me.

He walked me to the station that day for the first time in a while, saw me onto the train with all the bags, settled me into a seat. I remember my body being jostled about by the movement of the train, rattled along. I closed my eyes. Somehow I got myself and those parcels back to the room in Shepherd's Bush.

~

Walking in London in the dark, I wanted to go further afield, out of the city, to the hills, the plains, which must have existed out there somewhere. But I was too scared, I kept looping around the same familiar streets. I felt numb. Sounds

100

were not what they were before; they were muffled like echoes. My hands were always cold; flesh was cold. Smells did not exist either, not really, although one night I was sure I smelt the river, and it was a bad smell, awful, there was something rotting in it, and I saw it before me, a mass of brownish water coming at me, over my head, and I could not breathe. And this pain, this terrible pain that I had not yet glimpsed or caught the shape of, was everywhere but not upon me. It was as if I were holding it out in front of me with two bowed arms, and walking, walking in these loopy circles.

~

Papers arrived from Australia. I showed them to Edward, who said he would show them to his lawyer. After eating in the tavern we went to the college – he had to collect a book – and I waited for him again on the brocade seat and fell asleep, and this time when I woke in the bed it was morning. He was sitting very upright in a chair at the foot of the bed making notes in a periodical, and when I saw him I began to cry, for where was I? He came over, sat next to me and he said, 'There, there. It will all be all right,' patting my leg through the bed cover.

He was not looking at my face, and the words sounded wooden, and I knew he did not think they were true either, and that they never would be, and I was relieved by that because at least someone else had an understanding of this darkness, this terrible truth – that everything was not fine, and this did not have to be explained, apologised for, excused or denied.

~

When he proposed again it was very different from the first time. We were in the teashop and I had just said I should probably set off for the station. His voice was business-like, but he leant towards me and took both my hands, and I remember feeling his shaking. I accepted without flourish. Good, he said, and he leant right back in his seat as if he could relax for just a moment.

I didn't hear from him after that for several days. I thought he must have changed his mind. So I got on the train to Oxford one morning and went up to his room in the college.

'Hello,' I said at the door. He looked very surprised, and not at all pleased. 'Can I come in?'

He stood up, running a hand through his hair. 'Yes, do,' he said eventually.

I looked around the room: papers in neat piles on his desk, pens lined up, the chair pushed in.

'Working hard?' I said.

'Always working hard.'

'What are you working on?'

He didn't answer that. I went to him, reached up, put my arms around his neck.

'Keen for some distraction?' I said.

'Yes,' his smile perfunctory. 'Then I'll need to get back to it, unfortunately. You oughtn't to have come all this way. You've wasted the money of a ticket.'

Oh, don't be so ridiculous! I wanted to cry out. We're about to be married!

The world had changed around me. I had experienced a great loss, everyone else had gone, and I was scared; I needed someone to hold onto. That is what I thought.

30.

London, October, 1950

'Hamish Residence,' Hetty said.

'It's me. Alice.'

'Oh my god. How are you?'

'Oh, well, I'm —'

'A friend,' she called out, her voice muffled, her hand over the receiver. 'A friend,' louder. 'I'll just be a minute. No, stay there. No, please stay seated, I'll be half a minute.' And then she was back. 'Sorry.'

'How are you?'

'Terrible. I'm counting the days.'

'Oh, Hetty. I'm sorry.'

'*You're* sorry. What about you? How are *you*?'

And when I hesitated, then said, 'I'm fine,' she said, 'Where are you living?'

I told her about the room Fiona had found me. 'I don't know what I would have done without it.'

'You would have worked out something.'

'I'm not sure . . . I've been —'

'It's a difficult time.'

'Hetty, I'm marrying Edward.'

Silence at the other end of the line, and then a bang and a scream, but there was something wrong with the way it sounded, with its timbre, as if there were something quite different beneath it. 'Damn! Just a second —' a loud clatter of the receiver, footsteps walking quickly, then exclamations.

103

After a long time footsteps came back to the phone. 'I'm sorry, Alice.'

'Everything all right?'

'She fell. She's a damned idiot. I told her not to get up. She did it deliberately, she does this sort of thing. Because I was talking to you. She's barking mad. And now we'll all be dancing around her, around the clock, and I'll be up again all night. What about Australia?'

'What? Oh. Well . . .' and I looked outside the phone box to the streetscape of London, the dry brown leaves whisked about by the wind, everyone with their hands in their pockets, heads down. 'I can't go back, Hetty. It's not just that there's nowhere to live now, nothing to live on, it's . . .'

'That they're gone.'

'Yes.'

'But surely there must be —'

'Look, this is what I've decided.'

'Really?'

I started to cry.

'What about London?' she said. 'Keep the room.'

'She's coming back.'

'Share it with her.'

'I'm sure she'd love that.'

'Get another room.'

And eat what? I wanted to say. And keep warm – how? And even if I ate the walls and dressed myself in the curtains, how to be a concert pianist then? How? Sneak around the Royal College pretending I had never left? Leap up on stage during a concert?

These people, I thought, these people with their families and their means, however meagre, and their futures like smooth, cleared roads laid out in front of them, these people who know nothing of what it is to have nothing.

'I have no money. I mean none, Hetty. There's nothing.'

'Really nothing?'

'Really.'

'Christ.'

'Quite.'

Silence.

'Are you practising?' I asked her.

'A bit. I used to put the mute on and do it while she listened to her wireless programs, but that didn't last long. Then I knitted her some earmuffs and I slip them on her when she's sleeping, which is quite a lot, and get going in the attic. You should see these things I made her, all fluffy, multi-coloured. And when I'm doing all this I sometimes think: who is the madwoman here, exactly?'

'Funny.'

'And you?'

'They let me use a room at the college. I've been playing a lot.'

'I'm glad to hear it. You're brilliant, Alice. Maybe you could . . .'

'What?'

'Maybe teach?'

'Teach?'

'At a school?'

'Like a boarding school? I'd rather shoot myself.'

'I know.'

'I want to perform. I want to be a concert pianist.'

'I know. You have to. We all knew that; we all know that.'

Another pause.

'Alice, is he still . . . odd?'

'What do you mean?'

Silence.

'He's been very good to me,' I said. 'He buys me tea and distracts me with walks and galleries, even though he's very busy with teaching and so on ... especially when I wasn't very ... I mean ...'

'Oh, Alice.'

We're in love; I didn't say it. We've grown close; I didn't say that either.

'I think I'd like a family of my own one day,' I said quietly, and that was true. Perhaps I had started to have an inkling of how significant love was, giving it as much as getting it. That there was something beyond ourselves, as individuals, that really mattered. But the instinct was also immediate. I didn't want to feel like this anymore, so alone and with no home, so frightened; I couldn't feel like this anymore.

'When's the wedding?' Hetty said, a new hardness in her tone. 'I'll see if I can get there for it.'

'You don't have to. It wasn't why I was calling,' although it half was, and then the phone started beeping and I had to put more money in, and the coins clunked down, got swallowed up, the pile in front of me diminishing, but she couldn't see this, of course.

'It's very hard to get away from this asylum,' she was saying. 'I mean, I leave her for literally one minute and she's done something ridiculous, fallen on her bloody head, or something. Speaking of which, I should go; you can probably hear that noise, that's her version of moaning, if you can believe it, variations on a theme of —'

'Yes.'

'Maybe for just a day or two I could get my sister to ... Listen, what's the date of the wedding?'

~

She did make it in the end. She arrived in London in a great rush the day before, excited to be there, and the joy of seeing her, Hetty, at the station in her old hat, her brown coat, her way

106

of talking: look at you, she kept saying, look at you with your posh clothes and your new 'do, because by then I'd had my hair waved. She gave me a lace nightdress with little ribbons in bows on the shoulders.

31.

Oxford, October, 1950

The wedding was at the registry office on a Friday. Hetty
was a witness, and one of Edward's colleagues, a man with
a moustache, I don't remember his name. The four of us had
lunch afterwards in the dining room of the Randolph Hotel,
trout scattered with almonds floating in a pale lemon sauce; it
tasted of nothing. When we finished we stood outside on the
pavement talking.

There was a chilly wind that day that snapped our skirts
around our legs, threw back jackets. I was holding onto my hat,
telling Hetty I would take her to the station; I didn't want her
to go, wanted to keep her close, and when the taxi came I was
about to get in beside her but Edward held my arm and said, No,
we need to get back, and he picked up my bags and we went to
the house in North Oxford.

It was furnished by then, of course. There were fancy hooks
inside the door for coats and hats, a phone table in the hall with
a built-in chair. He put my suitcase down inside the door.

'Why don't you wait in there,' he said, pointing to the front
room, and he walked past me into another room. It was what
he used to say when we went to his rooms in the college. What
was he up to? The Steinway was still in the front room, but
now there was a chaise longue, armchairs, some pictures on the
walls – a still-life, a farm with a plough. Everything looked
antique, although genuine or reproduction I wasn't sure. I stood
at the window then sat on the edge of the chaise longue.

I had mostly spoken to Hetty during lunch, he had spoken to his colleague; in the taxi we hadn't talked at all. He was probably tired. I was tired.

'Why don't you make some tea,' he said, coming in. 'The woman stocked the kitchen.'

The woman?

'Housekeeper,' he said. 'I dismissed her yesterday,' and then he left again.

I went down to the kitchen, which smelt like bleach, as if it had been swabbed, and I found what I needed, made the tea, sat at the kitchen table watching the steam coil out of the spout. The kitchen was very cold; it was always cold in that room.

I went up the hall and poked my head around the doorframe. It was a big room, his study, with floor to ceiling bookshelves in dark wood, the volumes lined up row upon row. The huge desk, also dark wood, faced the door. There was a window behind it, Edward's head and torso a dark shape in front of it.

'Tea's made.'

Papers in front of him; he was working.

'Why don't you unpack,' he said in a cool voice, not looking up. 'You'll find a chest of drawers in the bedroom. Then we can have some supper. She left some food in the pantry.'

I walked quietly up the stairs with my suitcase. The chest of drawers was small and I needed to hang things, but the wardrobe was full of his clothes (immaculately laundered, facing all the same way). I arranged my things in the drawers; I would sort out the wardrobe situation later. I changed into a warm skirt and jumper, some thick stockings. I looked around. There was the big double bed, made with tightly pulled linen.

I went back downstairs, found half a loaf of brown bread, some milk, eggs. We ate in the kitchen, and while we were eating it was as if he were concentrating hard on something else, something in his head, perhaps, or a sound outside on the street.

'You must be very busy,' I said.

'Yes,' he said.

'How many weeks of term are left?'

'A few. But it's always busy.'

I was starting to wonder if I had done something wrong. I took our empty plates to the sink, washed them, put them on the rack, as if this were all normal, as if I had done it all before, as if the sink were already as familiar as my own hand, and when he was about to get up I turned around and said, 'Is something wrong, Edward?'

'No.'

'Are you feeling all right?'

'Yes. Why do you ask?'

'You're very quiet.'

And then he looked at me and he said, 'Nothing is wrong. We are married. This is a relationship, and relationships, you will soon find, work best when certain arrangements are understood. Like all relationships this involves an exchange. You will need to adapt to the fact that I work most of the time. At the moment I am doing more work than usual in order to make up for the time you wanted me to spend with you at the start of term and over the summer. Married life is completely different to courting, an entirely different relationship. As a wife you will, of course, be occupied very soon with your own tasks.' He took a last swig of tea, put the cup down on the table, and went back into his study. 'Why don't you play something on that piano?' he called from inside the room.

His summary had left me breathless. I looked out at the dark garden and thought, I am going to laugh, I really am, and where is Hetty or George or Mary or Hilary to laugh with me? At the same time, I was feeling some horrible thing shift around inside me. I felt it had a shape or, rather, that it had taken the shape of the inside of my body. It distracted me, that shape, that mass of darkness, it weighed me down, it made me slow and quiet, it made me want to lie down and go to sleep. It stopped me from running after him, hammering on the door and saying, How ridiculous. Take that back. You sit down and discuss this with me or I'm leaving at once. I did none of that. Instead I thought this speech was not unlike one of his speeches about the buildings and sights he had shown me in Oxford. It was something that could be looked at, but could be walked away from.

That night I got into bed wearing the nightdress Hetty had given me. He came up the stairs, went into the bathroom, emerged wearing pyjamas and turned out the light. Then he took off his pyjamas and got into bed. He started kissing me, but it was different from those times in the park – he was rushed, and rougher, and then he stopped kissing me, got on top of me and started pushing the nightdress up. The heaviness of him was very surprising, I remember it like yesterday. I reached up, put my palm on his cheek, tried to kiss him again, but he ignored that, got the nightdress up all the way and pushed himself into me, and kept pushing hard. When he finished he rolled off, lay there panting, then got out of bed.

I heard water running in the bathroom. I stayed very still. Then I sat up and turned on the bedside light. He came back in, stepped into his pyjama pants and buttoned up the shirt, sitting on the edge of the bed with his back to me. He got under the covers and said goodnight. I turned off the light and lay in the dark, looking at the slit of light at the bottom of the window, which the curtain did not cover entirely.

All the concern he had expressed about me, the way he had looked after me, complimented and encouraged me; not to mention the words spoken that morning. It was as if all that were a mask, a chimera, and this disregard, this contempt, was

111

what lay beneath. Or else it had been an aberration, an anomaly so awful it was best forgotten.

I moved over in the bed, close to the edge, and lay there for a long time, my heart beating, forgetting, drawing ever further away.

32.

Oxford, October, 1950

The next morning he got up and left while it was still dark. I lay in the bed pretending to be asleep. When I heard the front door close and everything went quiet, I got up and went down to the kitchen to make a pot of tea. A navy cotton apron was hanging on the hook on the back of the kitchen door. I put it on and started cleaning; I wiped the glass in the windows until it squeaked, pushed a cloth across a floor until it shone back at me.

I can see now why I was drawn to the catharsis of a clean surface, of limbs moving strong and fast. The claim of command, however transitory and unreal, that a mop can bring. Here I was, newly married. I wiped and wiped; swish, swish. Then I washed myself fastidiously, got dressed, did my hair and face and sat down at the piano. And I played. My god, how I played. I played all the pieces I knew, one after the other. Afterwards I was myself again; it helped me breathe.

I looked around the house, examining it. Then I put on my coat and walked up the street on one side, and back down the other, taking it all in.

When he came back in the evening I told him that it was a good piano. He nodded. Then I said that I had done some cleaning; we were standing in the front room at the time and he looked around and, with a half-smile on his face, he said, 'What about that?' pointing to the mantelpiece.

I looked at the mantelpiece but I saw nothing.

'There,' he said, pointing at it again. I still couldn't see anything. 'There!' a little louder, 'You've missed a spot, see?' And he went close to it and pointed again. I looked at it, and back at him, and I saw a flash of something terrible, which I could not yet name, but it frightened me.

'You're blind,' he said, and he walked out.

33.
Oxford, October, 1950

The night after, he came home in the evening and walked straight down to the kitchen, where I was standing at the stove.

'Is dinner ready?' he said.

'Hello. Not yet. Soon, though. Are you hungry?'

'Dinner needs to be ready at seven.'

'Oh. Why?'

But he'd left the room.

When it was ready I called him and he sat at the table, looked at the food in front of him, his face expressionless. He started to eat. When about half the food was gone, he put down his cutlery.

'You do realise,' he said, 'that this is quite disgusting?'

I looked down at the food, shocked. I had almost finished mine. It was a basic meal, I can't remember what it was, but it was all right, I thought.

He ate some more, pushed back the plate and left the table.

I found this sort of behaviour unfathomable. The only way I could understand it was to assume that he was used to the rules and fare of High Table. I hadn't done much cooking; I'd spent most of my life in institutions too. Maybe I still had a lot to learn, but I thought that what I cooked wasn't bad.

He was particular about a lot of things, it turned out. How they were to be done, how they were to look. He wanted his shirt to be ironed in a specific way and ended up writing it down for me. And if there was a wrinkle it had to be done again.

'Edward,' I laughed, when he pointed out a crease for the first time. 'You're being ridiculous.'

'I think you'll find,' he said, entirely serious, 'that the idea of wearing that thing you've ruined is ridiculous. You'll have to do it again.'

His face had a rigid look, that intense glare.

And he continued finding fault. The cleaning, for example: when he came in, if he was in a bad mood (I quickly realised there was a correlation) he would immediately inspect something, the kitchen floor, say, and point out where there was dirt or disarray. Once, he opened the cutlery drawer and saw that I had rearranged it. This enraged him.

'This,' he hissed, taking up all the forks in one hand, the knives in the other, clattering them back into different places, 'is where the forks go!'

I didn't say anything. I had moved the cutlery because it was what I'd seen at home, what made sense to me every time I washed them, dried them, put them away.

'Are you listening to me?' he said.

I turned to look at him, said nothing.

'*Are you listening to me?*' he roared, and he slammed his fist down on the bench over the drawer.

I jumped, frightened.

'All right,' I said, in a voice as mild as I could make it, 'all right.'

He ended up writing me a list that detailed all the housekeeping tasks, how and when they should be done, and the time each task should take. The things I felt about this officious document. Of course he didn't have any idea how to do those jobs either, so he often overestimated the times considerably. I completed them as quickly as I could and spent the rest of my time doing what I wanted, then braced myself for his return in the evening.

As his lectures on housekeeping got longer, I learnt to look

116

as though I was listening. I had a way of angling my head, my body, positioning my eyes, when in actual fact I wasn't taking in a word, I was listening to music in my head, or a conversation I was having with someone, or a letter I was writing. Sometimes a few words found their way through: stupid, he would say, or slovenly, or hopeless. But I would blot it all out.

Twice a week he didn't come home in the evenings because he dined in Hall. This was a relief. But it wasn't supposed to be what you felt when you were just married, was it?

I wrote letters but didn't send them. To Hetty, to my mother, to God. I didn't know who to ask. Was this behaviour normal, to be expected? Would he settle down once we had both got used to things? Was I doing something wrong? He seemed to be very anxious about his work. He would come home obviously preoccupied, then sit in his study at his desk for most of the night, pulling at his hair.

At the time, he was pioneering a radical form of laissez-faire economics, but it wasn't going as well as he wanted and some of his manuscripts were being rejected by journals and publishers. In those post-war years of high growth and low unemployment everyone was Keynesian. He did have some colleagues who championed his work, but at this stage they were mostly subordinates. He'd studied with Friedrich Hayek at the London School of Economics and spent some time in Cambridge (where the department was evenly divided, for and against Keynesianism). He visited Cambridge a few years later when Milton Friedman had come out from Chicago. But he had fallen out with Hayek (over the term 'conserva-tism': Edward embraced it, Hayek did not) and was scathing of Friedman, who moved between bureaucracy and academia, honing his ideas. Edward remained in academia and felt he was far superior. He thought he had come up with a radical free-market approach to economics that amounted to a whole life philosophy, and people were simply not recognising its brilliance. He used to tell me about it. He would beckon me into his study when he was in a favourable mood and talk to me about it, mostly in technical terms that I did not understand, but sometimes in ways that I did, and I remember thinking: this doesn't sound right to me. Once, he showed me a page of graphs, one axis on top of the other, and he pointed to them and said, 'The whole world, and everything in it, is explained by that.'

I passed his study one day and he was standing by the desk reading a letter. He was holding it in both hands, had his head right up close to it. When he finished I noticed that his hands were shaking. Then he placed the letter down on the desk and put both hands over his face. I nearly went to him then, but suddenly he swung around and with huge movements swept everything from the desk onto the floor, including a cup of tea, which threw a brown stain right across the carpet. I must have started because his head whipped around. Just in time I stepped out of view and went straight upstairs. I found the letter later when he was out: another manuscript had been rejected. I picked up the pieces of broken china, scrubbed the tea from the carpet.

~

I played the piano a lot. After I finished the housework I went straight to it. Oh, that Steinway, it was a glorious piano. It was new. I had no idea how he had come by it.

After my practice I'd go for a walk in Port Meadow, a large area of open common land bordered on one side by the River Thames. I'd walk out of the bottom of North Oxford, into Jericho, then up Walton Well Road to the entrance; it took me no time at all to find it. At that time of year Port Meadow was a wet expanse (it had a tendency to flood; sometimes in winter it even iced over and people skated on it). Horse, cattle and geese grazed upon it. I would walk out into the middle and look up at the sky, which was so high, vast and grey. Then I'd return to the house in time to cook the dinner.

(I fantasised about these walks later. What if I'd kept walking all the way through the meadow instead of turning back, out into Wolvercote, where I'd eat dinner at the Trout, chowder and ale, perhaps, then get on a bus, and then a train, a boat. Or what if I'd said hello to the gypsies who camped in the meadow rather than ignored and avoided them; what if I'd gone right up to them and started a conversation and they'd invited me to join them and I'd sneaked out at dawn the next day and become a traveller, leaving Oxford at the age of twenty, a big sun rising over the spires, making the ice shine on the road.)

I kept trying with the cooking, the dinners. They seemed to me to be important, more so than the state of the floor, or the laundry. Coming together at the end of the day, sharing a meal. But it was not only that. Sometimes after dinner he'd asked me to play for him. We'd walk up to the front room together, he'd pour himself a snifter from the tray in the corner, sit down in one of the new armchairs. He would sit listening, sipping, and when I finished he would nod and say something like, 'Thank you, that was very nice,' then get up and go into the study. They were quite beautiful to me, those moments.

I read the little recipe books over and over, I studied them. Sometimes I shortened my walk at the end of the day to cook something more complicated (I never shortened my practice). There wasn't much interesting food back then to work with, and it wasn't only that there was still rationing and restrictions and shortages, it was also because he was so mean with the money. He would count out the housekeeping on a Monday morning and shove it across the table at me, muttering, Bring me the receipts.

One day I decided to try a dish I knew he liked. He'd mentioned it once or twice in the summer when we'd had those glorious picnics in the South Park. Maybe, I thought, I could make a dish so well he could not fail to enjoy it, and he would be happy; I would make him happy. The ingredients took up most of the week's housekeeping. I took all day to prepare it. I put a lace cloth I'd found folded at the back of the linen cupboard on the table, and two crystal candlesticks, which the man with the moustache had given us as a wedding present. Then I went out and spent another penny on two tall white tapered candles at a little store on Walton Street. I began to feel a small fizz of anticipation. I could picture in detail what a successful evening meal for a newlywed couple looked like – it was familiar to me, even though I'd never had one.

When he came home and saw all this, his eyes narrowed and he said, 'What is this?'

'Dinner.'

'Is it ready?'

'Not quite.' It wasn't yet six forty-five; the dish was still in the oven.

Without saying anything, he went into the study.

'It's ready,' I said at the door when the time came (seven precisely).

'I'm busy now, it will have to wait.'

I stood there, flabbergasted. Then I started to panic, for what was I to do with the meat? How did you keep it warm without continuing to cook it?

In the end I took the food out of the oven, served it up on the plates and, keeping the oven on, put them on top of the stove, where they would stay warm.

When he came in I put the plates on the table, he looked at

120

the food for a second and started to eat. At this point he would usually say something derogatory, but he said nothing that night, not for the entire meal. He finished, wiped his mouth, pushed his chair back and went back into the study.

I took the dishes slowly to the sink and stood there thinking, What on earth am I going to do for meals for the rest of the week? Thinking, in another place, in another time, there could be another couple like this, and later in the evening when the dishes were done, she would sit in a chair in the front room looking at the window, and he would appear at the door with two cups of tea, one for her, one for him. They would sit beside each other, sipping in silence. Then he would get down on his knees before her, lay his head in her lap and start to weep, and he would beg forgiveness and plead with her to play something for him. And when she acquiesced and went to the piano he would listen attentively, as if his life depended on it.

I washed the dishes, wiped down the stove-top.

It was no good, I thought, all these stories I made up in my head; they were no good.

34.

Oxford, November, 1950

I left not long after. I packed my things after he went to work one morning, walked to the station, the small amount of housekeeping money that remained for the week jangling in my coat pocket.

I watched the trains come and go. The station guard came over to me and asked if he could assist with anything. No, thank you, I said primly, I'll just sit here for now, if that's all right with you, and he went away. No one bothered me after that; it was almost as if they were used to such a thing. I paid tuppence for a cup of tea, a penny to use the lavatory. I sat watching the drama of people arriving and departing, trying to work out what to do. At one point I started to think about Australia, being on that pier in Tilbury, stepping onto the boat, feeling the tug of it as it sailed away from the shore, and then the buoyancy of the ocean.

I don't know how he knew where to find me. That evening he walked onto the platform and stood there looking at the tracks. When I didn't move he came over and picked up the suitcase. There wasn't anger in his gesture, neither was there tenderness, it was matter of fact, as if this were yet another task in a long day. Wordlessly, I stood up, followed him out of the station and into a taxi.

When we were in the taxi he reached over and took my hand. I started to cry then. At the house he opened the front door, put my suitcase down at the bottom of the stairs, took out a hanky, held my chin in one hand and carefully wiped my cheeks. Then he kissed me on the forehead. He said, I have made a very big mess of things. I have really ruined them. Down here, he said, pointing down the hall.

I went into the kitchen and saw that he'd been trying to cook some chops, and that he had let the potatoes boil dry on the stove. I picked up the saucepan of burnt potatoes, but he said, No, I'll do it, you do some practice, and my heart leapt. I went to the piano and started to play, although I was still listening to the sounds coming from the kitchen.

He told me to come. He had set the kitchen table with the plates of food: wilted cabbage, some nearly raw sticks of neatly sliced carrot and the cold, singed chops. We ate it all; it was late by then. I got up from the table, picked up the plates, he went into the study.

That night he read in bed before going to sleep, and when the lights were off he reached over, found my hand and held it for a while, then he moved his body towards me and held me in his arms in the dark.

The next evening there were no cruel comments about the house or the meal.

It took about a week for it to all start again.

Perhaps we could call this part 'the honeymoon'.

35.

Oxford, November, 1950

I was running a damp cloth slowly over a windowsill. I was thinking, for a moment, that it was not unlike practising scales.

'It's not good enough,' he'd said the night before. 'It just won't do. It doesn't measure up.'

He'd come home late; his face was grey. The mutton stew had been simmering on the stove too long and had dried out, but I served it anyway because it was all there was.

'You look tired,' I said. 'You must have been working very hard.'

He didn't answer. He looked at the stew, tasted it, threw down his fork, which skittered, tines up, across the table towards me.

'Inedible,' he said. 'And what have you done with your hair? It looks peculiar.' He reached across, picked up the fork, took another mouthful. 'Disgusting,' he said, and he picked up the plate, held it for a second then dropped it. It broke into pieces on the floor, although the stew, strangely, stayed in the same shape.

'Clean that up,' he said, pointing to it. I sat there looking down at the mess. Jumped slightly when I heard the front door bang.

When he came in the next evening for dinner I did not speak. I served him something, quietly. He ate carefully. Then he looked up at me and said, 'This is nice. What is it?'

'It's a chop with roast onions, mashed potato and gravy.'

'Very nice. Thank you.'

I was speechless. I remember looking at the meal, making a quick note of the various things I'd done, wondering what had made the difference. I thought as I ate: yes, I suppose it is quite nice. I remember realising my entire body had been clenched. I sat up a little, swallowed another mouthful.

I became increasingly nervous when I cooked the dinner. This exhibited itself first in a fluttering in my stomach, which I mistook for hunger. But I was slightly short of breath too, my heart would race, my hands shake. Jesus, Alice, I thought, pull yourself together. It's a clutch of carrots boiling, for goodness sake.

I tested them gingerly with a fork. I tested them again, but gently, so that I did not break them, ruin their shape. I was making sure they were cooked just right. I was perfecting them. (Again, a bit like doing scales, I thought.)

I didn't rush through the housekeeping anymore; once, I spent the whole morning on my hands and knees polishing the floorboards in the hall so they were perfect. When he came in that evening, I made sure I was at it again.

'Working hard, I see,' walking past me into the study. Then: 'Come here.'

I sat down in front of the desk, careful not to move or touch anything. He told me that one of his papers was to be published in a prestigious journal; I congratulated him. He told me the reasons he detested a colleague whose office was next to his. Why the man should be sacked; how he was going to make sure this happened. Then he took me out to dinner. The night after, he was horrid again. I realised that it had been a long time since he'd asked me to play the piano.

~

He yells at me and says harsh things. He smashes plates. He is particularly, overly particular. He used a glove on a shelf to see if I had dusted it properly.

I played Prokofiev today, the Toccata. You should have heard it. I thought the keys were going to bruise or singe, my hands beat them so hard and fast. You should have heard the ring of that piano, the reverberation of those strings. It's a Steinway, did I tell you? When I sit on the chaise longue sometimes, resting between playing, it looks like a bull readying itself to charge.

I continued to address them; I never sent them.

36.

Oxford, December, 1950

How long can a pianist play to an empty room? To the view of a quiet street? It took about a month until I could do it no more. And then I waited. I waited for a favourable mood. I prayed for something good to happen in the editorial offices of economics and political journals around the country, around the world. I prayed for Edward Haywood to be feted, at least momentarily.

In he came one evening, and he was whistling. Nothing recognisable, but still.

'Dinner's ready.'

'Good,' and by some stroke of luck I'd made that chop and roast onion dish again. He sat down; he even smiled when he saw it. He tasted it. 'Delicious.'

It was as if I couldn't help it, the feeling I got then, responding to compliments, still performing for applause, examining its timbre. As he ate he told me about his victory at work that day.

'Edward,' I said, when his stomach was surely full. My hands were shaking again. 'I'm wondering if you might be able to introduce me to some other musicians in Oxford.'

'Why would I do that?'

'Well ... I would like to start doing some concerts. Start to get going with things.'

'Really,' he said. 'Start to get going with things.'

'Yes,' thinking that already this didn't sound good. I took a sip of water, tried to calm myself.

'Why do you want to do that?'

'Well,' astonished I needed to spell it out, 'as I said, I would like to get on with my musical career.'

'I don't know any musicians. I only know economists.'

'What about the other people who ran the Summer School?'

'None of them know anything about music, I can assure you. Holding that thing was just for the money it brought into the college; we'd had a lean year.'

'But all those maestros . . .'

'Visitors. Obviously,' he snapped, and now he was frowning deeply.

I knew that I should stop now, but this was too important. I kept going. I tried to slow my breathing, the way I did before a recital, except that I'd never been this nervous before performing.

'I was also thinking you might be able to help me arrange an introductory recital in the Holywell Music Room,' and looking at his face I said quickly, 'or even a room in your college.'

He got up suddenly, the chair leapt back, hit the floor.

'And why would I want to do that?' Glaring down at me.

And then I was going to kill him. I was going to get the knife from his plate, smeared with that blasted gravy, and plunge it into his heart. Instead I said, 'I am a pianist.'

'What?'

'I am a pianist.'

He glanced down at his plate, peered at the stove to see if there was any left, and then he went back to work.

I sat there for a long time, thinking, recovering.

I decided that I wouldn't let his attitude matter, that I would do it all myself. I would find out from other women in this place how things worked, wives of people like Edward, who were sure to know. I needed some friends. I needed a lot of things.

37.
Oxford, October 10th, 2005

Chopin, the 'Revolutionary Étude', was pouring into the house. It was a deluge, a flood. I was spinning down the stairs, a dervish in the air. Before I reached the ground floor it had stopped.

I stood in the front room feeling sick and lay down on the floor. I wondered if I had entered that stage in the process of starvation when the body starts to eat its own organs. So far the hands and ears had gone, probably also the mouth. What was next? Ah yes, I should have guessed, that feeble throbbing, a faint flick; the heart was next, the heart, of course.

The cold was immense and it was everywhere, it was like wet cement poured on top of me; the floor was painfully hard, pressing itself up into me. I got myself slowly upright, shuffled into the library.

Lighting a fire took energy, but energy was given back, for just a bit, and I progressed. Gone now was his entire oeuvre on rational expectations and their applications (four-and-a-half shelves; all the scholars had wanted them). Gone were the three shelves of government reports (and what a thrill it was to see those coats of arms on the covers flare up before dissolving). No, it was not too hard to sit in front of a fire burning books and papers about conservative economics. Filing the music was hard. That's what was killing me. Lifting those scores. Writing the labels. Tucking them into the file boxes. You'd never believe the energy this took. And making the phone calls, of course.

I wished I could have found my Chopin book then and looked at that étude. I remembered seeing a small child play it once in a concert hall at the Royal College, some startling prodigy, her little body so animated, so definitive at the piano.

I went out to the phone. It felt as if my body were slightly in front of me, then behind me, then below me, then above me. Battling with the very air I breathed. I was going to do it. I cleared my throat, called the number, but as soon as he answered I hung up. I sat in the hall, smelling smoke.

38.

Oxford, December, 1950

Since marrying Edward I had not been to his college. At that time all the dons were men. Wives, along with other members of the public, were allowed to enter the college grounds (except at times when they would disturb the scholars, such as before exams) but were not allowed to attend college meals or enter the common rooms. Once, a special dinner was held for Fellows, and their wives were invited by the Master's wife to the Lodge. The women were served buns and coffee and invited to look through a slit in the wall at the men feasting in Hall.

The term I arrived, the college's governing body had debated whether wives should be allowed to dine in Hall once a year. The argument against this proposition was that the presence of wives would dramatically lower the standard of conversation. They would speak of nothing but nappies and chores. But there was a growing feeling among the Fellows that this exclusion looked outdated, and that progress, or at least the appearance of it, should be respected. That term the yea vote won. So out we wives duly trotted one Friday evening to spend a night at High Table, aprons put to one side, as if we had been waiting forever for the occasion.

The night before, I asked Edward about the dress code; he went wordlessly up the stairs, into the bedroom, over to the chest of drawers, where my clothes remained, pulled things out, dropped them onto the floor.

'These are all creased,' he said, frowning.

He inspected things quickly, picking them up, dropping them again.

'There is nothing here,' he said. 'I'll have to get you something.' And out he walked.

I picked up the clothes, folded them all, put them back.

He bought me a pair of shoes and a black velvet frock, quite glamorous. That evening we walked to the college in the dark; winter was nearly upon us. I was feeling very nervous and to my surprise Edward took my arm.

I was worried about having to make conversation with men like him and getting something wrong. But I was also worried about meeting the other wives, because this mattered to me very much.

We walked through the college gate, Edward's black gown flapping behind him. Through the quads, the cloisters, into the Hall, huge and dimly lit. Like Edward, the other academics wore black gowns over their suits. I saw a row of pale talking heads suspended above the black murk of the table. Until my eyes adjusted to the dim light of the place it was as if those men possessed no bodies at all.

Edward and I were seated apart, which relaxed me momentarily. But the wives were so outnumbered that we were nowhere near each other. I'd been placed between two men who, deep in conversation, appeared not to even notice me sitting down.

'It was that committee Hebdomadal Council created last year,' one of them said as I lowered myself beside him.

'What committee?' And my other neighbour leant across me. Quickly, I leant back.

'They're the ones who did it. It's all their fault.' Like a snarl.

The conversation went on and on – what had been said, what had been put into the minutes, it seemed to have something to do with new admission standards for the colleges. I sat silently, looking around. Pictures on the wall opposite showed previous college masters: an old one of a man in a curly wig holding a globe and scroll; a modern one in broad brush strokes at the other end, hands held loosely in his lap, one of his fingers curled, as if beckoning to someone.

Staff pushed trolleys alongside the table, large white soup tureens on top. They served quickly, expertly, silver ladles flashing. Conversation continued unabated. Sometimes a man leant slightly to one side to let the ladle reach his plate, or he lifted an elbow. It was as if it had been choreographed, these movements: the person dining never looked at the one serving, yet seemed to know exactly where they were.

I watched a woman further down the table, caught her eye; she looked away. I watched the way she kept her hands in her lap as her soup was served, thick steam drifting up in front of her face.

Then it was our turn, our bowls were filled, and, oh, that soup, how delicious it smelt. It was thin, clear and brown, a consommé, and when I took a mouthful I felt a ripple of pleasure, for despite its appearance of watery simplicity its taste was intense, multi-layered.

Silence around me as I sipped, then one of my neighbours glanced in my direction; the other one did too. I realised with a jolt that they were expecting me to say something, that this was when I was meant to speak: while they were eating. I put down my spoon, opened my mouth (I had prepared several erudite conversation topics; I'd been studying the papers closely). To my horror I found that I couldn't remember anything about domestic politics, international affairs, European philosophy or that new play in London. All that came to mind was a comment about the delicious liquid cooling before us, which I knew was the wrong thing to speak of, absolutely.

'Who is your husband?' one of them asked me.

'Edward Haywood.'

He nodded, head still bent, spoon moving back and forth. I noticed his lips quivered slightly just before the spoon went in. There was a small patch of dark bristles below his left nostril. He picked up his napkin, mopped at his mouth.

'Children?'

'No. Not yet.'

Nodded again.

'Hobbies?' tipping his bowl back to scoop up the last of the soup. When I didn't say anything, he glanced at me, then back at his bowl. He'd missed a bit. He tipped it back again.

'Do you have ... interests?'

He was looking around now, at his elbows, at my elbows. What was he after?

'I'm a pianist.'

Ah, he wanted more bread, and he'd spied some, a bread roll on the side plate in the vacant place opposite me.

'And how long have you been doing that? Playing the piano?'

He heaved himself across the table, grabbed the roll in three fingers and reeled back; it was an astonishing move.

'A long time,' I said. 'About seventeen years.'

He laughed a bit at that, not kindly, tore the bread roll open, pressed a square of butter, hard, into the gash.

'Are you any good at it?'

And he put the whole thing, the entire roll, into his mouth. He must have realised straight away he'd made a mistake, his mouth could hardly hold the thing, let alone chew it. He sat there frowning, jaws struggling to work themselves around the lump of hard crust, to get to the soft, buttery centre. It would have helped, I thought, if he had a dislocating jaw like a snake.

'I recently completed my studies at the Royal College in London on a scholarship,' I said, trying not to watch. 'But I must say,' and it was strange, I was suddenly speaking to this man quite honestly, 'I've started to doubt myself, which I hope to get over soon. I do so hope it's just a phase. I have this dream, you see, of becoming the next Rubinstein or, even better, the next Rachmaninoff. I suppose we all —'

But he had started to choke, he was making hee-haw sounds like a strangled donkey, and then he jerked up in his chair and clutched at his throat. I was just about to whack him on the back when he croaked and a piece of half-eaten bread flew from his mouth and landed in front of us on the table. It was wet, shiny. It was covered in a brownish green sheen. It looked like a slightly-over-the-edge oyster, and we both stared at it, appalled, fascinated.

~

Dessert.

Another room, smaller, an oval table, a box of cigars and cigarettes passed one way, port the other.

This man had thin strands of hair stuck to the top of his head with hair cream. He had a cigar, which he hadn't yet lit; he was rolling it in his fingers and little bits of tobacco were falling onto the table. He pressed a finger to them, put the finger to his lips, licked it.

'Did you know,' he said, and his voice had that ripe, end-of-an-evening timbre, 'that there has been some recent research on musical performance and sexual attraction?'

I looked around for doors through which to exit.

'It found that the first two rows of every concert hall are always filled with women.'

'That was a consistent observation?' I replied.

'Obviously,' loudly. 'As I said, it's published research.'

'And in all these cases,' I asked, 'the gender of the performer was . . .'

He frowned. 'Male,' he grunted. 'The theory,' voice mellow again, back on track, 'is that musical performance is akin to a mating dance. The raising of the peacock's feathers, if you will,' and he grinned, and it must have been something about the position of his lips because I could see every one of his yellow teeth. 'They tell me,' he breathed, and now he was leaning in close, I could smell the stilton from the cheese plate, 'that the pretty little colonial one likes to tickle the ivories.'

I froze. My eyes darted around like searchlights in a dark field. I saw two women conducting a whispered conversation behind an elderly man who had fallen asleep at the table; his gown was folded like a blanket across his considerable girth. The women were rising, their heads still together, they looked as if they were suppressing laughter. They made their way towards what looked like part of the wall, but no, there was something there, a handle, a panel, they pushed at it. A door.

'Do excuse me,' I said, rising as regally as I could. I scuttled off after them.

~

Leaning on each other laughing, bent over double, sniffing, wiping their eyes – when they finally recovered they started talking at a thousand miles an hour and I stood beside them slowly washing my hands, thinking about how I could break in, introduce myself. They left the washroom; I dried my hands fast, jogged after them, back through the cloisters.

There were rectangles of light on the black grass in the quad: the windows of the Hall were lit up, bright; the staff must have been cleaning in there. The women went to a different door this time; I followed them in and found myself in a room that resembled a large sitting room. There was a thick carpet on the floor, armchairs arranged in circles, the heavy curtains were drawn. People were drinking coffee, brandy. In the middle of the room, Edward sat talking to an elderly man. They both rose when they saw me; Edward introduced me to the College Master.

'Did you enjoy the dinner?' he asked. There was a slowness to him, a tiredness, but also a contentedness, a serenity, which was different from the other men.

'Yes,' I said, noticing Edward out of the corner of my eye, looking at me with frowning concentration. 'Yes, thank you, it was —'

'I hear you are from Australia. How are you settling in? I do hope you are not too cold, we do try . . .' he trailed off.

'Cold? Oh, I'm used to it, you see I —' but it didn't matter, the Master had caught the eye of someone entering the room behind me; Edward was looking over at whomever it was too. As they moved away from me I saw that the room had a fire and went and stood in front of it.

I watched the skin beneath my nylons go red and blotchy. My shoes were new and very uncomfortable. I was wondering if anyone would notice if I slipped one off, for just a minute, when Edward came up behind me, put a hand on my shoulder and said, 'You look pretty.'

~

When Edward stepped away a minute or two later, a man came over and stood next to me. He peered at me for a second from behind his glasses, then nodded and smiled. He looked like a mole who had just popped up out of the ground expecting it to be spring.

'I hope I'm not interrupting a thought,' he said.

'No,' I said, although by now I was wary.

'You're Alice Haywood?'

'Yes.'

'Excellent. I thought I just saw you here with Haywood,' and he turned, as if to see where Edward had gone. 'Sorry. My name is Frank Porter. My wife, Elizabeth, asked me to look out for you. She couldn't come tonight. Bad cold. You're new to Oxford?'

'That's right.'

'Excellent,' he said again. 'Well, at least I've got that right,' and he laughed. I smiled too. 'Elizabeth has taken over the "welcome to college" tea. I don't know if you've heard of it?'

I shook my head.

'I hadn't either, which isn't much good. I should have, given I've been here for . . . Anyway, it's a get-together so women can meet one another. This year Elizabeth is hosting, and she asked me to make sure you'd received your invitation.'

I stared at him, nonplussed. It seemed this was an entirely benevolent overture. 'I haven't. But I'd love to come.'

'Excellent . . . Now I wonder what happened to your invitation . . .' and he pursed his lips. 'Never mind. I can tell you all about it.' He smiled again and gave me the details and their address in North Oxford. 'Oh, I can't wait to tell Elizabeth. She'll be so pleased. And now that I've found you, I think I might sneak out. She's quite unwell and,' he glanced around, 'these dinners are a bit interminable, aren't they?'

But before he left, he stood there beside me for a while, holding his hands out towards the fire, too.

'That feels lovely,' he said, 'doesn't it?'

39.

Oxford, October 11th, 2005

Brahms, the Intermezzo in A major, was trickling in from somewhere, nowhere. I got up slowly from my place in front of the fire, went into the front room. For the first time I was able to admit that I was behaving like a person lost in a desert who has started hallucinating. A shimmering oasis, palm trees, frosted jugs of lemonade, ice blocks chinking. And it is a piece for the end of the world, that one. If you were given the choice between the world and it, you would choose the music, I am sure of it. It is a piece that is all coda, the whole of it saying, here, rest, lay down your head. And the way it was played, such beauty, such ache. I leant against the wall, my body curved into the shape of an ear, a clef. Listening, leaking.

The Brahms finished, I went over to the window. There were a few leaves left on the bottom branches of a tree in the street, piles on the ground beneath. They looked like severed hands, fingertips curled in one last tremulous embrace. A small child walked past, kicked at the piles with her little boots, making the leaves fly and circle and fall into different patterns. But I couldn't see a parent. I got up quickly and looked down the street as far as I could, and there she was, the mother, pushing an empty pram.

Quentin Kidd came out of his house, my neighbour on the right. He waddled down his path carrying two bulging bags of rubbish. We hadn't spoken for some years. Before he retired he was a lecturer at Edward's college; he wrote plays as a hobby, and pantomimes, even had a few staged. Edward despised him, probably because of his rumoured homosexuality, but also because he never thought Quentin much good at what he did. I watched him squat, place the bags beside the gutter, then ease himself upright and limp back in.

I got up and found a blanket in the cupboard under the stairs, a whiff of mould to it. I held it around my shoulders, shuffled past the phone to the kitchen for a sip of warm water. Then I sat in the hall cradling the receiver in my arms.

40.

Oxford, January, 1951

One bright winter's morning, not long after the dinner, I walked with Edward into the economics department. I was nervous, but also excited.

He showed me the anteroom outside his office, with a desk and a typewriter. He informed me of the similarity between a typewriter and a piano keyboard.

'I've never used one of these before,' I said. I hadn't expected this. 'I don't know how those machines work.'

He gave me a handwritten paper, many pages.

'Well, give it a go,' crossly. 'It can't be hard.'

Perhaps he thought such a thing came naturally.

He went into his office, closed the door. I looked down at the pages of his writing, then at the first word: The. I found the letter T, pressed my finger down, nothing happened. I pressed it again, hard. Bang! The noise! H. Bang! Again. E. Bang! Edward put his head around the door, frowning.

Sorry, I mouthed.

How was I supposed to make the machine work quietly? And then I finally recognised the sound I could hear. It was women's fingers flying over typewriter keyboards, creating a steady, even patter. They were so expert the sound they made blended into the very structure of the building and disappeared almost entirely.

I sat up straight, looked again at the paper, the keys.

When he came out later he leant over the machine, inspected the wonky paragraph I'd managed, reached over, ripped the paper from the roller, screwed it up and threw it onto the floor.

'Hopeless,' he hissed, 'I can't use that. What's more, you ruined the morning with that bloody racket,' and out he stalked.

I stayed there, not moving. After a while I heard footsteps, then a group of men passed by the door. The sound faded. I kept sitting there.

A while later I heard them come back. One of them put his head around the door and said, 'Haywood in?'

'No,' I whispered, and I felt, suddenly, as if I might cry. He looked at me strangely and left.

And instead of thinking: this is unfair, and he is monstrous, I was starting to think, no, I am not very good at this, not at all, I must be such a disappointment. And to start to think such things, that was almost the worst part.

~

A lot of the wives did secretarial work for their husbands. Some were also research assistants, a few collaborators. Stella, for example, whom I met at the welcome tea, was married to Giles, an archaeologist. They had no children and she went on all the digs, even co-wrote the books (just his name on the cover, which only changed much later). Enid, married to James, had been an anthropologist herself but had given it up when they'd had a family. ('Better one of us be excellent than both of us mediocre.' Also, when she'd had too much sherry: 'If only I were a book, then he might see me.') She edited his work, gave him a lot of help. Josephine, still working as a teacher, spoke four languages and wrote poetry. Helle was German and had been a nurse; after raising five children she set up the county's first foster-care program. These were just some of the women I met through Elizabeth.

Elizabeth herself (whom everyone except Frank called Bess)

was a bit like Frank but even better. She had big glasses and a big smile, which was strange in that place. There was something about her that instantly relaxed me, and we got on very well. Her parents had been missionaries and she had trained as a religious teacher, but she wasn't sure what she wanted to do; she was doing this and that, she said. No children at that point. She spoke of Frank often, and warmly.

Several of the women were involved with charitable works, and this interested me. I thought I could do something for others less fortunate, and get to know the town better. Perhaps I could also find out about the arts scene, for music and charity often go hand in hand. I could establish a performance reputation in Oxford before making it back to London.

I asked Bess about it, and she said, Oh, you need to talk to Hilary, she organises the volunteer rosters; that I should call on her and perhaps take a little posy, which seemed odd, but down I went to her place one afternoon, one of those huge houses on the Banbury Road, a little clutch of forget-me-nots tied with a ribbon in my hand.

Hilary didn't even invite me in. She stood at the door and said, 'You want a place on one of the charity rosters, I expect?'

'Yes, please.'

'Well, I warn you,' she barked, 'it might take years.'

'Years?'

'We run highly efficient services here in Oxford. There are simply not enough poor to go around.'

I nearly laughed right there on her doorstep. You didn't have to leave the house to see poverty in Oxford; St Ebbes, a slum, was mere feet from some university buildings. But then I looked at her face, and thanked her and handed over the posy, and I was glad I hadn't laughed, because she seemed a bit sad looking at those flowers, and puzzled, and her hands took them so greedily.

~

Later that week Bess heard that the college organ master had shingles.

'Quick,' she said, calling around, 'go and tell his wife Hazel you play the piano. Don't say you're good at it, that would be fatal. Just say you happen to play.'

'Why shouldn't I say I'm any good?'

'If you don't say anything, she'll know that you're extremely good.'

'What?' (I hadn't yet learnt those rules of the place, how things were said.)

'No time to explain. Go, go. There'll be other people wanting it. She lives in that crumbly terrace around the corner with the sick elm out the front, you know the one.'

I got the job filling in for the organist for the rest of January and into February. Most afternoons I'd accompany the choir, stopping and starting on the nod of the conductor. I asked about pay at the end of it, and the conductor gave me a look and said he'd ask the bursar, and the bursar told Edward.

Roaring into the kitchen, throwing up his arms. 'You crass colonial! Knee-deep in the mud, not even trying to crawl out of it, no idea of etiquette. Shut up until you learn something. You're an embarrassment.' Throwing the dishcloth, shoving a chair, which tipped and fell backwards onto the floor. 'Pick that up!' and I was shrinking then, I was shrinking from all of them.

~

I could have taught the piano, but where? In that house? With him there? In any case I didn't want to. I wanted to play the piano myself. I wanted to perform, not bow out.

41.

Oxford, October 12th, 2005

The phone rang, the noise exploding into the house like shattered glass.

'Hello, Mother.'

I didn't move.

'Hello?'

'Hello, Richard,' clearing my throat, trying to breathe steadily, to breathe at all. Straight away he asked if I was getting out much and if I had seen Bess lately.

'She's so busy these days.' My voice came out in a husky whisper, I cleared my throat. 'Looking after Frank; Parkinson's, you remember,' staring at the carpet.

Then I asked after Martha and he told me she had left him, moved out, which upset me. They hadn't been together long, perhaps a year or two, but she had seemed to adore him.

'When? When did she leave?'

'Oh, I don't know. Possibly after Christmas.'

'Possibly? You don't remember?'

'I mean that it was over by then anyway so it didn't matter, but I don't particularly want to talk about it.'

'But that was ... months ago! You've been without someone all this time?'

He didn't answer.

You need someone to love, is what I wanted to say, someone to love you, and you need to love them well – deeply, completely, equally. Do you think you could love someone like that, Richard?

'Mum, has the library been in touch?'

I realised then why he was ringing. I was quiet.

'The Bodleian. About his collection.'

'No, I don't think so.'

'Really? That seems very odd. Are you sure?'

'I think so.'

'Could you let me know when they do?'

'Yes.'

'Are you all right? You sound like you've got a cold.'

'Oh, I'm fine. I probably have got a cold.'

'Are you warm enough? Have you got the heating on high?'

This was killing me now.

'Oh, you know me,' I managed to get out, 'I'm always cold.'

'You're not to worry about the bill or anything like that.' He even had the grace to sound embarrassed.

'Thank you, Richard. You're kind to think of it.'

'No, no,' suddenly brisk, 'no risk of that,' and we were fencing now, we were diplomats going through the various genuflections, hands together, hands apart, bowing, ducking, never meeting one another's eyes.

'Well . . .' he said, finally, typically, 'I'd better be off then.'

I sat by the phone for a long time. Then I picked it up and rang Bess. I ended up asking her to meet me for tea, a suggestion so ludicrous it shocked even me. She started going through her diary (her charity work, her book club, the asylum seeker welcome meeting, belly-dancing class, babysitting one of her many grandchildren).

'What about tomorrow, then? We could try that new French place on Woodstock Road with all the cakes in the window.'

And before I could back-pedal, having realised what I had done, she was describing to me where the cafe was, but she couldn't remember exactly, so she called out to Frank. 'Frank! What used to be where that new French place is on Woodstock

Road ... French! What? No, that's not right ... Patel's? But wasn't that down near the ... Oh, I see ... Oh, right, yes, well in that case ...'

'Bess,' I erupted (I am dying! I am dying!), 'Bess, I must go. I'll find it.'

I hung up. I felt as if I'd had an out-of-body experience. The thought of it, sitting in a new cafe on Woodstock Road with Bess, declining French pastries (sorry, dying from starvation, actually). I would have to ring her back to cancel. But what would I say?

I got very worked up about this, pacing around, banging myself on the head, until I decided that I simply wouldn't turn up – but then she would probably come around to see me. Could I be dead by tomorrow, solve it like that? But there was still so much to burn and sort. I spent a tormented night.

In the morning I washed and dressed for the first time in many days. I put on good clothes, even the string of Venetian glass beads Bess had given me once for my birthday. I would not be attending the cafe, but I still hadn't worked out how to extricate myself from the arrangement. I felt sick, sweaty.

In the end it didn't matter. Bess rang a few hours before we were due to meet: Frank had had a fall and had just left in an ambulance. She was about to drive to the hospital. She was upset; he'd had a few falls before, but nothing this bad. I kept saying to her, It will be all right, Bess, he will be all right.

When she hung up I sat holding the receiver until it started to beep. I went to the window and sat down. I took the beads off, held them in my lap.

At dusk the students cycled back up the street; there was a slight incline I'd notice when I watched their legs, the way they lifted themselves from the seat. I went to the phone, dialled the number.

'Hello, hello, hello,' he said, 'is that what you want to hear me say? What is it you want me to say?' but tiredly, as if he already knew there would be no answer, and then he hung up too.

42.
Oxford, January, 1951

My first performance in Oxford didn't take long to arrange after all. It was an item in a charity concert to raise funds for a homeless shelter destroyed by a fire in the kitchen. It wasn't much, but it was something. Maybe I would meet some people there who knew of other opportunities.

At the meeting to organise it, Hilary told me that I was to go last, and I should play something sweet to finish. Or spectacular, Bess said, smiling, sitting beside her.

I chose the 'Dance of the Wild Horses' piece from boarding school; a sentimental choice, and auspicious, I thought. I assumed Edward would come; I hoped my performance might even rekindle some of the admiration he had expressed during the Summer School. Perhaps it would prompt him to ask me to play for him again after dinner. But he told me he was too busy to attend; he might be in London or working in his office. I was disappointed but did not show it.

One man played Chopin, laboriously. A woman sang folk songs, clear and true. Another sang an aria, and the whole time her eyes were fixed on the stained glass at the back of the room. After a few more items it was my turn. I walked up to the piano in the silence, sat down, pushed up my sleeves. My fingers started rumbling the low quavers of the opening line.

What went wrong first? The accents in that first line, which are meant to make the music sound like distant pounding hooves? I didn't get the emphasis quite right, and then when

149

the melody was introduced I was going too fast; I missed a note and my hands began to stiffen, as if tired. It was at this point that I started to hear something in the room other than my playing. A voice, very near, it was as if a demon had crawled onto my shoulder and was speaking directly into my ear. You are hopeless, it said. You are useless at everything. You are incompetent. You will ruin even this. And, by the way, your outfit is embarrassing. I was distracted by this, I started to swat at the voice and lost my place for a second; my hands stiffened even more. I started using other parts of my body to compensate, hunching up my shoulders, hardening my back, which was bent in its effort to contribute. I flung my whole body at the keyboard trying to keep up with that mad pace I'd set. The voice amplified to a shout, and single insults (Hopeless! Useless! Stupid! Incompetent! Liar!) exploded in direct competition with what I was playing. I skipped to the end, ripped the last glissando up the keyboard and down, caught a knuckle on the edge of a key, tore the skin, a streak of blood appeared across the keys. I crashed the final chord.

There was a pause then a smattering of applause. Hilary stood up at the front and with one arm directed people to the silent auction at the back of the room. They all turned their heads to look.

I raised my hand to my trembling mouth, tasted blood, closed the lid of the piano with the other.

43.
Oxford, February, 1951

Into the meadow. The wind held the scent of snow, everything was frozen. When I got out to the middle I started to spin, arms out, head back, turning, turning. The sky fell down beside me, under me, the vegetation was a blur, the grazing animals smeared, the horizon a jagged zig-zag, the ground beneath me jumped up, and when I fell I banged my hip and shoulder hard. Instead of getting up I rolled over, onto my back.

The wet of the meadow started to seep through the material of my coat, into my sweater, my shirt, the rest of my clothes. It touched my skin, tentatively at first, but then it was all over me. It had entered my blood, surrounded my bones, infiltrated the marrow where it stayed circling, breathing its ice, making itself known. I was so cold, I was nothing; and when I felt him, two fingers plucking at my hand, I curled into myself and covered my head. Then I tried to scramble to my feet, but my frozen limbs were slow, so he held onto my arm and was pulling at it, trying to help, supporting my back. At last I was standing before him.

I recognised him straight away. I'd seen him on busy weekday mornings standing in front of St John's College with a sack at his side. He did not face the street, but rather the high college wall. He always had his head to one side, smiling a little, as if he were listening to something. He was homeless, probably mad. He was wearing a three-piece suit with holes in it so huge I could see the meadow right through them. His hair was long, greasy, stringy.

I could smell him now, sweat and grease and dirt, the unwashed tang mingling with the smell of the meadow.

A clucking sound came from his lips, and he moved his hands, as if he were worried about the mud on me, but when I moved to reassure him he scuttled off towards the long grass and bushes at the edge of the meadow, close to the train tracks, and I realised I had not even thanked him. I had thought, to begin with, that he was going to harm me.

I walked back slowly to the house, thinking about the gentleness with which he had treated me; maybe he had seen me walking in the meadow before, although I had never seen him. A lightness to my walk now, I reached the house in no time, not even noticing the hill. Edward was there already. He appeared not to notice the mud on my clothes as I stood at the door.

'Where have you been?' he said.

'The meadow. Walking.'

He looked at me, narrow-eyed, walked towards his study. 'You're late,' he said, over his shoulder.

I went upstairs and ran a bath. I was sitting on the lid of the lavatory, marvelling at the mud on my clothes, when I heard him coming up the stairs.

'I fell,' I called out. There was no reply. 'I fell in the meadow.' Still no reply. 'Someone helped me up, they rescued me,' I said, louder.

Perhaps he could not hear me, what with the pounding of the water, the closed door. The room had filled with steam, the mirror was foggy. I turned off the taps and got in.

44.
Oxford, March, 1951

I was doing the dishes, my hands fumbled under the suds for a plate, and I dropped it as I was lifting it onto the rack. It fell on the floor and broke into several pieces. Looking down at it I found that I did not have the will or energy to clean it up, this broken thing. I could see in my head what needed to be done, the bending to pick up the larger pieces, getting out the dustpan and brush, sweeping up the flecks and putting it all in the bin, hiding it in there beneath other rubbish, this evidence of waste, destruction. I felt overwhelmed by an immense tiredness; I could not clean it up, not yet. Instead I sat down at the table.

It was March, the house was silent, frigid with cold. Edward wouldn't allow the heating on during the day, it cost too much money; it came on when he was at home. For the last few weeks I had been teaching myself a new piece by Brahms, the Rhapsody in G minor. After that disastrous performance I decided that I needed some new repertoire. I had a Brahms album; I had always liked that Rhapsody.

Edward no longer liked me to practise in the house when he was there. He said it was too loud and distracting. Even if he wasn't working he preferred me to refrain because it shattered his thinking. It was all right, I thought, because he wasn't there much anyway. I could still practise during the day and when he was out in the evenings.

It had not taken me long to learn the notes of that piece; when I started it, I could already hear it in my head. That morning

I played it through then sat looking at the music. How could I know if I sounded any good? How could I know with just my own ears listening to myself? I'd always had a teacher to tell me it was ready, or needed more work.

I found some recordings of the piece in Edward's record collection in the study, listened to them, then chose the one I thought sounded best, from a recital in Carnegie Hall. I played it again and again. I went back to the piano, mimicked what I had heard. I slowed it down, brought out the bass more, did the accents heavily, changed some of the dynamics. I sat looking at the music again. I still couldn't tell if it sounded any good.

I got up, put my coat on and went for a walk.

I had given up looking for the homeless man. I hadn't seen him since that incident in the meadow, and I was glad about this, mostly. I had probably scared him, I thought. Occasionally I wondered if he was hiding somewhere watching me, but I never had the feeling that I was being watched, never had the impression of hidden eyes upon me.

The cold was terrible in the meadow that day. Instead of walking out into the middle I walked over to the canal and watched the quick flow of the dark water. There wasn't a bird on it. It was too cold to be out. I returned to the house.

When I got back, Edward was there already; he was home early, I could hear him in the kitchen. At that moment I remembered the broken plate on the floor that I had not cleaned up. Immediately, I considered turning around and walking away. How was I to face this?

But I did go down the hall, and there he was squatting on the floor in his suit, the tie hanging to the floor, with the dustpan and brush, sweeping up the broken plate, and I started to apologise, to say, I'm sorry, Edward, I'm very sorry, and he looked up and I knew then that he meant to hit me, and I turned and ran.

I ran down the hall into the front room and he shouted, 'You come back here.' He came to the room, grabbed my arm, wrenched me around, and I said, 'No, no, please, it was an accident, it was a mistake, I am sorry, I am very sorry, it will never happen again, I promise, I promise.'

And he shook my arm hard and said, 'You did it deliberately.'

'No, no, no, honestly, I didn't, please, I didn't, I wouldn't, I wouldn't,' and by then I was crying, really crying, and he kept hold of my arm for a bit longer, then dropped it, turned, left.

I stood there, the world orbiting around me, stood there with the piano, the silent piano in the corner. Stood there, and the Brahms came into my head, the swirling bass, the accents on the triplets, the dipping, lifting melody. I started to sway a little, back and forth, rocking on my feet, playing that music in my head.

45.

Oxford, October 14th, 2005

I was bent over the fire anticipating the sight of demand and
supply curves buckling, blackening and shrivelling before me
when I realised that I was holding instead an album by Brahms,
and just in time I snatched it back. Then I found on the desk an
economics paper, an off-print from a journal, among the sheets of
music. I started to panic. In my dying state was I filing economics papers instead of music? I looked in the boxes, pulling things
out to see properly; all the scores I had so carefully arranged
came hurtling out. I found no economics papers among them,
but I didn't trust this, not entirely. I started poking in the ash
looking for traces of burnt music, expecting to see singed clefs,
shrunken quavers, whole blackened lines of melody, vanish-
ing harmony, and while I found no evidence of this the episode
frightened me, and I wondered if I should eat a bit to allay my
confusion and get the jobs done properly.

One might think some apposite music would have arrived
then, Fauré's Requiem, for example, to send me off, even
a nice Schumann impromptu to sweep me away, but there was
nothing, no music at all, just a truck roaring up the street then
reversing by inches all the way back down. Beep, beep, beep.

~

Richard rang again that night, just two days since his last call;
it should have warned me.

'How are you, Mum? Are you all right?'

'What?'

'I said are you all right?'

'Yes, fine. Are you?'

'Sort of. I keep getting prank calls, actually.'

I froze.

'Someone rings up then hangs up. On the land-line.'

'Oh dear.'

'Yes. It's been disturbing. So I finally asked someone about it.'

'You what?'

'I said I asked someone about it. You're quite deaf, you know.'

'I'm not,' I muttered.

'What?'

I said nothing; he sighed.

'Apparently you can dial this number that tells you who rang your land-line last; I never know these things. Anyway, when I dialled that number it said the call was from you.'

I was sitting absolutely still. Rivers of sweat were flooding into my clothes.

'Perhaps your phone is faulty,' I said.

'No. I did ask about that, given I've received quite a lot of these calls.'

I stared at the window, a blank square of light, closed my eyes.

'So I thought I'd ring up and see how you are,' he was saying, 'see how things are going.'

'Well, I don't want to waste your time,' I managed. 'I know you're very busy.'

'All the time in the world at this end, Mum.'

I was feeling faint, as if floating; no, spinning; no, vertiginous.

'Perhaps someone is coming into the house and using the phone,' I said.

'Like who?'

'Like a robber.'

'You're suggesting a criminal is entering the house and prank-calling me from your phone? Do you think that's likely?'

'Well, people do very strange things in this town, Richard, all the time.'

'Now that is true.'

'Perhaps I should go and check right now if I've locked all the doors and windows properly —'

'What?' sharply.

I didn't repeat it.

'I'm wondering if things have got a bit on top of you. Are you keeping up with the . . . uh, book club, or what is it? Arts circle? I think meeting with people can do a lot of good . . .'

As if having a coffee with a friend, meeting with a group for an hour or two, would make one whole again. As if I were two-dimensional and simply needed gluing back together.

'I'm quite all right, Richard. How are you?'

'It is quite obvious that you are not all right. You don't sound all right, and you're not acting all right, so what's going on? Come on, I'm not going to put the phone down until you say something.'

And he went on in this vein for some time, until out of sheer desperation, unable to find it in myself to say anything else, I said foolishly, 'I suppose I am a bit hungry.'

'*Hungry?*'

'Not extremely hungry, nothing like that.'

'When did you eat last?'

'I'm not sure. It doesn't matter.'

'This morning?'

'Er . . .'

'Last night?'

'Uh . . .'

'Do you have food in the house? When did you last shop?' His voice was agitated. 'How long has this been going on? I mean — are you really that . . . incapacitated?'

'No! Nothing like that.'

'I don't understand. What do you mean you're hungry? You can't just say such a thing and expect me not to react, not to worry and try to do something about it. I mean, for Christ's sake!'

I heard traffic in the background.

'Where are you?' I said.

'I'm at home.'

'In Bayswater?'

'Yes.' He sighed. 'That's where I live.'

I should have asked why he wasn't at his studio.

'Is it nice down there, the weather?'

'Uh, yes, warmish, unseasonal.'

'Have you been in the park?'

'Look, I'll order you some food, all right? I'll get it delivered.'

'No! Please don't go . . . to any trouble.'

'No trouble. That's what we're going to do, all right?' And he hung up.

He rang again not long after to say that an order of groceries would arrive that evening; also that he thought we should visit my doctor together, a suggestion I protested vigorously. I ended up hanging up abruptly. He rang once more, and this time I did not answer, because I did not know what to say, and the phone kept ringing, and I kept ignoring it, and it kept ringing, and I started to reconcile myself to the sound of a constantly ringing phone, an additional torture to top off these, my final days, but eventually I picked it up and put the receiver onto the phone table.

Richard's voice piped out.

'Mum! Jesus. Pick up the damn phone, for fuck's sake!'

'Hello.'

'Jesus! What is the matter with you? You need to answer, all right? You can't just not answer! What am I supposed to think?

159

Something could have happened to you!' He took a breath. 'I was calling to say that when the person comes with the groceries you don't pay them, all right? I've paid already.'

'You haven't really gone and bought — '

'Mum, this is not a big deal. I did it online. They'll just —'

'What are you talking about?'

'Do you not remember what I said? Do you not actually recall —'

'Of course I remember. Someone's coming from the . . .'

'From the supermarket, Mum, delivery people.'

'I know! I know!'

'And they'll bring it inside so you don't have to —'

'*Into the house?*'

'Fuck! Not if you don't want them to; just get them to . . . I don't know – put it on the porch or something. Then you'll have to take it all in yourself. Now, we must go and see your doctor asap. Edward said . . .'

And then the world froze over, and I lost all power of speech, the little I had.

'He said that . . .'

I held the phone away from me, as far as my arm would stretch, his voice tiny.

'. . . be worth getting some things checked and if necessary a referral to this particular psychiatrist who —'

'Thank you, Richard, I'll be saying goodbye now.'

After that I sat there thinking for a long time.

～

That night the food was delivered. A man unloaded a mountain of it at my feet. When he got back into the truck and drove away I closed the door. The food was out of sight.

But someone else would see it, wonder why it was there. I opened the door and dragged the bags down to the kitchen, which took a lot of energy, which I resented because I didn't have any.

I looked into the bags, wondering what he had bought me. I saw a packet of Custard Cream biscuits. I bent to get it and lost my balance, fell against the bench, hitting my shoulder and nearly hitting my head. I gripped the bench with both hands. Eventually I made myself a cup of black tea, one teaspoon of sugar.

The next night an additional load of food was delivered. What was Richard thinking? I stood staring at the man holding the crate in his arms. Where do you want it? he said, and I pointed wordlessly to the mat. Right you are, he said (exactly the same as the night before; did he not remember doing all this just twenty-four hours earlier?). I thanked him, dragged the bags down the hall and into the kitchen, where, with the previous delivery, they covered the entire floor. After some thought I dragged them all out of the back door and locked it.

But I knew that even in the cool weather all of it would start to rot and stink; and I couldn't put it in the rubbish, there was too much. I thought about giving it to Quentin anonymously, leaving the bags on his porch in the dead of night, a mysterious gift, but he would probably interpret it as harassment. I could burn them, but what about the packaging? It would create terrible smoke, an almighty fume that would billow black and green into the sky like a banner, saying, Here is the woman responsible, here.

In the end I took all the bags back inside, there seemed no other option, and put the food away in the pantry, cupboards and fridge. I did this in a near-deathly state of starvation; it was exhausting, lifting all those things. And the stuff he had bought me! Sausages, a pineapple, a chicken, a packet of jam tarts, bacon, tomatoes, cucumbers, spaghetti, a sack of oranges, which I hid in a bottom cupboard.

Later, I started to think about the food again. Even its

presence in the kitchen troubled me. I went downstairs and opened the fridge, got out the first thing I saw, the pineapple, found the biggest knife and stabbed the fruit through the middle. I thought I might cut it up into bits, get rid of it that way. The knife got stuck, I couldn't push it further in or pull it out, and I stood there with my hands on the knife looking out at the garden as the pineapple bled onto the bench, the juice pooling around it in a sticky circle. I took my hands off the knife, went back upstairs.

The worry about the food remained, it elbowed itself forward. I went down to the kitchen again, got out another knife and starting grabbing things from the fridge and cutting them up, just to do something with them – reduce them I suppose was the thinking – and soon I had made an almighty mess; there was chopped food everywhere. I staggered up the hall and rang Richard.

'There is too much food,' I said when he answered. 'You must stop ordering it. I have a total of forty-eight sausages.'

'Mum, it is two a.m.'

'Two a.m? Is it?' I was mortified. 'I'm very sorry. I'll go now, I'll . . .' There was a sound on the other end of the phone, as if he was moving, covers shifting.

'What's all this about sausages?'

This was a big mistake. The hunger – I was doing things I wouldn't usually do.

'Look, nothing, really, I just wanted to say, well, no more orders, please. There was a special offer on sausages this week, you see, so in the second order they delivered a great deal more than the first.'

'The second order?'

'The one today. After the one the night before.'

'I didn't order a second delivery.'

'Well, it came – the evidence is all over the kitchen.'

'They must have made a mistake. I'm sorry. I'll make sure they haven't charged us twice.'

'All right. I mean, you have to admit that is a lot of sausages.'

'Yeah. Absolutely. Heaps. I guess, just throw them out. Don't let it bother you,' and his voice, maybe it was because he was sleepy, but it was so soft, and I began to quietly weep.

'Oh, Mum,' he said. 'Mum.'

'I'm very sorry, Richard. I didn't realise it was so late.'

'Never mind, I wasn't sleeping anyway.'

'What were you doing?'

'Nothing. Looking at the ceiling.'

'Are you all right, Richard? Are you really?'

'Yes, I'm fine.'

And I realised then that there was no point, that I had squandered all my chances. I seemed completely unable to speak the truths I needed to get out.

'You go back to sleep. Maybe get yourself a warm milk, or something nice to read, nothing too stimulating. I'm so sorry to have troubled you, I feel terrible about phoning at such a time. So kind of you to have —'

'Not at all, Mum, not at all.'

I remember getting up the next day, creeping down the stairs, throwing away the chopped-up food, sitting at the front window and being almost unable to move after that. Just my eyes, resting on the tree outside. I watched a wind pick up, the leaves flitter, the small branches start to waver, then the whole tree swayed, and when the wind dropped it was just the leaves again, plucking the air. There was no one out there, the place stood so still, except for the occasional cyclist passing. The exertions and tensions of the previous days had sped things up. Death felt near, an invisible stalker, impatient. And I was about to go and ring him, tell him what I needed to, finally set things right, talk to him properly, mother to adult child, but

I couldn't manage it yet, I couldn't. I still didn't even know what the right words were. And if I couldn't do it, then it was wrong to disturb him.

I found I no longer cared about burning the rest of Edward's library, which was vast anyway, far too big. Let them put it all under lock and key, in golden cases lined with dark velvet; why had I ever thought such a thing mattered? I couldn't do the filing either, I had no capacity to lift or sort a thing. So the chores would remain unfinished, and what sad, unnecessary chores they were anyway.

I went to the piano, locked my fingers around the keys, lifted them, sank them down and played a minor third, a C and E flat. The interval sounded softly. I have lost my heart (lift up, sink down), I have lost my heart (lift up, sink down), and how pathetic it was, how pathetic in its inadequacy.

46.

Oxford, June, 1951

My next concert in Oxford was the Rachmaninoff Concerto number 2 in C minor. The invitation to perform this extraordinary work came out of nowhere, towards the end of the academic year.

The concerto is one of the most difficult in the piano repertoire. Rachmaninoff wrote it after a period of depression and writer's block, following the disastrous reception of his First Symphony. (He was found after the premiere in Moscow crouched beneath the theatre's stairs with his hands over his ears, blocking out the booing audience.) Eventually persuaded by his family to see a therapist, his treatment was a great success and in 1900 he wrote the second and third movements of the concerto quickly. Then in the spring of 1901 the famous first movement walked onto the page.

A visiting music scholar at Edward's college, a specialist in Romantic repertoire, was planning to conduct the concerto in the Sheldonian as part of his program of study, but the soloist had pulled out. The scholar brought his problem to lunch one day at High Table. Did anyone know a suitable pianist in Oxford? And Edward offered me.

I didn't know why. Maybe he was feeling guilty, although Edward never felt much remorse. Maybe he was trying to help me, but that also seemed unlikely. Maybe he thought my performance would make him look good, but in actual fact I think any success of mine at that point would have been threatening to him, made him feel inadequate. No, Edward always liked to have the answer to a question, especially if no one else did. The possibility that he was not thinking of me at all when he offered my services, that it had nothing to do with me, did not occur to me, but it should have.

I'm told the scholar questioned Edward about this wife of his and her musical qualifications in front of his High Table colleagues, which would have clinched it. I could just imagine him, the flashing eyes, the words articulated oh so carefully. I think you'll find she'll do it nicely, he would have said quietly, his voice full of ice and scorn. That night he handed the score to me.

'That silly ass Fincher wants to conduct this in the Sheldonian and he can't get himself organised. So you're doing it.'

'Sorry?'

'What do you mean "sorry"? You're the soloist. Here's that concert you wanted. In the Sheldonian.'

I looked at the score.

'Are you joking, Edward?'

'No,' irritated.

'When?'

'What?'

'When is the concert?'

'October,' he said, heading down the hall.

'October of this year?'

He didn't say anything. I got up, went down the hall.

'October of this year?' I said at the door.

'Of course,' he spat.

Four months, an impossible time frame in which to learn the work.

I took the score with me into the front room and sat down with it on the chaise longue. I knew it well to listen to, but I had never played it. I imagined, for just a minute, performing this work in the Sheldonian. I pictured myself on stage in a new concert gown, the orchestra behind me, the conductor by my side, then afterwards in the foyer holding a big bouquet and being plied with more flowers.

Edward left the next day for a fortnight in Cambridge. With no teaching commitments in summer, he was often away (it became a time I looked forward to with eagerness, which I was careful to hide). I would not perform the concerto, of course, it was clearly not feasible; I would have to extricate myself from the arrangement when he got back. Edward would have to tell the scholar it wasn't part of my repertoire. A terrible thought; I pushed it to the back of my mind. In the meantime, I had the score; I decided I might as well have a look at it.

I ended up playing it nearly constantly for two weeks. Parts of it seemed to fall easily beneath my hands, naturally, I began to think. How I loved all those passionate swells and dives. Those grand old arcs of melody, both hands spread wide. The melancholy of the work, the driving bass notes in the first theme of the first movement that keep the beat and provide that constant, driving momentum, while everything else swirls around them – I liked it all. The intensity of it, the high emotion, the unbridled fervour. It was something to aspire to.

The fortnight passed quickly. The night before Edward returned I sat with the score, away from the piano, and had a close look at it, all of it, not just the parts I enjoyed playing. It went on for pages. It required technique, stamina and interpretation that would challenge the best of pianists, and I'd hardly learnt any of it. I realised someone needed to be told, and quickly, that I would not be performing.

When he got home I stood in the bedroom watching him unpack, then I followed him down to the study, made him a cup of tea, handed him the paper.

I was feeling unusually strong, bolstered, perhaps, by that two weeks away from him. I'd seen a few of my Oxford friends.

It was as if a part of me had started to grow back, emerge again. And what a joy to realise it was still there, just underneath, waiting.

'You know that concerto,' I started.

'What concerto?' looking at his desk.

'The Rachmaninoff, the one you . . . the one I'm supposed to be performing.'

He looked up.

'The one you *are* performing in the Sheldonian. Yes, what of it?'

'Unfortunately it isn't possible. You see, I have never played it before. It isn't part of my repertoire. To learn it in time to perform in October is impossible. It's an enormous work. Monumental.'

Silence. He was staring at me.

'I'm sure that someone else could be found easily,' I said. 'It's such a desirable invitation.'

'The arrangements were very clear,' he said. 'The commitment was made.'

'Without consulting me.'

'What?'

'You didn't ask me before saying I could do it. I would have told you, if you had asked me, that it wasn't part of my repertoire.'

'I thought,' he said, very carefully, 'that this is exactly what you had asked for. That a performance of a Rachmaninoff concerto in the Sheldonian might be exactly what you wanted.'

'Well, yes, partly.' (In fact, I would have been better equipped to perform a Beethoven concerto, but this wasn't the conversation we were having.)

'So what, exactly, is the problem?'

'It is just as I said. There is nowhere near enough time to learn it.'

'Oh, now, we both know that's not true,' and he looked back at his desk, started arranging papers.

I didn't understand.

'You see, I spoke to some colleagues about it, as well as Fincher, who is an accomplished pianist, a scholar of the Romantics, and they all agreed that it was possible. The Music Master, for example,' he cleared his throat, 'the Oxford Chair of Music, said it was achievable, if the pianist had sufficient skill and self-discipline. The Organ Master agreed. Furthermore, a visiting Russian scholar, who dined on two occasions with Rachmaninoff himself, said that any pianist with adequate training should be able to do it, if they wanted to, if they had the stamina. So, I repeat, what, precisely, is your problem? Is it that you are not good enough?'

I couldn't believe what I was hearing.

'I need to work now,' he said. 'I suggest you start studying that music.'

Oh, how young I was then. How my sense of what was right and wrong was so pliable. I was starting to doubt, you see, my own assessment of that music. I was starting to think I might have overestimated things, that I might be able to perform it after all, if I just worked a bit harder, was a bit better.

It does not seem unreasonable now that I thought such a thing back then. I still believed that the people who were supposed to be right about things could be trusted. Wasn't the entire town of Oxford predicated on the basis of that knowledge? It was convenient if the truth, the answer, was to be found in one place, and I didn't have to look for it myself, didn't have to search and determine and question forever. It felt hard – dangerous, even – to be right about things when other people thought I was not. To be right about things I didn't particularly want to be right about (as I said, I really liked that music).

169

Also, I wanted to do something that meant something to someone else, to do something that mattered, that helped. Most of all I wanted to love, and to be loved. And I nurtured some hope, a forlorn little stub of a candle, that the possibility of this sort of love still existed between Edward and me. If I worked hard enough, if I was good enough, I could be loved, and love back.

Never mind that the love of the performer up there on stage, blurred under the lights, far away, was not the sort of love I was after. Never mind that what I yearned for was love that cared, that was near, that was the truth, that was four arms tangled up together, holding each other up.

So I decided to spend a bit more time working on the concerto and see how I got on. I would probably have to find another way to extricate myself, other than through Edward. And because he was away for the rest of June, and I had little housekeeping to do, I immersed myself in the music and progressed quickly. When my hands hurt badly after hours of constant playing, I kept going, working as hard as I could.

Then he got back and all the housekeeping and meals had to recommence; and I couldn't play when he was in the house, my progress slowed markedly. I started to think again about how I was going to get out of it. I thought about contacting the conductor myself, suggesting he ask the Royal College for a replacement, giving him names, even arranging it all and presenting it to him as a fait accompli. And every time I planned these things I prevaricated, thinking I would just give it one more day, or two, or three, see if I could get a bit further with it, for they had said it was possible, hadn't they? And I thought I was good.

～

In August Edward didn't go away as planned; he worked in the house instead. I stood in the morning at the sink, listening to

170

him moving around upstairs, pleading with him in my head to leave, then pleading with God to make him, then hearing him walk down the stairs into his study.

After several days of tiptoeing around the house doing chores, the concerto roaring, soaring and crashing in my head, I could bear it no more. I crept into the front room, pressed the soft pedal down with my left foot, and started, very quietly, to play.

'What are you doing?' he shouted, exploding into the room, bending over me, jabbing me with his words. 'I need quiet, absolute quiet!' and he slammed back into the study.

I sat on the stool, heart thudding.

Later, I started to play on the table in the kitchen, the score in front of me, my fingers pummelling the wood. He came in.

'What on earth are you doing?' amused, and suddenly in a much better mood (perhaps his work was going well). He poured himself a glass of milk, drank it standing up.

'You are working very hard,' I said.

He kept drinking, looking out the window.

'I'll do some practice this evening,' I said, 'if that won't disturb you terribly. You'll remember I have this concert in October.'

He jerked around, put the glass down hard on the sink.

'I am working hard,' he hissed, 'because I am about to deliver a highly confidential report to the government on unemployment.'

I started to feel hot.

'What a worthwhile piece of work,' I stammered. 'How is it going?'

But he had left the room.

After that he disappeared up to London again and I could practise whenever I wanted, but by this point I was dispirited, and my anxiety was stratospheric. I found it hard to eat, sleep was sporadic, my dreams frightening. I vomited once or twice thinking about the performance; sometimes I found it hard to breathe when I sat at the piano. I felt inadequate when I played, as if no matter what I did I was always failing. I always felt rushed and was no longer thoughtful about the way I approached things or expended my energy. It was as if I were drowning in the work, as if it were a huge body of water and I was struggling upwards in vain, never breaking the surface.

When Edward came back and I knew that my practice would be curtailed again, I felt terror. I had spent the day of his return in a frenzy of house-cleaning, laundry, shopping, cooking. It was evening; he was reading the paper.

'Edward, you know that concerto I —'

'What? What concerto?'

I gaped.

'The Rachmaninoff you —'

'Christ,' rustling the paper noisily, 'you're not still on about that are you?'

I would not let this put me off, I would not.

'Edward, when you asked me to do it I said that I did not think it possible in the time frame. Since then I have been prac-tising extremely hard, in the time that I have, and I'm very sorry to say this but the answer remains the same. While I very much want to do this, I mean I would dearly love to, it just . . . it simply can't be done.' And I felt tears gathering in my eyes then; I was exhausted. He looked at me, curious, almost.

'Do you know,' he said, 'what weakness is?'

'Perhaps not.' I was shaking now.

'Weakness is crumbling and flailing about when the hurdle has become a little higher.'

'I don't think that description quite matches this situation. In the first place the hurdle is rather more like an enormous —'

'All of those men said it was possible.'

'All those men are not trying to do it themselves, and in these

172

circumstances! What is their evidence? I have a feeling they set you up.'

This stunned him.

'You!' pointing, furious. 'You are the one who is weak and lacking!'

And it was so unkind, and I was so worn out, that I started to cry properly, big hot tears sliding down my cheeks. Crying for everything that was ruined and not working, and he was staring over the paper at me in a way that I did not understand, except to see – I could not help it – that there was pleasure in that look, definitely.

'I thought you said you were a pianist,' he said. 'I thought you were supposed to be good.'

And I cried even harder.

'Come on now,' in a different voice entirely, almost matronly, 'pull yourself together. Come on. Blow your nose,' and he handed me his hanky. 'We'll have some tea.'

We tramped down to the kitchen; he started looking in cupboards (he never made the tea). I told him where to find things. He poured milk into my cup, spooned in sugar (which I didn't take, it didn't matter).

'There you are. Drink.'

'It's a bit hot.'

'Of course it is.'

'Edward —'

'No, no,' one hand up, 'not until you've drunk your tea.'

I drank it, scalding my mouth. I rearranged my face.

'I'm very sorry, but I think we very quickly need to —'

'You see, you've started to panic. This is what some people do in such situations. You need to treat this like an exam. You have done an exam, haven't you? Perhaps at school? Well, what I tell our nervy undergraduates is that if they've put the work in all year and not been lazy, they'll be all right. They just have to go in there,' and he held his hand close to his chest, then shot it forward like a spear, 'and do it.'

'I have been working extremely hard, when I am able to,' I said.

'You'll have no problem then, will you?'

He got up; I took the cups to the sink. Standing there, washing them out, what arose in me was a rage at him, at all of them, so huge, and with it a determination to succeed so enormous that it was bigger than me, and I felt a rush of new, boiling, seething energy. I would do this concert, I thought, even if it killed me. And as I was putting the cups away I thought, for just a second, and would that prove them right or me? I decided this didn't matter, I would not be distracted by semantics, I would just get on with it.

The next morning I knocked on the door of a nearby vicarage. The church had a hall that I knew contained a piano because I had heard it being played sometimes as I walked by. I told the vicar, a middle-aged fellow with floppy hair and an earnest smile, that I was a pianist from Australia looking for somewhere to practise, and this man, this kind man, said, Well, you must use our hall, we love to hear music, and we would love to help you. And just like that, he gave me the key.

So whenever Edward was in the house and I needed to play, I went up the road to the church hall. And when Edward said, What are you doing, where are you going? I said, I'm going to work very hard on that concerto, you'll remember the concert is in October. And he'd look at me, a bit unsure, as if trying to decide whether to stop me, and I would just walk out. And once or twice I'm sure he followed me, maybe he even stood under one of those big trees on the other side of the road and listened for a bit, just to verify it; I decided that I didn't care about that either. I got back in time to make the dinner, so he couldn't complain.

I hammered at the concerto. I attacked it with hands and axe and pick and saw. The music was a stony, arid, weed-choked field that I had to clear and plough and plant in order to eat. How I hated that music by then. How I hated its bloated intensity, its clichéd themes, its predictable arches.

Late summer turned into September, the days were still warm, the parks in full green glory, and I saw none of it. I did the housework in a frenzy, then cloistered myself in the front room or the hall and attacked the concerto again. My hands hurt terribly by this point; my fingers seemed to move too slowly on the keys, even missing notes. I did not stop, I could not stop. I shook my hands out sitting at the stool, and kept going.

~

When the conductor got in contact through Edward in late September to arrange a rehearsal with the orchestra, I could play it. I knew all the notes. Not that that is readiness to perform such a work. For example, I was still striving so hard to play the solo part I could not really concentrate on the ensemble work.

The rehearsal went badly for other reasons. The lead violinist stopped playing frequently to argue with the conductor about entries, fingering, interpretation, all petty points, and whenever she did the whole thing had to stop. In fact the entire string section seemed to be waging some sort of war with the conductor, who resorted to bellowing at them to keep quiet and play, although I noticed he couldn't resist taking them up on some points. And then the rehearsal was over, people were filing into the chapel for evensong, and that was it; we hadn't even reached the end.

I sat at the piano watching the musicians pack up. Then I got up, put my score back in my bag beside the groceries I'd bought on the way over.

I went back to the church hall with its bare wood floor, its white-painted walls, its spinning dust motes and those cheaply

175

framed religious pictures on the walls (Jesus in robes with a glowing heart; a crowd of men with mouths open in surprise; men looking up towards Jesus with hands clasped and sad eyes), sat again at the old upright and played the concerto over and over. I was trying to make it part of myself; I was trying to tie myself to it in order to free myself from it.

47.

Oxford, October, 1951

The morning of the concert. I woke, lay in bed not moving, then remembered what was about to happen. I got up quickly to use the lavatory.

Downstairs, Edward was playing opera music in his study. The church hall was occupied on a Saturday morning; choir practice. The opera continued. Why do opera singers never hit the note squarely? I thought. Why does the orchestra shimmer around the voices, there, but never quite accompanying? The light was hard, bright. I watched a man walk past below with a dog on a lead, swinging a stick; on their way to the meadow. The clocks of the town started their slow, unsynchronised chime.

I was standing at the basin in front of the mirror washing my hands, when I noticed that the little finger of my right hand was curling slightly inwards. When I tried to straighten it, it didn't respond. I pulled at it with my other hand, but it returned to that odd curled-up position. I dressed and went downstairs, put the kettle on the stove, sat at the table, looked at my hand again. Now the fourth finger was doing it too. I stood up quickly and shook my hand vigorously. I looked again; there was no change — both fingers were bent.

The kettle whistled; I picked it up, held it poised. I was about to tip the boiling water over myself, but something stopped me; something within me considered this and dismissed it. Instead I walked up the hall to the piano.

177

I played a C minor scale. The two fingers played their notes slowly, as if with hesitation. I played a rapid passage of the concerto up the top of the keyboard and they could not keep up at all. It was as if something had been cut, a tendon, or a synapse, something that links thought and action.

A beat of silence, and then another.

There was no front room anymore, no body within it, just space around me, white and airless space, a mouth opening to the shape of an O, no sound coming out. The view of a hand, three fingers straight, two fingers curled; the view of a piano.

'It's breakfast time,' he said at the door, frowning. 'What are you doing?'

I was lying on the chaise longue.

'Have you been sleeping? It's breakfast time. Get up. What is the matter with you? You look terrible. Sick.'

I got myself to a sitting position.

'Something has happened to the fingers on my right hand,' I heard a voice say.

'What?'

'Something has happened to my fingers, the fourth and fifth fingers on my right hand.'

'You're panicking again.'

'I can't do the concert, Edward. We're going to have to —'

'Ah,' he said, 'ah-hah,' and now he was smiling, wagging his finger, 'a little ploy, I see, to try again to get out of it.'

'This is not an excuse, Edward. I cannot play. I have damaged my —'

'Show me.'

'Looking back, I can see now that —'

'Show me.'

'One is not supposed to practise like —'

'Show me your hands.'

'One is simply not supposed to play the —'

'Show me!'

And I stood there, both hands up, palms facing him, ten fingers raised to the ceiling.

'You're clearly hysterical. They look perfectly fine.'

I stared at them. I stared at him. They did look fine. Had he performed some sort of black magic to prove his point?

'You're seeing things that aren't even there. You're beside yourself. You need to do something to take your mind off things. That will help.'

I recalled then how George and Hetty and I used to lark about before a performance. Rather than do another run-through we'd tell jokes and have a drink, perhaps something to eat, and I wondered if he might have a point. So when he said, Come in here, I'll give you something to do, I followed him. And when he gave me a big jar of copper coins to sort and count in his study, that is what I did. I sat on the rug in front of the fire, which he had lit, even though it wasn't cold, and I counted and sorted the coins several times to make sure I had things right, then I made patterns with them on the rug.

When he got up from his desk and sat in the armchair reading, with his legs stretched out, I stayed on the rug. And when he wasn't looking I examined my fingers, and they still looked fine, as if what I had noticed before was either exaggerated or imagined. And I did think about getting up and testing them again at the piano, but some strange inertia kept me sitting on the rug beside him, that little fire at my back.

And the day ticked away, and the fire burnt down, and soon it was time to dress and go to the theatre.

~

Backstage, the noise was darting around me in small circles, coming then going, coming then going, the musicians were laughing, talking, playing, tuning. I looked down at my hands. Both fingers had curled inwards again. I turned to him.

'Look, it's happened again. Look!' putting my hand to his face.

He grabbed it.

'Stop that. You're mad.'

'You have to see.'

He frowned over my fingers for a second.

'You're doing that deliberately. Straighten them out.'

'I can't, I tell you, I can't. I would if I —'

The conductor, all flapping tails and mutton chops, red in the face, bustled over like a rooster; he shook Edward's hand.

'Three minutes, Mrs Haywood, and we have a full house.'

I lurched to the door, I almost fell. Edward grabbed my arm.

'Pull yourself together. Pull yourself together, for Christ's sake. You go out there and do what you're supposed to, and you do it well.'

Members of the orchestra were staring at us. I was embarrassed, I was ashamed. I was standing backstage with only three functioning digits on my right hand. He left. The orchestra fell silent, formed a line, then they filed out, and soon I was walking onto the stage.

I remember looking up and seeing the ceiling of the Sheldonian Theatre beyond the lights, the painted sky, the cherubs gambolling in the clouds with ribbons, a scene depicted many years ago and over-painted repeatedly. I remember looking at the grey-brown clouds, the smudged cherubs with missing smiles, bodies in fragments.

I sat at the piano, my hands on the keyboard. A white baton danced before me, two black arms were thrusting, jerking, the baton was hitting the air harder and harder, a seething face behind it. My hands, with their missing fingers, clattered up and down on the keys, and when it was all over I went to the lavatory and hid in there until the theatre was empty.

~

I crept out of the toilet. I pushed on a heavy door, let myself out into the night. Keeping close to the wall of the theatre I crept around its perimeter. Then I sat on the steps in the shadow of the railing where I could see people pass. I did not have my key or bag; I didn't think I'd need them.

From where I sat I had a good view of the White Horse pub across the street, the bar below street level. I watched two men buy drinks, chink glasses, laugh at something then look away from one another and around the pub.

In the end I walked home, slinking up the back streets. I knocked when I got there; there was no answer. I went around the back, climbed in through the kitchen window, clambered over the bench. Then I checked the house in the dark; he wasn't there.

48.

Oxford, October, 1951

In the waiting room there was a baby in a pram lying still. Its eyes were wide open but were rolled back, looking at nothing. A few seats down an old man bent and hacked into a cloth he held in both hands.

The doctor was old, tired. He diagnosed a conversion disorder, focal dystonia produced by hysteria. He feared my hands could deteriorate further. Performance was clearly the trigger, so that had to be avoided, but any piano playing was a great risk (he said sadly) because it could make matters worse, even impede basic functioning. I must not play at all, he said.

All right, I said, because I had no intention of doing so anyway.

~

That week after the concert I was a creature without a shell again, and this was when he came back to the house. I wish I could have found it, that hard little home that fitted me well, to tuck into. But I couldn't find my shell, couldn't rustle up an adequate substitute fast enough. Or maybe it wouldn't have mattered what I was like that day; it would have happened anyway.

I was sitting at the window. I had not left the house since I visited the doctor; mostly I had been in bed. When he came in, making that noise with the key at the front door, I did not move. He turned the light on; for a few seconds I closed my eyes against it.

'This place is filthy,' he said.

It didn't matter to me anymore, you see. I felt him move behind me, heard him go down the hall, into the kitchen, then come back.

'Get up,' he said. 'Get up and look at this mess. I've never seen it in such a state – it's abominable.'

I got up and stood before him, my head spinning. I was not sure I would be able to remain upright. I noticed, vaguely, that he was still wearing his travelling gloves, the tan ones, soft, fine leather, he was running his index finger over the mantelpiece, but I was not taking this in properly, the possible consequences. He inspected the finger of the glove, rubbed it with his thumb, got out his handkerchief, spent some time cleaning it.

'Come here.'

I didn't move. I had run so hard, for so long, and got nowhere, and where was there to run to anyway? I did not know, I could not see, and when he came for me he drew back his gloved fist. He hit me hard in the stomach, below my ribs. I doubled over, clutching myself, fell to the floor. A few seconds then the pain hit me.

He stepped over me; I heard him pick up his bag, go upstairs.

When I could breathe again I sat up. I was sure there would be blood, that it would be gushing from me, from this great, gaping wound, the pain was so intense. But there was no blood on that new carpet in that grand old house with the antiques in the rooms and the paintings on the walls and the smooth, white ceilings, and the man upstairs unpacking his suit; there was nothing at all.

49.

Oxford, October 15th, 2005

I was in bed having a conversation with myself about where to position my body, because there was no getting out of bed now, I could not even lift an eyelid. Such a weight.

As I began to drift I heard the scales again, the technical work, and I was home, my mother was sitting beside me, telling me to do this one and then that one, it was a random drill and I was following, arpeggios next, up and down, hands all over me, pummelling me, shoulder, clavicle, head, spine.

When the music came it was my body that reacted first, that sudden jolt of recognition, bile jerking into the throat. I spat it onto the floor beside the bed. What I could hear clearly, although it was very soft, was the repeated bass note, the grand pianissimo to fortissimo crescendo, the beginning of the Rachmaninoff Concerto in C minor, number 2. And then it stopped.

I lay still, barely breathing. It started again from the beginning, the bass note beating, beating, the treble in its heightening response. Like a spectre I rose from the sheets, got down the stairs, clutching at the wall with my hands, and navigated the house one last time, brushing things with my hands, checking it all once more – the gramophone, the sound system, the piano – for sound, for life. Then I propped myself up at the window and once again dragged my gaze over next door's rain-slicked porch.

50.

Oxford, October, 1951

He beat me badly after that a few times a year. Never a blow others could see – he was clever about that. A belt around the legs or across the back; a kick on the bottom that sent me sprawling; a punch to the abdomen. He was strategic about it too, always in control. This was no flying off the handle, no striking out while drunk (he never drank much, Edward). This was considered. This was action and consequence. This was explained and justified.

My face was slapped because I had made a mistake with his laundry. I was screamed at and kicked because I was late with his dinner. I was hit for not answering quickly enough. When it was particularly bad he tucked me up in bed afterwards and brought me a cup of sugary tea. Sometimes he sat beside me, holding my hand, and explained things to me.

It was just that I was so hopeless, weak, stupid and lacking. Some of it I couldn't help. Women were like this. I was sick (women sickened easily). I needed assistance, correction, instruction; my lack of a decent education was a pity. I needed to do better. All the wives he'd seen did better than I did. He was worried about me, me and my illness. I could get sicker.

(I think this is what he must have told them after the concert. My wife is not well. She needs a lot of looking after. This recent bout came on suddenly, just before her concert, and it has been a great shock to me. Thank you, yes, it is a terrible burden.)

Women, he said, had trouble understanding things and speaking the truth. It was partly hormonal, partly the way their brains were structured; they had an immature understanding of the world. I needed to try harder to get things right.

There was another philosophy as well, linked to his academic work, something about the world consisting of self-interested individuals. The stronger and superior will naturally rise to the top, he intoned. (Sometimes at this point he brought me ice wrapped in a tea-towel to put where I said it hurt; he was indulging me, he knew it didn't really hurt at all.)

The Steinway was covered with a shawl, a vase of silk flowers was put on top: anemones — red, white and deep purple-blue, with black centres (a Union Jack in abstract miniature, I once thought). It turned out they were a bad choice of ornament; they collected the dust terribly.

51.

Oxford, November, 1951

Speech was dangerous. I became a tight-rope walker.

'Baroque, this piece of music,' he said, listening to Mozart.

'Oh yes,' I said (it wasn't, of course). But the tone must have been wrong; he looked up sharply. 'Oh yes,' I said again, better, it seemed. 'Absolutely.'

'It's warm,' he said, another time.

'It is, yes,' I said, although it was freezing.

Another time he asked me, 'Have you seen a demand and supply graph?' drawing something out of his wallet.

'Uh . . .' trying not to look at the wallet.

'Well, is it yes or no?'

'I think I've seen one,' quietly, not yet knowing the consequences.

'And what about the blanks on either side of the graph, have you noticed them?' And now he was smiling.

I waited, not looking at the wallet; looking, perhaps, at the wall behind him.

'That is where you are. Not even on the graph, not even between the axes. You are off the page entirely. You ought to think about that. Now, there's a shilling. Spend it wisely. And give me the receipts.'

~

I was limping slowly around the house. There was a letter from Hetty, who was still in Edinburgh, saying she would be in London, and why didn't I come down for a few days, we'd stay in a hotel, see some concerts, have a lark in the capital. And he wouldn't give me the money. He wouldn't give me the money for the train ticket, or the place to stay. He said Hetty was obnoxious and to be avoided. I didn't know what to tell her; I felt so ashamed of this situation I had got myself into. I told her I had something else on that I couldn't get out of, and she thought, no doubt, that I was brushing her off, perhaps even that I considered myself above her now, enjoying the easy life, married to an Oxford professor.

~

I was polishing the floor. I was ironing shirts. I was dusting a shelf of volumes on economic theory. I was thinking about Australia, a place so far off it might as well have been a fantasy. I was thinking about playing the piano again, which I would do, I thought, as soon as things got better; I'd find a really good doctor, a modern one, to help me, fix me.

I had my head in a kitchen cupboard, I was wiping a cloth in the crack between the wall and floor. I was searching for something, I was hiding from something. I got up, put the cloth down, walked out the front door.

52.

Oxford, December, 1951

I sat on the platform, bag beside me, in my pocket savings I had scrimped from the housekeeping.

I had written again to Hetty and asked if she might need some assistance in Edinburgh. She wrote back saying she didn't, and I could tell by the tone that she was still offended about London. You can visit if you like, she wrote, but you can't stay here, she'll think you're an intruder, which would be funny for about five minutes, then horrible, so not worth it. Why don't you get Edward to pay for a hotel?

My letter to George was returned (he was in Europe by then, I found out later).

My letter to Rachel in Whitby was unsent. I couldn't work out what to say, what words to send to that happy, bustling house on the hill.

My letter to my mother's cousin in York was oblique, but she wasn't stupid. Marriage is a challenge, she wrote back. You must have fortitude. Sometimes men are bad-tempered, but it usually passes. Try to get things right. I do recall you were not one to be humble; perhaps this requires some correction on your part. We would gladly host you and your husband for tea.

A train clattered in; I watched the people get off and get on. I felt the money in my pocket, enough for the train ticket and a week in London, at a stretch, until I could find something else, a job, it didn't matter what. It had taken a long time – weeks – to save even this, and had felt dangerous (it was dangerous).

Bess had given me a stew recipe that used virtually nothing, tasted all right and lasted for ages.

Thinking of Bess lifted me.

At the end of the day I got up and went back to the house.

53.

Oxford, December, 1951

Bess had come to the door a couple of weeks after the concert. She said she was part of an arts circle with a group of women, all college wives. Every month on a Tuesday they met to discuss artistic matters, usually around a theme (classicism; romanticism; impressionism; the avant-garde), and she invited me to join them at the next one. I said no (the thought of it, facing such people after that concert, facing anyone, talking). But she returned and asked me again a few days later.

'The problem is,' she said, pushing her hair behind her ears, 'I'm down to lead a discussion on music and nationalism and I don't know a thing about it. Alice, could you suggest some New World composers I might mention?' And later, after I'd given her some tea and a few names and thoughts: 'Well, you'll have to come now, won't you, you've practically done the whole thing for me. None of us know a jot about music; you don't realise how much your presence would be appreciated. You'd be doing us a great favour.' I knew what she was up to.

I got to her place early, helped her set up. When the doorbell rang it was Stella, who had just returned from a dig so she couldn't have been at the concert.

Enid next. She got away on Tuesday afternoons by leaving her children with a woman down the street (whose children she looked after on a Wednesday when that woman went to her fencing club).

Then there was Penelope. 'Oh yes, Alice Haywood,' she said, when Bess introduced me, and she looked away, and I knew she'd been at the concert, and just as I was about to vomit right there on the fringed rug, Bess said, 'Alice will add some much-needed musical expertise to our circle.'

'What luck!' Penelope said. 'We certainly need it.'

These women did not sit, hands in their laps, watching, holding everything back. They sat forward, spoke passionately, argued intensely; ideas really mattered to them. Their intelligence was like electricity zinging across the room. Stella argued with such impeccable logic it bored through everything, until Enid sailed in and eloquently rebutted. Once or twice when Penelope made a point she raised a fist in the air.

A question about music came up that day to which no one knew the answer; the conversation went round and round. Finally I thought, oh well, here goes, and I told them what I knew, and that was it, I was part of it.

We spoke for hours. Frank came home and stood at the door of the sitting room, smiling in that way he had, his eyes nearly closing behind his glasses. He disappeared and came back with glasses of sherry filled to the brim, also a bowl of nuts he'd roasted himself, passing them around on a tarnished silver tray.

When we heard whistling and pots clattering in the kitchen, Enid whispered, 'What's he doing now?'

'Cooking dinner,' Bess said. 'Well, I can't cook, can I?'

'What does he make?'

'All sorts of things. Baked beans on toast —'

'That'd be right.'

'Irish stew, shepherd's pie, braised celery, roast pigeon, and on special occasions a thing called paella, which is quite delicious. He got it from a book by Elizabeth David. He's devoted to her recipes.'

Silence.

'Well, you're too busy to cook, aren't you?' Penelope said.

'Doing what?' said Bess.

'Saving our souls,' I said, out of the blue.

'Oh no,' she said, 'we're all doing that, every one of us together, including you,' turning to me.

We met for years. Sitting here, I still miss it.

I never told any of these women about Edward. Once, I planned to tell Bess, but there was a conversation that day in our arts circle meeting about a failed Oxford marriage. The divorce had affected the man's career badly, one of the women said, and they all nodded. They spoke of the woman involved without sympathy; she'd always been difficult to get along with, someone said. She was a neurotic, another person added, and no doubt terribly hard to live with, too. No children, either, said another, then trailed off, because a few of us sitting there still had no children. And Bess listened to all this, occasionally nodding. She was a great supporter of the institution of marriage; hers was happy. I realised then this was not a conversation one had. One did not speak badly of one's husbands in a way that was serious. Marriages were sealed boxes.

I learnt a lot about how to live in Oxford from these women, and I made some good friends. I kept expecting Edward would try to prevent me attending; perhaps because the other husbands supported it he didn't.

When we finished that first evening, Bess and Frank stood at their front door waving and smiling, shoulders touching, and I walked home in the twilight virtually hugging myself. Then into that grey and silent house, and there he was in his study, angry about his dinner, even though I'd prepared it and left instructions on how to heat it.

54.
Oxford, 1953

I made it onto the charity rosters. I started helping at a soup
kitchen run by one of the churches on St Aldates, joining the
other women in the kitchen on a Saturday afternoon, scrub-
bing out the huge pots caked with overcooked stew and barley.
The men sat at long tables eating with their heads close to their
bowls. It moved me to watch them eat; they were so engrossed
in their food, the old ones, in particular, the way they silently
relished it. There were never any women among them; I don't
know where the homeless women ate. The more gregarious
ladies doled out the food at the counter. The young priest ate
among the homeless, his freshly ironed sleeves rolled up, his
clean hair neatly parted. At the end we lifted the huge pots back
onto the racks, still warm from the wash, and I walked home,
glancing behind me now and again, half-expecting one of those
men to come up behind me and tap me on the shoulder.

~

Over the summer, when Edward was away, there were dinner
parties at Bess and Frank's house (hummus, ratatouille, cucumber
soup; back then he had to go down to London to get his ingredients), picnics in the parks, walks in the countryside. I still wasn't
pregnant, another sadness among many (our barrenness was my
fault, of course; I was faulty all the way through). Sometimes
I looked after other people's children during the holidays, those
were times I cherished. We'd sing and cook, go for adventures

in the meadow, play down by the river. But I was never entirely at ease during the summer; sometimes Edward dropped in out of the blue. Even if he was supposed to be in America, he might suddenly turn up. But there was still some release, and a lot of peace to be had. Autumn arrived too quickly; it was Michaelmas again, the start of another academic year. He came home for good, the town filled up with bicycles going fast, students, academics.

~

We went to a dinner party at Bess and Frank's once during Michaelmas term. It was unusual, the timing of it; perhaps Frank was in denial that summer was really over.

'What was it like, growing up surrounded by orange trees?' Frank asked, drawing me into the conversation, for I had been unusually quiet. (When Edward wasn't there I talked a lot.) And perhaps he was keen for stories of a sunnier place.

I glanced quickly around the table; was I the only one who could tell how uncomfortable Edward was with this turn of conversation? Indeed, with any conversation that had me at its centre?

'Hard work,' I said, keeping it short.

Frank thought I was joking and laughed.

'Hard work?' he said. 'I'll say!'

'I don't think there was much water, Frank,' Bess said, shrewder.

'It was mallee land before they cleared it for citrus,' I said. 'Mallee doesn't need a lot of water; it can tolerate drought. So they had to bring the water in.'

'Oh,' said Frank. 'And there I was imagining an idyllic child-hood. Children basking in perfumed groves of citrus, eating fruit with dripping fingers.'

'Well, we all ate fruit, of course, but in order to grow it my parents had to dig furrows along the lines of trees most mornings for irrigation. The water was brought from the river in big open channels and you dug the furrows to bring the water from the channels to you. I knew of two children who fell and drowned in those channels.'

'Oh dear! I have learnt something new, haven't I? I never imagined.'

One of Frank's friends sitting at the end of the table said he'd heard of mallee: it could not only tolerate drought, but also fire and marauding animals. Its roots stored food underground and could sprout again and again.

Frank had cooked paella that night, he'd been up to Covent Garden again to get his ingredients, and when the dish was set before Edward he huffed and frowned, until Frank finally said, 'All right there, old man?' which made me nervous, because Edward was so clearly older than the rest of us but didn't like it pointed out.

'What is this?' he said, barely getting the words out.

'It's paella, old chap, brilliant stuff. Mediterranean food from a sunny climate. Happy food, you see; Alice knows all about it. Tuck in.'

Edward glared at his plate, his fork, and I started dreading leaving, the night ahead. And Frank went on and on about Elizabeth David, how she'd lived in Greece and was evacuated to Egypt during the war; how, when she came back to England she was so appalled at the state of the food she viewed it as a violent insult to humanity. She published her first book in England before anyone could even get hold of most of the ingredients.

When we got home that night Edward hurt me, and all thoughts of Elizabeth David, oranges, mallee and paella scattered.

55.
Oxford, May 15th, 1972

I had been anaesthetised. I woke in a white place, clouds billowed around me, I was smiling.

I heard the rattle of cutlery on crockery, the curtain around the bed was whisked aside. There was a nurse with a trolley, a neat smile. She gave me tea and buttered toast, and this was nice, but there was something else I desired with all my heart.

'In a minute,' she said.

And then he was brought to me, wrapped in a blanket.

I was forty-one; I was resigned to my inability to have children. This was a miracle to me.

He had a shock of dark hair, big brown eyes. He was my mother, my father, the siblings I had never had, the extended family I had never met, but most of all, best of all, he was none of these people, he was himself, and he, tiny being, was staring up at me, into my eyes, as if to say: There you are, at last.

I held him to my face and smelt him. I was waking up, I was awake.

56.
Oxford, 1972

Richard's birth coincided with the oil crisis, a waning economy and heightened attacks on Keynesianism in academia as well as by the government and the media. Edward's work started to receive the reception he had always coveted. He was busy lecturing all over Britain and other parts of the world. He wasn't going to miss a moment of it; he had been waiting so long. As a consequence, Richard and I were mostly left alone during his early years. Across the Atlantic Friedman was busy with his popular columns and broadcasts, and Edward, envious of the man he viewed as the one to beat (despite, broadly speaking, being on the same team), worked even harder. When he wasn't away he was in his office writing, or at meetings.

On the rare occasions he was home he was mostly easier to live with. He found fault less, at times he even expressed gratitude for things I did for him. Other times he would revert and do cruel things, order me to ignore Richard when he was crying, but I was cleverer then, something finally mattered, and I would feign indifference, shrug, say, fine, let him scream the house down, and he'd give me a look of consternation and tell me to go to him.

So these were happy years. Caring for Richard felt like a dance, a synchronicity of movement and feeling. Sometimes we got out of step, then looked for our rhythm again, danced on. It emptied me out, it filled me up. With the other mothers and children we created a little community with its own sense of time, its own geographies, its own ways of relating. Caring, acceptance, generosity, patience, humour, kindness, creativity and love: these were the things we aspired to.

Richard showed such an interest in music that I started him young, which Edward didn't much like (You'll make him a nancy boy). But we did it anyway when he wasn't around. I taught him piano first, then organised violin lessons, because I wanted him to learn an instrument that was played with others, an instrument that, played solo, had the musician standing before the audience, not sitting with his head down behind a big block of wood. Before he went to school he was already making up little themes and variations.

Sometimes I pictured him playing with my parents, hide and seek among the orange trees, or down by the river fishing for yabbies, or learning to look for snakes before jumping over a log.

57.

Oxford, May 15th, 1979

When Richard turned seven, Edward came home for his birthday, which was unusual. We were standing in the kitchen, the three of us, singing around a sponge filled with jam and cream and strawberries, singing at seven little candles. Richard blew them out, he and I ate a piece, then another each, Edward refused any (he'd been on television earlier in the day; he wanted to stay trim for future appearances). Richard and I went upstairs and I ran his bath.

When I came back down Edward called me into his study and told me he had enrolled Richard at the Dragon School in North Oxford, where he would start in a few months as a boarder. I remember standing before him feeling as much shock and pain as if I had been hit again for the first time.

'No,' I got out finally. 'That is not right. It would not suit him.'

Edward was smiling in a way I knew so well by then.

'Not suit him, or not suit you? You think I haven't noticed,' and how bitter he sounded, how hateful, 'this thing you have going between you. It's sick. He needs to be removed from your clutches.'

I was aghast; I could not bear this.

'He is a child, Edward. He is seven. He needs his family. He needs love. This is what we all need, I think,' and I almost felt sorry for him for a moment, sitting at his desk, fiddling with the papers in front of him, pretending not to listen.

Edward's once lustrous hair had thinned, a bald patch at the front was steadily getting bigger. He spent a lot of time in front of the mirror every morning, arranging his hair over this bald spot. He was wearing a new suit, highly polished shoes, also new. These days he regularly advised Cabinet, appeared on television, chaired committees, gave plenaries. I saw in front of me a man who was so successful in many worldly ways, yet so lacking. A man who had missed seven years of his only child's life, who had no real friends, and who seemed to have no sense of joy, or peace. A man so convinced of his view of the world that he had to prove it, prove it, prove it.

'He is such a magnificent boy, our son,' I said, and while I was talking he poked around in a drawer of the desk. 'He is the most loving, intelligent, creative, affectionate —' but his lip was curling, and suddenly I knew that this was dangerous talk; I stopped immediately.

'Love?' he said sneeringly. 'Love? What would *you* know about that? You've never shown me any love or support or —'

'Edward, do not say these things, please.' I spoke quietly, not wishing to upset him more, determined to make him see sense about Richard.

'I've tried so hard to get you to see things; my God, I may as well have been talking to a wall you're so thick!' And so on, in the familiar way, but I let it pass over me, waiting for the invective to run its course.

'Edward,' I started, and I'd rehearsed this in my head while he was talking, 'don't you think that, as parents, we might try to improve on what has gone before? Don't you think that you and I might have done better if we'd had more of a chance to just be ourselves in our childhoods? Don't you think we might have found things easier if we had not been sent away so young?'

He slammed the drawer suddenly; I jumped.

'I don't care what you think,' he snapped. 'He's going. And if you want to talk about improving people, let's look at you, shall we? You, who moon about here doing nothing, not exactly a productive member of society, are you? You're a bad example. It will be good for him. It'll toughen him up, teach him the ways of the real world, rather than this namby-pamby nursery you've got here. It'll give him the best education around. Christ, it costs enough. Anyway, everyone goes there.'

'Not everyone,' I said. 'Many children go to the local primary and are very happy there. I'd thought Richard would do the same.'

He snorted; he was pretending to read the paper in front of him. 'That place? Don't be funny.'

'I've spoken to lots of parents whose children go there and they think it's excellent.'

'Ah, yes, the wisdom of gossiping women. We should go by that, definitely.'

'It doesn't cost anything.'

'Because it's rubbish.'

He looked up.

'Get out. I'm not talking about it anymore. The decision's made.'

I heard a noise in the hall, Richard; he had finished his bath, got dressed in his pyjamas. How long had he been there? I took him upstairs, read him a story.

~

Edward had bought Richard a ball (another first) and we were walking in the park the next day, before Edward left again. Richard ran off with the ball across the grass, he had spotted a friend, and as they played together, kicking it to one another, I brought up the question of school once more.

I tried every tactic I knew. I flattered and argued and cajoled, and nothing worked; I started to feel that I was making matters worse, Edward was seeing it as a challenge, a chance to stamp his authority. So I pretended to agree with him, to see if that would work, but it didn't; he thought he had won already.

When I took it up with him again that evening he exploded, and he hit me and grabbed the back of my shirt and dragged me towards the wall, and I knew he meant to throw me against it, with Richard right there, awake, upstairs, which he had never done before. I managed to struggle from his grasp, got out of the room; he didn't follow me. I could hear Richard in his bedroom, he had been bouncing his ball against the wall, and the ball had stopped and I knew he was listening, and I knew Edward knew that he'd been listening, too, and the thought of this, amid it all, made me sick. That Edward would do that to another person, his wife, and in earshot of his small son.

Up to the bathroom, wiping off the blood, cleaning myself up, running Richard's bath at the same time. Waiting until I stopped shaking before I went to get him. Richard walked to the bathroom stiffly, not looking at me, and I knew Edward's timing had been deliberate.

I should have left then, of course, and taken Richard with me. But I worried, I doubted. I worried about Richard's future, son of a single mother, a cripple, a woman who had not got on in the world. I knew Edward would try to stop me. I worried about paying for Richard's music lessons, his books, his shoes. I worried that Edward would prevent me from seeing my son at all. I had no belief in my capacity to survive.

I talked to Marjorie, whose sons went to the school, and she said it was terribly prestigious, academically excellent, and its music program was highly regarded. I talked to Edith, whose daughter was there. Boarding is good for them, she said, and starting them young is best. I knew this wasn't true, and I should have been more confident, done something more, but I kept doubting myself.

Was this about me keeping Richard for myself? I wondered, because I was lonely and I loved him so much, and loved to have him close — was I being selfish? Was it because my marriage was so terrible that I wanted him near? Would it be better for his education, including his musical education, to go to the school? Was this premature goodbye another sacrifice I must make for him gladly? All these questions circling, circling, circling.

When the time came and Richard was due to leave, I smiled and said, Oh, Richard, what a great school, you'll be so happy there, and his eyes took in my face, and he saw it all, but he smiled bravely anyway, and trotted off with his little cap on, and his new shoes, and his bag over his shoulder.

58.
Oxford, October, 1979

Sadness is demanding. It demands your entire body, the way it asks you to carry its burden; it makes you tire so easily.

I aged quickly after Richard went to school. My hair started to turn white, lines appeared on my face. My skin became finer and drier and seemed to detach from my veins and bones and pulse. My breath was shallower, I had to sigh sometimes to catch the small portion of air that I needed to keep going. Sadness curled me into myself, asked me to think upon it. Even if I forgot it for a moment, it was still there, calling me back to its cold arms, this terrible grief.

You stink, Edward said. You're like an old dishcloth. Surprised, I think, by how low I could go. Get up and do something, for God's sake. You have no self-respect. (He was right about that; I had disintegrated entirely.) He used me at will, wiping himself off, discarding me.

Bess called around. I had not shown up at the arts circle or my volunteer work. She knew I was crushed by Richard's absence; she'd seen many sad mothers, but she could not know or understand the extent of it. She caught me in my nightgown; I pretended I had the flu, easier for both of us. Somehow she got me to start coming on Tuesdays again; perhaps I was too tired to argue with her.

'All right,' I said, 'but I'm not talking about music or going to any concerts.'

'We're talking about Impressionism next time, and jolly old Monet.'

'No Debussy,' I said. 'No Ravel.'

'Just painting, Alice, just bits of pink and purple daubed on canvas by a Frog. No music. Although I don't know why; I find music to be so healing.'

It makes you feel, is what I could have said. That is the problem with it. I can't afford to feel anymore. If I feel all this I'll die.

~

Richard came home some weekends, and for the holidays, and when he did I put up a front. I got the house ready and I washed and dressed nicely. He was a different boy already. He was growing up, but it was more than that. He had taken on an abstracted air, as if he were coated with something, and those offhand manners, they were something I recognised all too well. Occasionally he'd hug me and start to cry, but then his tears mysteriously stopped, as if he had given them an order, an order he'd been taught (I'd been taught it, too). This was too much. I held him close.

I kept holding on. We made the most of the holidays. We swam with friends in the Isis, and I couldn't help but think that he might have been swimming across the mighty Murray–Darling, a rite of passage. Then he'd have sat on the bank with his friends, perhaps some fishing afterwards, a campfire, they'd eat what they'd caught.

I wrote to him every week. I wished I had wonderful things to write about, the glorious life I might have been living; instead I wrote about current affairs and what I'd seen in the park or meadow. Sometimes I'd include memories of our times together and imagine what we might do the next time I saw him. If I'd had the courage, I would have balled it all up in my hand and written: I love you so much. I love you more than life itself. You are a miracle to me, and a wonderful person. The things you feel are important, never doubt that. But I never did write that.

At first he replied frequently, in that dear schoolboy hand. Then the letters got shorter and came irregularly. He was busy with other things, which I told myself was good, surely.

After a while, if I tried to hold him when he came home, he'd pull away. Maybe it was just him growing up. Or maybe he blamed me for sending him away; by then he could see he wasn't coming back. Edward's decision had become mine. My acquiescence had sealed it. I don't think he ever forgave me; the rupture it created between us never healed.

Sometimes at night I thought about getting out of bed and walking to the school, sitting by the fence, as if I might hear him breathing in his sleep, that beautiful sound. Sometimes I imagined I'd hold up a sign as I sat there on the pavement. But what would the sign say? Maybe: *I am near.*

～

After the Dragon School he went to Charterhouse, Edward's alma mater, which also had an excellent music program (the best the country had to offer, several people assured me). He started spending his summers with friends, often in St Ives, Cornwall, where his friend Sandy lived. Sandy's parents were artists (his mother a noted sculptor, his father a painter, and both of them younger than me). When he was nearing the end of school he started socialising in the artists' circles down there (I read this in a concert program). I don't think it was just the art and music that attracted him though; this was his surrogate family.

When he finished school he was accepted at the Royal Academy of Music (more prestigious than the Royal College). What pride I felt then, and what fear. How my child continued to amaze and delight me (even at such a distance). Edward was appalled; he rang me from America screaming down the phone, great waves of the Atlantic lapping in my ears, said he wouldn't pay for any of it. But Richard had got himself a scholarship. He was enrolled to study viola and the piano, but in his first year he took an option in composition, and that was it, he's been composing ever since.

Success came early. A work premiered at the Proms when he was still a student, followed by a recording contract, and so it went. He received popular acclaim, as well as from the classical music fraternity, and continues to do so. He also has a lot of energy. He can conduct one of his nouveau symphonies for the BBC in the morning, collaborate with a pop star in the afternoon, go to some publicity event in the evening, then fall into his studio and work all night. He looks the part too: he's handsome, sexy, and dresses with eccentric style.

He didn't come home much when he was at college. He did bring his first proper girlfriend to meet me, a flautist called Marlena. She had long, wavy hair and a big mouth with large, plump lips. He was like a puppy around her, panting and jumping. She broke his heart, that one, and he was different with women after that, hardened, churned through them.

The Christmas before last he came home with Martha, an actor; the visit was her idea, I'm sure of it. He sat with his legs out, arms crossed, looking bored while she made conversation about things like the garden, which I'd cleared by then and replanted (bulbs, sunflowers, vegetables; I ended up sitting out there a lot on an outdoor chair I'd scavenged from someone else's rubbish).

Who was this man, I thought, sitting in the front room saying nothing while his girlfriend tried hard to be polite and make conversation? Who was this man, so tall, successful and good-looking? This son of mine whom I no longer knew but continued to love with a feeling so strong it nearly choked me.

Why was he sitting there like that while she talked? Why did he not lean forward, join in the conversation, tell me something about Martha, look at her when she spoke? Why did he ignore me when I prompted him?

I had stopped writing to him every week when he'd been at college for a couple of years; perhaps I could no longer bear the silence in return. I found out what he was up to by reading the papers and listening to the radio (pacing around the house as it played, so full of feeling; he wrote such beautiful, unusual music). Why he didn't invite me to concerts or tell me about them, I didn't know. I assumed he was ashamed of me. Maybe Edward had got to him, said things about me. Or perhaps he wanted nothing to do with our gaping wound of a family.

It was when Richard began receiving public recognition that Edward became interested in him. He started visiting Richard in London. He took him out to fancy dinners. I don't know how much that would have appealed to Richard, and I don't know what Richard made of his famous father – he never talked with me about Edward; I never asked. But I watched the two of them closely on the few occasions we were all together. Edward listened to Richard, I noticed. I knew only too well how Edward could woo people. He ignored me but was never as rude when Richard was around. Richard was formal with him, stiff. Wary? I wasn't sure. Once I saw a photo of them in the paper at some event and Edward was standing close to Richard (perhaps hoping some of that cool Britannia would rub off onto him) and Richard was looking at him with an expression I could not quite fathom. I studied that picture. Was it contempt on his face, or just uncertainty, or something else? I wondered to what extent Richard had his father in him. Could he love? Did he treat women well?

I wanted him to know how much love mattered, love that was giving; I wanted him to know that it enlivened you. I wanted him to know the truth of what had happened to his family, and why, so that he could make sense of things. I'd never even come close. Years I'd had to say all this, but I'd been scared, sad, defeated, and I was still putting it off. Picking up the phone, putting it down again.

59.
Oxford, June, 2005

It was a Sunday afternoon. Edward was back in town and had just left for the tennis courts, swinging his racquet. His legs were wizened, the hair on them curly and white, his knees like two pebbles. I could have told him he was far too old for such a thing, but he'd become health-conscious in his old age, exercised regularly on various machines, and still thought he could do anything. Characteristically obsessive, he'd bought a juicer for the kitchen and demanded I peel and chop all sorts of strange fruits and vegetables to put in it. The machine took all the best bits out of them, stripped them to a thin, warm juice; I would have told him this, too, if he'd been interested, if I could still tell the truth. It took a long time to clean properly, that thing, and when it malfunctioned he called me stupid.

He was not happy; contentment never found him. You could see in his body the disappointment, despite everything; the way his shoulders hunched, the mean twist of his lips. He expressed scorn and disgust for most others he encountered. I think he was envious of anyone who was happy. I never got a sense, though, that he knew what he was lacking and thus how he might fix it. Quite the contrary: it was always someone else's fault. He continued to lash out at me, and anyone who unsettled or offended him, as long as it would not affect his reputation. He was the sort of elderly man who wrote aggressive letters to his favoured airline, using all his titles, to complain about, say, the service on the Dubai leg. For a man of intellect he displayed a remarkable lack of curiosity about the world around him. He seldom asked questions. He boasted constantly. He never listened.

Richard was living in London and was established as a significant composer, but I had not heard any new work on the radio for a while, and when he didn't appear in the Proms program for a third year running I was worried, but did not know how to raise it.

I was still involved in charity work, mostly for the homeless. I was never the organiser, always one of the women in the kitchen out the back, or sitting in a cold hall behind a tin of petty cash. Privately, I resented that these activities were so often tied to a church. I had no faith, thought God was a lie.

I kept attending the arts circle, too, although sometimes I couldn't get out of bed, and this depression would last for weeks. Getting dressed became a distant location I could no longer reach. I kept the house as best I could for Edward and in case Richard dropped in (he seldom did); I rarely had friends around, I didn't have the energy. I knitted for charities and became quite skilled at babies' and children's clothes in modern designs. I had wanted a daughter; it wasn't to be. I worried perennially that Edward would sell the house from underneath me. I grew old. My hands never got better; then again, I never tried them at the piano. Playing was a distant memory, part of being a girl.

There was a rattle at the knocker that Sunday afternoon, unusually loud; Edward had been gone for about an hour. A young man stood there, a post-doc, who suffered Edward's company, no doubt in the hope that Edward could help his employment prospects (Edward had a reputation for writing make-or-break references; I suspect one could never be entirely sure which).

'Mrs Haywood?'

He was bending over to suck in air as if breathing through a snorkel. I invited him in for a glass of water. (It turned out he had run all the way from the courts.)

'I am very sorry. Edward, your husband, is dead,' he got out eventually.

I couldn't speak for a few moments. Then, 'I don't believe you.' I had outlived him? Not possible.

He blanched. I thought he was going to vomit. I turned around quickly, got the plastic salad bowl from the draining board, held it out to him, but he shook his head.

'I'm just ... I'm awfully sorry,' and the poor man, he was in agony. 'We thought we should tell you immediately. We shouldn't have done it like this, we should have found a friend.'

It was a massive heart attack. Edward was about to return a lob when he collapsed on the court, reaching up, back arched. Racquet dropped.

'It's all right,' I said.

All right? All right? I had outlived him! My ribs were creaking, my diaphragm expanding, I could breathe again. I could breathe! I started to feel light-headed, everything was white, bright, buzzing, singing. But the young man was asking me something, he wanted me to go with him to the infirmary. I spiralled towards the ground.

When we arrived, the two others who had been playing tennis were standing by the body, which was under a green sheet, talking about the game. It would have been a winner, they said, of the shot Edward had been attempting. If he hadn't died, that is, someone said. Me.

~

A funeral fit for a statesman at the college; a rehearsal the day before. Would you stand there, Mrs Haywood. Good. Now we all rise. Will your son be attending today? Just tomorrow. I see.

The eulogies were as expected. A magnificent mind. One of the best the country has ever seen. A lifetime of service. An example to us all. A list of his honours, positions, medals. Richard declined to speak; some of his music was played instead (a requiem he'd written for a pop star some years before).

A few dons came over afterwards, murmuring their commiserations, but not many. They were interested in Richard, though, those Oxford men, lining up to shake his hand, smirking up at him, so tall in his tight suit, his pointy shoes, his extraordinary hair. All the women looking his way, too.

Then, thank goodness, Richard touched my elbow, said it was time to go home. At the door I was taking the cups and saucers down already in my head; we could finally talk. Until I realised he wasn't coming in, he was just dropping me home. So sorry, have to get back to London. You'll be all right, won't you, Mother?

I went down to the kitchen and sat at the table. At one point I got up and put an egg in a saucepan on the stove, but I didn't light it, I just sat there watching it.

In the morning I was still in the kitchen watching it, the dawn reflected on the side of the saucepan. In my hands was the black patent leather handbag, peeling at the zip – a hand-me-down from Bess – which contained my purse, a hanky and the keys to the door. I got up, walked down the hall, but instead of walking out the front door I went up to the bedroom and closed the door.

~

The phone rang; mail dropped to the floor – letters about Edward's papers, wanted for collections, universities, museums, libraries. I replied to none.

Edward's solicitor rang, requested a meeting, earliest possible convenience. I went up to London, walked all the way from Paddington to save the money of a tube ticket. There was a wind in Hyde Park that day, circling, picking things up, putting them down – leaves, twigs, rubbish were all lifted, danced, dumped. It was in the solicitor's office too, I soon noticed; the blinds on the windows suddenly lifted and rattled, making me start. The solicitor told me that Edward's seams of wealth, of which I had no knowledge whatsoever, would be managed by a series of trusts. The allowance I had been left, I quickly calculated, would barely cover basic living. He took out a photograph of one of Edward's London houses (again, I'd had no idea). There were two cars in the garage, one a Jaguar.

I walked back to the train station, every bit of me shaking, realising belatedly that I had not eaten or drunk all day. With the few coins in my purse I bought a cup of tea at the station, and how extraordinary, I remember thinking, staring at the tracks, that the man could hate and humiliate me, even from his grave.

'Apparently I'm in charge of some bloody trust,' Richard said on the phone that evening, 'and I have to pay all your bills, or something equally ridiculous. Christ, he was a ... Anyway, I'll do it for now, but we need to get you some cards so you can manage for yourself, also change that fucking crazy allowance he's given you. I'll get onto it, all right? I've got to go now.'

More phone calls; I didn't answer. More letters; I left them on the floor. I rang Richard a few times but he wasn't there. Bess came calling, I watched her waiting on the doorstep, watched her leave.

He had died and I was free. Cue the Hallelujah Chorus. Cue the end of Beethoven's Ninth. Or cue nothing at all. It doesn't matter, just walk out that door!

But I didn't. I sat looking out the window or lying on the floor. The man had died, but I still couldn't leave, and I couldn't understand why.

The world kept turning, the arts circle met, the charity rosters rolled on, and I didn't do any of it. Instead I started to burn his papers and books, the ones that all the letters mentioned first, which gave me warmth, faintly, briefly. I was forgetting to eat, although this was not deliberate yet. Then one morning in late September, sitting at the window, feeling hungry (but dully, nothing sharp about it), I decided that if I wasn't going to leave, if I couldn't reach Richard, if I couldn't do these things, then I would like to die instead. There was nothing dramatic about the decision; it was just a soul quietly giving up. I remember looking over at my knitting needles, which I hadn't touched in weeks. There was a pullover on them, unfinished, for a baby girl in mauve and blue wool – perhaps someone else could finish it, I thought. I would leave the pattern handy.

I sat at the piano and struck a note with my finger: A, concert A, a sixth above middle C, and I heard an orchestra tuning up, long bows on open strings, perfect fifths splitting, opening, closing, surging, bowing, the woodwind, the brass, the growl of the double bass. A, A, A, everything playing that note until it, too, began to fade, waiting for the music to begin.

60.

Oxford, October 16th, 2005

I was on the floor in the front room listening to the first movement of the Rachmaninoff being played over and over. My fingers were moving against the carpet, my chapped lips opening, closing. I was very thirsty. The hunger might fade, but my God, this thirst.

When the playing stopped I lay in wait to see if I had died or if it would start again. The phone had rung once, twice, three times; now it was going again, and I could not get to it, I could not move, and this upset me. I began to weep, or was it raining, for when I inched my head to the left I could see drops on the glass.

The rain became harder; I could not hear the music. I gripped a wall, clambered onto the stool in front of the piano.

The rain skittered off the gutter, sluiced down the drains. A cyclist flew past the window wearing a jacket that streamed out behind her, flapping, rippling; dark wings. The rain diminished as suddenly as it had surged and the music surfaced through it.

I crashed my hands in fists onto the keys. The music stopped, but then continued. I pounded my fists over and over. The music stopped, then started from the concerto's beginning. I did this again and again, my arms shouting in protest, my hands shriek-ing. Every time, after a small pause, that music continued.

Instead of trying to drown it out I started to correct it. When I heard a wrong note I found the right one and played it back, one finger extended, over and over again, as loudly as I could. This made the music stop for longer, but the right note was always played back, as if in polite acknowledgement. I started to correct other things, not just wrong notes. Incorrect rhythm (I bashed the correct rhythm out on one note repeatedly), misplaced rubato, ill-judged dynamics and expression. I corrected it all. And everything I did the music listened to and incorporated. But this could not last, surely. After a while I noticed that the music was getting slower, the pauses more frequent, and after a long correction to do with the shape of a phrase (during which I had pulverised my finger) it stopped for a long time. Had it disappeared?

I sat at the keyboard, waiting, hurt finger at the ready.

I looked out at the dark road, slick with the rain still sprinkling down. I played the concert A a few times, just to be sure. But nothing came back, no music at all. It had finally gone.

The next morning, there was a knock on the front door.

II

61.
Currabin, December 17th, 2006

When I finished writing last night, I hid these pages beneath the newspaper on the kitchen table, came back out, the parrots were shrieking in the gums along the drive, and as if on cue my neighbour Shirley rounded the bend and bustled towards the veranda, a bottle of wine in one hand, a dish of her lamb casserole in the other.

'He never listens to me,' she said.

We both looked over at the paddock next door where Harold, her husband, was riding his tractor wearing a pair of large earmuffs. I don't know what he's up to out there; I thought you weren't supposed to work heavy machinery through this soil anymore. Yet every evening, there he sits, riding the tractor up and down. I've almost got used to the noise, *rrr-rrr, rrr-rrr.*

'Yes,' I said, 'that's what I used to think.'

'About my husband?'

'No, I meant about mine.'

We sat in silence for a bit.

'I suppose he's nice otherwise,' she said suddenly.

'He looks nice.'

The tractor was over by the fence, throwing up a huge cloud of dust that glowed golden in the falling light. I did think Harold was nice, actually, the few times I had met him, but what would I know? He'd come over with Shirley not long after I arrived, sat on the veranda and sucked slowly on a bottle of beer. He wanted to make sure I knew that there was a drip system on the property attached to a rainwater tank. He wanted to make sure I was using it to water the orange trees. We batted this topic to and fro politely; I have no intention of using it, I think the trees should be allowed to die.

The two of them are clearly having problems, which might explain Shirley's visits in the evenings, with her bottles and her casseroles (unfortunately not to my taste, although I don't tell her this because her intentions are so kindly, and, well, kindness, what else is there?) It probably explains the tractor, too, come to think of it.

Shirley and Harold have two children who live in Mildura and have families of their own. They have friends, enough work, are healthy and are involved in various good works in the community, yet this issue between them, whatever it is, is clearly making her most unhappy.

Now she stared at him, leaning forward a little. 'Do you think?'

'I don't know him. He just looks ... honest. I think it's the way he sits. But that could be rubbish,' I added quickly. 'You're the one who'll know best.'

She nearly left the rest of her bottle behind. I had to call after her to take it. She will be back this evening, I guarantee it.

62.

Oxford, October 17th, 2005

A young woman stood at the front door. She was thirty-something, tall, had long brown hair with a fringe, an attractive, open face.

'Hi,' she said. 'I'm the piano player from next door.'

The house was falling down around me. Doors were blowing off, walls crumbling, windows melting to pools, and there I was amid the structural ruin, a suspension of dust spinning around me.

'Emily,' extending her hand. I reached out and was clasped then released. 'I was wondering,' looking at me, right in the eye, 'if there might be a better time for me to practise.'

I stared, open-mouthed.

'Perhaps I'm too loud,' she said.

'Oh, no.'

'Sorry about all the wrong notes,' her expression neutral.

I looked down at her hands: unusually large, the nails were short. I wanted to touch that hand again, feel it, the flesh, the warmth.

'You know the concerto well. Have you played it yourself?'

After a beat, I nodded.

'Well, I just thought I'd come around and introduce myself. I'm performing it soon, you see, and I wondered if we might be able to negotiate some times when I could play ... uninterrupted.' It sounded slightly rehearsed, the way she put it.

'Where do you live?' I said, still not quite believing.

She blinked.

'Next door,' a little louder than before. 'I'm the one playing the piano.'

'But it's vacant.'

'Just the top part, the house. I'm in the basement flat.'

'Basement flat?' Such a thing did not exist.

'You don't have one? It's the old cellar. The entrance is down the easement. There's a gate.' She glanced over her shoulder. 'I suppose you can't see it from here.'

I looked at my porch, at hers.

'I moved in properly a few days ago, but I was coming and going before then for a bit, once I got the piano in. The thing is, I'm really quite woefully underprepared at this point and —'

'So you need to practise.'

'Yes,' shoulders relaxing, 'that's right.'

'Where are you from?' I said.

'Uh . . .' her gaze slid next door.

'I mean your accent.'

'Oh. A place called Orange Town, just outside Toronto. And you?'

'What?'

'Are you from here?'

I licked my lips. 'I'm from here.'

'Right.' Hands into her pockets.

'I'll be quiet,' I said.

'Thanks,' but she was frowning again when she left.

I closed the door, retreated to the chaise longue to think. I looked around. I was shocked to see the place still stood, unaltered.

63.

Oxford, October 18th, 2005

The next morning I was upstairs putting some clothes into a bag; I was packing. In order to have the energy to do this I had eaten several Custard Cream biscuits, an apple, also a packet of sausages cooked in the frypan and dipped in sauce. I was holding a vest, as my stomach considered all this food (producing a vast grumble and churn, pains shooting out every which way), which was so old it was grey, and it had a rip under the arm. Had I kept it as proof? Of that night he heaved me out of the back door and I grabbed the frame and resisted for once, wailing no, no, but he wrenched me off anyway and put me outside on the cement in my underclothes. It was freezing that night, then sleet started to fall. I scraped at the door like a dog, whimpering, in disgrace. It was as if they were the only options back then: out or in. I folded the vest, put it in the bag.

I heard her play the note, the concert A, several times: A, A, A. But I paused before I went downstairs and by the time I got there the note had stopped.

~

When she practised the concerto that evening I sat by the wall listening carefully. She was getting a lot of things wrong, so much so that I wondered if it was my recollection of the work that was at fault. I got out my old score, followed the music with a finger, turning pages, flipping back as she repeated passages. No, it wasn't me.

225

She didn't practise long; I'd have thought she would keep going for hours. I would have kept going for hours if I'd been playing like that and had a concert coming up.

~

The next morning: onto the good clothes, which had hardly been worn — the black velvet frock, the bolero jacket. Performance clothes, of a sort, for I had got better at those college dinners, it had not taken me long to learn the right way to talk; to make conversation that neither elicited nor required any response. Once, before a dinner, I'd walked down the stairs and Edward had said, before he'd even seen me, No, don't wear that, wear that other dress I got you, which amazed me. How had he seen me, was he omnipresent? Although, looking back, it was just because of the structure of the staircase — he could see me descending before I could see him, nothing more.

I heard her play a minor third, C-E flat. I got downstairs in time, but at the last minute I lost my nerve, veered away from the piano, into the study.

C-E flat, she played; the sound was muffled in the study. I picked up a bit of paper, watched the fire travel upwards towards my fingers.

C-E flat; C-E flat.

Then she played a short piece of music. It was modern and wan, it had a simple melody that dipped and lifted. It was very beautiful and I went towards it, towards the wall, and when she finished she played the concert A, and straight away, before I could think, I went to the piano and played it back, A-A: Hel-lo.

A few minutes later, another knock at the door.

'Hi there,' smiling.

No doubt about it, this woman was glowing. Her skin had the look of someone who exercises, sleeps well, eats well, works

226

well, has interests. Every movement she made was sharp; there was nothing defeated in the way she carried her body. This was a woman in full command of herself, I thought. Yet she didn't play like that.

'Has the wall always been like this, so porous?' she said.

I cleared my throat. 'No.' Quite the opposite, I could have added. Apparently no one ever heard a thing.

'I think the landlord only recently converted the basement into a living space. It was a wine cellar before then.'

'Is it dark?'

'Surprisingly not. They've made it into one big open space, studio style, and the entire back wall is glass, so the light pours in, and there's a view of the garden. Best of all, I finally have a place to myself to play uninterrupted and whenever I want.' Then she fell silent, as if she'd said the wrong thing.

I cleared my throat again. 'I must apologise for —' but she didn't let me.

'Ever since we spoke I've been meaning to come around again and apologise. I didn't say at the time that I learnt some very useful things when you played through the wall like that. I hope you'll reconsider and continue doing it.'

I didn't say anything.

'I must admit, I thought it was bothering me,' she went on, 'but I think I'm mostly bothered by this concerto at the moment.'

I still didn't speak.

'It's very hard, isn't it?' she kept on. 'I'm not getting anywhere with it right now. I've performed it before, but that was ages ago, when I was a student, and for a long time now I haven't been doing enough practice, I've been so busy with work.'

I found myself wondering if I'd dreamt her up; was this a ghost before me? The idea of a lie, an apparition, the music itself as an elaborate delusion; there was a weird safety in that.

227

'You know it very well,' she said.

Every single note.

Her open face was not guileless, there seemed to be knowledge there, perception, but it was not unkind. I didn't think it was something I needed to hide from. She was at a point of struggle, which she seemed to be dealing with calmly, maturely. But I didn't trust myself.

'When is your concert?' I said.

'Beginning of March, next year.'

It felt inevitable, that bolt of sick fear, and it must have been visible.

'Don't think I'll make it?' smiling.

I looked down.

'Well, I'd love to hear about your playing sometime,' she said, 'if you ever have the inclination. And please, if you hear me play something wrong, let me know. I need it!'

I nodded.

'Well, thanks,' she said.

For what? For keeping quiet?

And then, as if I'd spoken, 'For the music through the wall.'

The following week she continued to practise, although her efforts were sporadic. Why? I wondered. Because she was busy with work? Maybe, but she could play more in the evenings, couldn't she? Unless she was working then, too. Was it because she'd played the concerto before that her approach seemed lackadaisical?

Day after day she made the same mistakes without correcting them. And there was a lack of depth to the playing, as if she was skimming her hands over the keys, when the concerto required stretching to the extremes of dynamics – plummeting, soaring, reaching vast dimensions in the instrument. She was obviously an accomplished pianist, her touch was assured, her technique sounded excellent, but it felt, the way she was playing the concerto, that she wasn't really listening or engaging with the music.

I got agitated sitting beside the wall. I gripped the score in my hands as she made mistake after mistake. Countless times I nearly went to the piano to bang out the correct version with my finger, and when she played a passage in a lukewarm way, I found myself leaning into the wall, into the plaster, willing her to press her fingers in harder, harder.

One evening when, yet again, she was making the same obvious errors, I got up and beat out on one key the correct way to play a particular passage. She stopped playing immediately, then played what I'd suggested. We carried on like that for a little while, but it was always hard to make clear what I meant with one finger.

She was at the door again; I knew she would be.

'I've had a radical idea,' she said, and her eyes were sparkly. She was wearing jeans, a coloured sweater, shiny boots; her hair was shiny too. 'And this really is just an idea,' two hands up for emphasis. 'I'm not a professional musician, you see, I'm an academic, a geographer.' She paused, took a breath. 'Not being part of the music scene here, I have no one with a decent knowledge of the concerto to play it to. So what I was thinking was maybe one day I could come in and play the solo part for you, and you could tell me what I'm doing right and wrong. I'd really appreciate it.'

Edward would have said no. He would never have permitted it. If I'd arranged this without his knowledge and he'd come home while this woman was in the house an embarrassing scene would have occurred, and as soon as she left there would have been repercussions. The place had never been my home, to act in as I wished. But Edward was dead, Edward was gone. Perhaps I was finally starting to realise it.

'The house is untidy,' I said.

'I don't see mess. I don't even own a Hoover.'

'I'm not a piano teacher. I haven't played for . . . years.'

'The things you notice are important. It's not just random notes you're playing through the wall.'

'The piano is probably out of tune, horribly so.'

She shrugged. 'Sounds okay to me. You might be right, though. I'm not sure I have a great ear at the moment.'

'I think you do.'

We looked closely at each other for a second.

'I could come around one evening about six, if that would suit you. I don't work late on Mondays.'

I was tipping, I was looking over the edge, the fall was far. I started to feel the pounding of my heart.

'I'll see you then,' I said.

Oxford, October 24th, 2005

I had washed, dressed, powdered, twisted back my hair, and eaten a meal. The house was as clean as I could get it; respectable, at least. I was sitting in the chair I'd placed behind the piano. I was looking at a woman sitting at the Steinway, putting a score of the concerto onto the stand.

'How do you think we should do this?' she said, swivelling around.

'You could start from the beginning,' I said, after a pause.

'Good idea.'

She turned back, lifted her hands, the first line of the concerto stepped off the strings into the room.

~

She was Dr Emily Green, a Senior Lecturer in Human Geography and Fellow of Jesus College. Her parents were both academics: her mother a professor of geology, her father of law. Her brother was doing a PhD in coastal geomorphology on a tropical beach. She was a cultural geographer, she told me, and at the time she was working on a series of papers on the relative merits of economic and cultural analyses to understand geographical phenomena such as gentrification and inequality. I thought geography was about maps, I said, cartography, explorers. It still is, she said, in the sense that maps, cartography and explorers were always about space and power.

Her interest in social justice, as she put it, extended beyond the confines of her academic work. As a member of the governing body of her college, she was involved in a campaign to ban sexual relationships between Fellows and their students; mostly middle-aged or elderly men courting young female undergraduates dependent on them for their academic progress. (Alice, she said, they even divvy up the blondes and brunettes during the admissions process.)

She was also concerned about the university's aggressive acquisition of land in the city, which, in a town surrounded by a green-belt, was finite. The university's strategy was affecting housing prices, she said, and worsening the homelessness problem. She wanted the university to open up spaces like sports fields to the public.

Don't you get into trouble doing these sorts of things? I said. A bit, she agreed, but it's Oxford trouble; subtle but toxic. They do things like ask you about your referees. Doesn't that scare you? I said. Not really, I'm not going to stay here, she said. There are far better departments for my sort of stuff elsewhere. Besides, no one lives in Oxford forever, do they?

I noticed that her tone, particularly when she played legato, was like a voice. It was as if the instrument had sprung larynx, mouth and lungs and learnt to sing. I'd heard none of this through the wall. And her technique was unbowed by the work; this was not just because of the size of her hands. To give just one example, there is a sequence of chords in the development of the first movement which is huge and difficult and had caused me so much pain and trouble, yet when she played them she used an up-down motion of her wrists that allowed her to relax momentarily between each chord, preventing strain, which was clever, I thought. Another thing I noticed that day was the clarity of her touch, the way she was able to bring out individual voices in the work, despite its complex texture. But I did not dwell on these aspects of her playing that day, because what I noticed most was her interpretation of the concerto.

At the time, unsurprisingly, I associated Rachmaninoff with melancholy. His work is often said to be able to reach you at your lowest. (I even read of a man, a writer, who was prevented from suicide by simply listening to his music; he no longer felt alone.) But Emily was playing the first movement joyously, with obvious pleasure, revelling in the beauty of it. She was playing it in a way that could only be described as victorious, Beethovian, even, with suggestions of his great clarions of triumph over adversity, except that in the Rachmaninoff she had yet to establish any adversity. Combined with this there was a slippage at times in her tone; that voice-like timbre changed to something lighter, almost flippant, and wasn't helped by the numerous inaccuracies I had already noted. Overall there wasn't the intensity of engagement at the keyboard that the work required; this was part of what I had been trying to get at when I had been listening on the other side of the wall.

Sitting behind her, gazing at her hair sliding down the middle of her back, I listened to her play the last lines of the first movement, a pianissimo meno mosso section, a coda, which I'd always thought sounded like Rachmaninoff's pitiable anxiety tugging at his sleeve just when he might have achieved some relief from it. She flicked off the final chords, turned around.

'So,' she said, smiling.

I shifted in my chair, bent slowly to pick up the score.

'That was very good,' I said.

She turned back to the piano.

'I've been trying some different things with the interpretation. I'm not sure they really work.'

I didn't say anything. What did she want from me anyway? I wondered. Some quick praise so she could leave and get on with it? Her conscience assuaged by paying some attention to her lonely and decrepit elderly neighbour?

'As I said, I'd really appreciate your perspective.'

I'd actually been feeling excited. I'd powered through the housework, got dressed up, and now I realised, oh, what folly it all was. What did I have to tell her about this piece of music that would be of use? How could I even begin? I had nothing to say.

Her scarf was lying on the floor beside the piano; I noticed a faint lattice pattern in the silk. I would make a few comments, I decided, about the music, then I would never see her again, and that would be it. I roused myself.

'When the recapitulation starts, those big chords carrying the basic motif . . .'

'Yes?' flipping pages.

'You could play them more lightly.'

'Oh right, why's that?'

'Your part is the accompaniment there.'

'Is it?' She looked closely for a minute. 'So it is. Thanks.' She made a mark with a pencil. 'I always seem to have trouble with the section after that,' she volunteered. 'It always feels a bit out of control.'

'It's because you get faster there before the octaves begin, which makes them difficult. More difficult.'

'Do I get faster? You see, I didn't realise this . . .' She bent forward with the pencil. 'This is very helpful. What else?'

'Your runs could be crisper. You could use a lighter pedal, a flutter pedal, and more strength in the fingers. Aim to hear the edge of every note. It's easy to remember that with Bach or Mozart but the temptation with Rachmaninoff, the Romantics in general, is to go to mush.'

'Yes.'

'One must avoid that entirely.'

'Yes.'

'Especially with this work.'

'Oh, I agree.'

I looked at her, trying to tell if she was mocking me. That open face seemed sincere.

'You could maintain,' I said, 'a greater sense of the rhythm throughout. Like a heartbeat. Duh-dum,' and I thumped my chest. 'Duh-dum. All that rubato you use, the feeling this, the feeling that, demonstrating the beauty of it, you risk losing the thread. And you'll certainly find it difficult when you have an orchestra in tow. If you keep a continuous beat at the foundation of the work you'll bring the audience with you, as if you have roped them to you. Your playing will be addictive.'

'Do you think?'

'It was how Rachmaninoff himself played,' I said, defensive. 'A hallmark of his technique was his rhythmic drive.'

'Oh, I believe you. It's just that I sensed something big was missing, and I think this might be part of it.'

'It's a question of balance,' I said, looking away. 'Rhythm versus rubato. Tightness versus looseness. Head versus heart.'

She was nodding.

'Rachmaninoff was a controlled man, most controlled.'

'Is that so?'

'He was cold. Diffident. When he performed, he hardly moved. Just his hands moved, and from them, ah,' (I was demonstrating) 'passion flowed. Rubinstein was the same, you know; I saw him once, in London.' (Oh shut up, shut up.)

'Did you!'

'Like a statue when he played, a stone. Detachment,' I said, getting up, 'it's not a bad thing to remember.'

66.

Oxford, October 26th, 2005

I was at the front window. I saw a man walking a dog, a big boxer; the dog had its chest right near the ground and was straining so hard against the leash it was choking itself. The man was being hauled along behind it.

I heard her start to play the concerto. She was playing it exactly in rhythm, and I mean exactly, as if to the tick of a metronome. It sounded absurd, it was absurd, and wrong, absolutely. I sat there trying to ignore it. After a couple of hours it stopped and I saw her pass the window. I drew back, fast. The knock was light, conspiratorial.

'Hi there. I just wanted to thank you for the other day,' and she was holding up a large metal pot. 'It's soup.'

The aroma was billowing out, the steam. I could think of nothing to say. I reached out, the handles were still warm.

'Actually, it's also bribery. I wondered if I might be able to come around again sometime. I found our conversation so helpful, Alice. I used a metronome after we spoke and I've realised the extent to which there *is* this pulse all the way through, just like a heartbeat, as you said. It's such a percussive work.'

I nodded.

'It uses all these different aspects of the instrument, all these different sounds, as if there's a whole orchestra under the lid.'

I nodded again.

'Well, what do you think? Should we meet again?'

'That sounds fine,' after a beat.

'Great,' smiling. Then, 'Are you sure I'm not troubling you with all this?'

'No.'

'Good,' instantly relaxed.

'You know,' I called, as she opened the gate.

'Yes?'

'The rhythm.'

'Yes?'

'Rachmaninoff's rhythm – it varies. It isn't metronomic. It's the sense of rhythm that I meant, not something literal.'

'Oh, yes, I know, I looked it up after we met. I was just using the metronome to get a sense of what an even beat was like, but come to think of it I could have just held my hand here.' She pressed two fingers to her neck.

'I don't —'

'The pulse.'

'Oh. Yes.'

The soup was studded with vegetables and short, thick noodles. I ate it that night, the entire pot.

67.

Oxford, October 31st, 2005

When she played the first movement for me again, the Monday after, the music was transformed. Transformed: I am being hyperbolic. She retained some of her ill-judged rubato and deeply unfortunate cheerfulness of expression, so the mood was still wrong. There were other problems too, but she was playing it with exactly the sort of rhythmic drive I imagined. I had heard a little of this through the wall, but nothing like what I was hearing played before me. I was seized by her playing; I could have got up and danced. I tapped my hand on my knee, listening to her great swells and dives as she rode that music like a wave; it crashed down in a great wall of water, and then surged up again, over and over.

'Any thoughts?' she said as she turned to me when she finished.

It was a long time since I had talked about music; it was a long time since anyone had listened to what I had to say. Perhaps it was her playing that so emboldened me. Perhaps it was the way she had listened to what I'd said, and with such positive consequences; yes, perhaps it was the music that opened me.

'Did you know,' I began, 'that this is one of the most difficult pieces in the entire repertoire for piano? You need to be a virtuoso to perform it.'

'Do you think?'

'So they say.'

'Were you a virtuoso?'

'No.'

'Am I a virtuoso?' smiling.

'No. Not yet.'

'Oh dear,' still smiling, then, 'I wonder what makes a virtuoso?' and still that lightness of tone.

'You need to practise more. You do – what – a couple of hours a day?'

She thought, nodded.

'It's not enough. You also need to do more technical work, particularly with your left hand, which coasts along sometimes, I've noticed. You don't grip the keys with it enough. You're aware Rachmaninoff had a formidable left-hand technique?'

'I've read that, yes.'

Outside, clouds were moving quickly across the grey sky, the bare branches of the tree had started to rattle.

'Your problem is not only technical, which can be fixed if you do a lot more work. Your problem is interpretative.'

'Yes.'

'Yes?'

'I agree. I'm confused about the interpretation of this work.'

'Well, where do the climaxes lie?'

'You mean here? On this page?'

'On that page, in that movement, in the whole work. What is your destination? What are you aiming for? You need to keep that in mind when you are playing it. There should be no distractions, it needs to be a single, focused mission.'

'Hmmm,' she said.

I started to climb the tree outside, gripping the branches in my hands, wedging my feet against the trunk.

'You know Rachmaninoff's compositional output was relatively small,' I said.

She didn't say anything; she just kept looking at me.

'Some say he was heartbroken about being forced to leave Russia after the Bolshevik revolution; a rather romantic explanation,' I found myself declaiming. 'In fact, he didn't have the time to compose. He had to be a concert pianist to earn his living. He disliked the life of a performer, all trains and practice, he said. He only had the summers to compose. At the end of his life he realised that he'd made the wrong choices about how he'd lived and he regretted it deeply. People who visited him before he died wrote that he was the saddest man they'd ever seen. Anyway, the upshot is that we're left with less Rachmaninoff.'

The clouds were racing each other now, the branches of the tree had started to clatter, I was at the top of it, I was reaching up to the sky. Who was in there, talking so eloquently in that room with the piano? Not Alice Haywood.

'When he performed,' I said, 'except for the occasional memory lapse, he never made a mistake. He was the most accurate of pianists.'

'Right,' she said, and then she frowned, turned back to the music. 'But I'm not sure how this matters when it comes to interpretation. This work is about grand emotional expression, surely, not single-mindedness or perfectionism. It's pure expressive romanticism, a rebuttal to Enlightenment thinking, all the rationalists and pragmatists, with their hypotheses and proofs and truths.'

I didn't understand.

'In order to interpret a work correctly,' I said, and this was straight from music school, 'you need to get to the spirit of the composer, their moods and intentions. You need to understand those fully in order to express the music accurately. Rachmaninoff had to leave his country forever, he was a famous performer whose talent had given him a career he hated, but he needed the money so he had to do it. You know his audiences would demand his C sharp minor Prelude, and if he didn't play

241

it they would start to chant? He loathed that piece in the end. So yes, I suppose you could call that emotion.'

'It's an interesting question, isn't it,' she said, 'this notion of the right interpretation and the truth of the composer's spirit, how to translate that into music. I mean, surely these things are arbitrary and subjective. It's one of the things that's always puzzled me about classical music scholarship, this idea that one has played Debussy incorrectly because it's not how minstrels would have sounded in Paris in 1910. But who really knows what they sounded like? And why does it even matter? I see there are parameters. Bach, for example, played with a lot of rubato is wrong, but even then does it necessarily sound bad? Not to those who have a schmaltzy C major Prelude played on an electric keyboard at their wedding. And why should they be wrong? My point is that even if I were to play with his biography in mind, his spirit, as you say, which I happen to think is not compulsory, I'd still question your interpretation of it – in this work, anyway.'

'Oh yes?' I was out in the street, I was up the tree, I was looking down the road.

'Oh, absolutely. I mean, you talk about sadness and regret, but this was composed in vastly different circumstances. He had recovered from his nervous breakdown and writer's block and this concerto flowed out of him, just like that, he was healed, and it received glorious praise. It launched him, launched who he was. So I think it's about the triumph of hope over desolation, music over silence, life over death. It's the music of resurrection, surely.'

I eyed her.

'Resurrection.'

'Yes.'

'I think it's a myth, that story,' I said finally. 'I think they make up those sorts of things to fill programs and musical dictionaries. How could they possibly know?'

242

'They do research, presumably.'

I sniffed.

'Well, you believe the stories about him being the saddest man alive. Why can only misery be verified and trusted?'

'Disregard the rest of his life,' I said. 'The piece could still be about the humiliation of that first performance of the symphony, or the loss of his ability to compose, or of entering a place of darkness so complete that you are nothing that you thought you were; you cannot even lift your body from the floor. It could still be about that.'

'Possibly. I suppose it's all in the music,' and she looked back at the score.

I didn't speak for a while.

'When did you play it?' she asked.

'Oh . . .' looking out the window. 'A very long time ago.'

Silence again.

'I wonder . . .' I hesitated. 'What would have happened if there was no family estate for Rachmaninoff to flee to, no great doctor, no successful treatment, just Moscow scorning and discarding him?'

'You're making an argument about privilege.'

'Or happenstance.'

'Both?'

'A disastrous reception of the first symphony, which becomes the only symphony, a young Russian unable to do what he loves, alone in Moscow, hearing music in his head that remains forever silent. Why did it not happen like that?'

'I don't know. I suppose circumstances dictated otherwise.' She lifted a leg, uncrossed her knees. 'Or perhaps he just wanted to compose very badly and nothing was going to stop him, he just needed some help. Everyone needs help from time to time, we're all human. We need connection, recognition. It makes us who we are, partly, the way others see us; it brings us into being, or does the opposite, of course. I was just teaching on this, actually.'

Silence. A car went past in the street.

'What if the help doesn't arrive?' I said.

'You don't think it does, usually? Don't we look for it over and over, whether we know it or not?'

You are young, I thought. You have lived a blessed life. You have no idea how the rest of us live. You will never play Rachmaninoff properly. I got up and went into the study to the file boxes.

'Take these,' I said, handing her Moszkowski's *Etudes de Virtuosité* and his *Three Concert Studies*. 'They are good technical preparation for this work.'

'How kind of you! I'll copy them and return them to you ... same time next week?'

When she left, I lay down on the floor with my arms stretched out, palms up, looking at the ceiling. Then I got up, sped down the hall, out the back door, and stood in the little square of garden, staring up at the dark-blue sky, searching it.

68.

Oxford, November, 2005

She started coming every week, usually on a Monday. She always played the concerto through, and then we discussed it. It was what she used to do with her teacher in Toronto, she said, before a major performance. Between these sessions I listened to her practise on the other side of the wall, and thought about what she needed to work on. Her visits gave me a reason to eat, because I had to have the energy for them; I would get on with dying once her concert was over.

She was practising longer and more intensively. She did an hour or so of technical work in the morning before she left for the university, then practised the concerto when she got home, and often into the night. It was as if she were teaching it to herself from scratch, pulling it apart, examining it, putting it slowly back together. I heard her play one hand of a section, then the other hand, listening carefully, assembling it again – one hand, both hands – until she played the whole section through. Then she did it all over again. Line after line, section after section, page after page: inspecting it, contemplating it.

In mid-November she started working on the technically most difficult parts of the concerto. One Monday when she played it through I marked each bit that wasn't perfect and took her through them.

'God, Alice,' she said afterwards, rubbing her face.

'You can do it,' I said. 'All the other bits are better than I've heard it played before.'

I wanted her to know the concerto as well as Rachmaninoff himself. When you listen to his recordings you can hear him bringing themes and accents that sound almost singular, like anthems out of an apparent morass of notes. He makes the piano sound at one minute sonorous, at another percussive, at another like a single voice, at another like an orchestra, then silvery bells, then lightning and thunder. I wanted her to have that power, to feel that freedom of expression. I wanted her to get so far beyond the technical complications of the work, make them nothing, so that she could play it exactly as she wished. I wanted her to make it an extension of herself. I wanted the notes to be within her so that all she needed to do was think about how she wished to execute them. Yes, I will admit it: I wanted to hear her do what I had not. But it was not only that.

I started to wonder why she was working as an academic, given she was such a consummate musician.

I asked her one day, as she was rushing off to mark undergraduate essays (the topic: famine, its political causes and consequences).

'I need an income,' she said. 'I need to eat. Besides,' trying to stuff her score into her already bulging bag, 'I like it, most of the time. I like to work on things I believe in, I think it's important.'

'Don't you find it dry?'

She slung the bag over her shoulder.

'There's actually a lot of emotional amplitude in academia. It's just hidden and comes out in strange ways.'

'Like what?'

'Extreme views; irrational beliefs masquerading as some great truth; quibbles over nothing that last decades. I think a lot of academics hide themselves behind intellectualism and apparent objectivity, whereas a lot of the time it's really just a power trip, about getting authority and keeping it.'

I didn't say anything. She looked back at the piano.

'You can't play this music and hide, though, can you?'

I was taken aback.

'Maybe you can,' I said.

'I don't think I can, not if I want to play it properly. That was the problem before, you know, I hadn't engaged with it enough. I wasn't listening properly, I was holding back. Out of practice, I suppose. I've realised recently that in my work and life at the moment I can pretty much forget my feelings if I want to, pretend they don't even exist. But when I play this . . . well, it's the opposite. I can't fail to be moved. For the thirty minutes or so this concerto lasts I can just let go.'

Not long after this she rearranged her teaching commitments so she could practise harder.

~

Sometimes, on a Monday, we listened to other music. Other versions of the concerto first, then things like Bach's double violin concerto, Saint Matthew Passion, the Adagio by Samuel Barber. Then she started bringing around her beloved pop.

'Alice,' she joked the first time, 'you can't tell anyone about this, all right?'

'Why not?'

'Because it's officially bad music taste.'

She pressed play.

Cyndi Lauper, 'Time After Time'; Whitney Houston, 'How Will I Know' – 'The eighties, Alice, a golden age of pop.' Then the Waifs, 'London Still'; Ryan Adams, 'Desire'. Then a song with a fast beat called 'Missing'. She turned the music up loud, put her arms up, moved her head and hands, soon she was dancing. The shelves in the study started to shake, the floor vibrated, the dust rained down, and I looked at the floor, embarrassed, thrilled.

She played me a lot of that music. Madonna, Dire Straits, Billy Joel. All the 'bad music' she could find. Like sweets, she said, like fizzy wine. And everything she played I liked.

I think she started to become for me something like music itself, or what music was becoming for her, a means of liberation, a returning to oneself. She played for me, she spoke to me and listened to me. And it was satisfying to be working anew at something I had failed at so spectacularly. The feelings I experienced when I knew that I was helping her were incomparable; I was helping to prevent her from making the same mistakes I had made. She was always thanking me, too. I was connected with music again, yes, but in a way that was not unsettling, unlike the music through the wall, which had prompted such torment, doubt and recollection. I could shape this music of hers, transmute it.

I felt propelled by an energy that had me pacing about the house, particularly after she practised. I was restless inside, impatient, repulsed by those old grey walls, the floors and ceiling, that still stood around me. One night when she was playing next door I opened the front door and stood on the step. Out there her playing was even louder. The air was cold and I puffed in time with the concerto for a while, watching the beat emerge in white puffs of breath in front of my face. Then I walked down the steps and out the gate.

I walked on dark pavements, beside unlit gardens and slabs of black lawn, hearing her playing in my head, treading its beat into the path. A car pulled in front of me, a garage door slid up; a woman rode past on a bicycle, legs pumping hard, and everything was in time with that music, everything. I walked up Woodstock Road, right to the top, stopped to catch my breath, and watched cars circling the roundabout and entering the ring-road that encircles the city. I watched a runner jogging up the other side of the road. She, too, got to the top, flopped over, touched the ground, then turned and jogged back.

I started walking back down side streets and back streets, wherever took my fancy, down streets of identical houses, down laneways paved with stone. Past a church with a noticeboard out the front, white letters pressed into black background: He Bled for You. When I got home there were bags of food on the porch with a receipt resting on top; I took them down to the kitchen, packed it all away.

Richard had bought me three bags of oranges now, all of which I had hidden. I pulled them out, peeled a bagful, and roasted the fruit in the oven coated with sugar, honey and juice. The second bag I juiced, put the jug in the fridge. I boiled the last bag without peeling the fruit and made a cake with the pieces, mixing them with eggs, sugar, butter, flour; it rose lumpen, monstrous, moist.

~

I started leaving the house between Emily's practices and going into town, walking in and out of shops already festooned with Christmas decorations. I used the credit card Richard had got for me; my first purchase was a clutch of green and purple grapes in a little plastic box, which I ate on a bench outside the store, shivering with the cold, eating them one by one, feeling their solidity explode inside my mouth.

I bought some new clothes: first some things to keep me warm on my walks – a pair of red gloves, a purple scarf, a soft green sweater – and then some underwear.

Sometimes I went into one of the new cafes that seemed to be all over the place, with lines of students at the counter, rows of cakes behind glass. I'd order something and sit in the noise and warmth, solitary and undisturbed, yet not alone. This, I thought, was a very different Oxford from the one I had known.

I started to walk in the mornings in the South Park, where the puddles were already frozen, the grass crunchy with frost, and a mist sometimes hovered, tall and thick. One day a group of runners burst out of the mist, streamed around me, ran on. I walked to the pond, ducks slid across the icy water, ripples broadening behind them, down to the river. Through the kissing gate, onto the boardwalk, where all around I could hear the dripping leaves, the flow of the river, the rush of the lock. Two swans glided upstream, their breasts pressed into the water.

69.

Oxford, December, 2005

By now Emily was playing parts of the concerto as if she were surfing it, as if the music were a wave coming towards her and she was pushing herself towards it, standing up, balancing, becoming part of it, part of the wave, part of the water. The first day she sounded like that I walked into town with my head high, the green and gold leaves of the trees on St Giles fluttering against the pale-blue sky.

I went into the Covered Market, saw branches of holly in buckets, and Christmas lilies, petals just parting. In the mall a man was busking on a piano that had its front removed, he played it with his wrists arched high. I rounded the corner into Broad Street, the buildings were golden in the early fall of light. Through the courtyard of the Bodleian Library, past the Radcliffe Camera, towards St Mary's church I walked, and the shapes of those buildings, the trinity of square roof, round dome, triangular spire, how perfect they seemed, as if someone had thought it up and made it so.

When I got back that evening Quentin Kidd was in his front yard, and when I greeted him he did a double-take. Hello, Alice, he said, drawing closer, his face moving like a boy's. We spoke for a while about the mild day, the news, his garden, and then his writing. After that we spoke more often and I even started to wonder if he lingered outside when he saw me returning from a walk.

I talked with others who lived in the street too. Henry, the handsome man across the road who spent hours tending to his front garden; Caroline, the American with a bright-pink bicycle. I had tea with Bess a few times, and with some others in the old crowd. Sometimes sitting in the house at night I could almost sense the proximity of these people, sitting just a few streets over, or even closer, perhaps next to a fire or heater too.

I contacted Richard and we had conversations about nothing significant, but it was something, a start. There were so many things I had to tell him before I died, I knew that, but I was feeling less urgency. Perhaps I felt that when the time came I would simply be able to say them after all.

And always this restless energy kept beating, beating, beating.

I caught the bus to different parts of the town, as far as they went. Up the Cowley Road, the bus slowly emptying out until it was just me, the driver and an elderly woman with a shopping trolley. The last stop was a housing estate; I got out with the woman and walked around until I reached a tall fence with traffic behind it; another part of the ring-road. Back at the bus station I could smell the chippy, that delicious scent of the hot cooking fat in the pans.

I was happy. I was happy listening to Emily practising next door, hearing her improve. We no longer disagreed about the interpretation, she had incorporated a lot of what I had spoken about, so the breadth was there now, but it was still very much her own. My role was to help her play as best she could; I didn't insist on my interpretation, such as it was, and maybe that was changing anyway. Meeting with her regularly was a great pleasure, and meeting with others, old friends and new, that was an awakening in itself.

I was walking to the edges of the city and back in the dark; I was packing things away in the house; I was burning Edward's papers and books, when I remembered; I was cooking and eating (oranges, fish, apples, cake). I visited the Botanic Garden, the

252

modern art museum, even a tourist attraction with a little train and displays with buttons to push called 'The Oxford Story'. I listened to a radio station that played pop songs like Emily's.

'Why is that music so catchy?' I said to her, after I'd listened to an eighties pop marathon on the radio one Monday morning. 'I feel uplifted when I listen to it. Is it the harmony, do you think? Or the beat? Or the way it's so familiar? It's like reading a murder-mystery, isn't it, all that evil solved within two covers. They always end on a perfect cadence, those songs, don't they? And nothing's evolved in this type of music, they're the same structure as Elvis Presley.'

She laughed and said she thought I was right.

The winter deepened; dark afternoons and black nights were accompanied by the beauty of her playing on the other side of the wall.

One night the air held the scent of snow and when I woke in the morning it was drifting down in front of the window. I heard children laughing, looked out, and there they were, a whole band of them in coloured hats and mittens and coats playing in the snow-smothered street, building a person with sticks for arms and one of their own hats on its head. Then Emily walked onto the pavement and I tapped on the window so softly she can't possibly have heard, but she looked up anyway and I waved, and she waved back and smiled and held out her arms, as if to say, look at this, see this, and I nodded, so beautiful.

The phone rang, it was Richard standing in a street in London, something to do with the lawyers and money for me. He said it was snowing, and I said, yes, it's white here too, and, oh Richard, it's so beautiful! And he laughed and said, What's happened to you, Mum? You're so happy. And I couldn't breathe then, I couldn't breathe. I remember it now as the pinnacle of my happiness, that moment, that morning, that day; I could circle it on a calendar, I could note the time. What more could I want? I thought.

70.

Currabin, December 18th, 2006

It is midday. The stumps of the orange trees have started to shimmer in the heat as if considering a magical disappearing act. The sweat slides in slow tracks down the backs of my legs. They said on the radio this morning that elderly people should remain indoors (something about our kidneys). I walk a slow circuit from table to kitchen tap to lavatory.

Most people here have given up on oranges. It's grapes now, which are no better in terms of requiring water, but they fetch a higher price. Harold and Shirley have gone fancier still with walnuts, espaliered plums. She asked me about the drip system last night; I lied and said it was turned on in order to get her to stop talking about it. It's not that I feel malice towards the oranges, it's more like empathy.

Now the sun is dimming, a breeze has crept across the veranda and lifts a strand of hair, a loose piece of paper. The track of sugar ants just beyond my left foot has started moving faster across the tiles, so perhaps it will finally rain. The stumps remain steadfast, though. When there is a storm here there are two types of lightning: sheet lightning, which illuminates whole sections of the sky, and fork lightning, which reaches down like a claw from the heavens. I was taught this as a child, standing beneath the roof of a tin shed, following the pointing finger of a neighbour, and when the rain rolled in and drummed on the roof, drowning out his voice, drowning everything out, I remember starting to shiver.

71.

After one of our Monday sessions, Emily asked me why I no longer played the piano. I could have told her a story about arthritis, but instead I told her the truth. Well, partly. I told her about the paralysis that had affected me during my own performance of the concerto.

She was troubled by this. She took my hands in hers. She said it was extremely sad, a tragedy, indeed a great injustice that someone with my knowledge and passion for music would suddenly be unable to play, and so permanently.

'Can the doctors not do anything?'

'Nothing.'

'But medicine changes so quickly, doesn't it? Perhaps you could try again if you haven't seen a doctor in a while. I could come with you,' she added. 'Sometimes it helps to have someone else there.'

I said nothing.

'At the time, what was the advice exactly?'

'That I must stop playing the piano because to continue could cripple my hands completely.'

She didn't like that.

'To just leave it like that! Have you tried to play much since the concert?'

'Only,' and I held up one finger.

'Maybe you should just try,' she said. 'I mean, how could it hurt? What is the worst that could happen if you tried, just for five minutes?'

After she left, I remained standing at the window. I started to feel the presence of the instrument beside me. I had always felt that the piano looked like a bull ready to charge, yet now I admired its steady planes, the flat top, the curve of the side. It reminded me of the landscape of my childhood: there was a boy who used to ride around the district on a bicycle with no handlebars, and I thought now, standing by the piano, that he hadn't needed any, for there were no hills or sharp corners, it was a straight, easy path before him. Perhaps this is our perception at the beginning, when we are children. What different countries I entered when I became an adult, a woman, when I had a child. What could equip you?

I pulled on my new scarf and gloves and walked to the meadow, across the grassy expanse towards the canal. A couple of cows stood watching me, swished their tails, then loped off to join the herd. When I got to the edge of the canal I stood for a long time looking at the black, brackish water. A longboat chugged by; it had a line of neatly pegged washing on its deck. A woman sat below it on a deckchair, face to the sky, wearing sunglasses, although the day was grey. The water swelled around the boat and settled back down. All I needed to do, I thought, was simply play the piano? All these years, that was all I needed to do? Ignore the advice and just play? A rage swept through me then that was so sudden and extreme it frightened me. I turned quickly, away from the canal, and walked back to the house. I decided that if Emily were to raise the matter again I would tell her I was reconciled to not playing. I also decided that I would forget about our conversation, about her suggestion; yes, it would be better to do that.

But Emily did not forget about the conversation, and I did not say my line about being reconciled. The next time she came around she brought a stack of papers and put it down on one of the front room chairs. I thought it was something to do with her work, but as she was leaving she waved her hand in the direction of the stack and said, 'I've been doing a bit of research. These are papers on musicians' focal dystonia. Apparently treatments have really improved since you were diagnosed. It's fascinating reading.'

I left them there.

The next time she said she had watched a video on her computer of a woman with the condition doing some simple hand exercises that had helped her to play the piano smoothly again, and then she demonstrated them.

The session after this she said, Any thoughts? while wiggling her fingers, and I said, Oh, not really, and she gave me a half-smile and averted her eyes, which I didn't like much.

That night I did have a look at the papers, but it was all medical jargon, academic-speak, and I soon abandoned them. I sat down at the piano and looked at the keys, so many of them laid out in front of me, a cadaver's grin. The score of the Rachmaninoff was on the stand and I raised my hands slowly, closed my eyes. I heard the first line of the solo part of the concerto in my head, moved my hands forward as if about to play, but I got up instead and walked around the room.

I sat down again, looked at the music, raised my hands, got up again and walked about. This was how it proceeded for some time.

Finally I pretended to myself that it was nothing, that it didn't matter a bit, and I sat down again at the piano, glanced at the music, heard it in my head. I remembered my mother's words about the piece 'Andante', how one note will always follow another, that they will come, and I moved my hands towards the keys, and at that moment the fingers on my right hand contracted, as surely as if someone had taken my hand in theirs and closed them as one would a door.

I sat at the piano for a long time. I started to think of the meadow, of the canal. Of entering the dark of the night and walking across to that black water. Rehearsing what I would do, stepping into it, feeling my body sink, weighed down by my sodden coat, which would be impossible to struggle out of, my mouth filling with the sour water, my lungs, all of me saturated.

I got up. That is it, I thought, that is the end; we cannot talk of it anymore, and I would tell her so when I saw her next.

72.

Oxford, mid-December, 2005

I didn't tell her when I saw her next. She left for Toronto a few days later. It was a long-planned visit, three weeks over Christmas, but somehow I had forgotten about it; I suppose I hadn't wanted to remember.

Immediately, the house went quiet. Then the centre of the city as the students left, and staff went away. The park emptied of runners and women with prams. The house grew colder and darker in the midwinter freeze. One day I went into town and bought boxes of the highest wattage lightbulbs I could find and screwed them into every socket I could reach, which did make the house lighter, but lit up like that it looked even worse, the smudged grey walls, the cracks that had emerged in the front room, the frayed carpet, the gloomy furniture.

My walks and outings started to tire me. I would find myself in a strange street, staring at a house with a tatty wreath on a door, thinking, What am I doing here? I'd return home exhausted to cook a meal I did not want to eat; I just wanted to slump, slump in that house, my faithful mausoleum, and do nothing at all. The blackness that had almost overtaken me seemed close again. It lurked in all the dark places: the inside of cupboards, the bottom of saucepans, in the long weeds and grass between the house and the shed. How easy it would be to pull it on again, I thought, like a pile of soiled clothes lying in the corner on the floor. I could feel the foul tug of them over my head and up my limbs, smell their stench. To have it return like that, so suddenly and unexpectedly, after such happiness, was almost worse.

I forced myself to eat. I tramped to the frozen park in the mornings. I sat next to the wall and imagined Emily playing. I put the radio on and listened to pop songs.

I decided that my short-lived enthusiasm for life had been dependent on Emily's presence and that this indicated another fault in my character, a grave one, and then everything that had gone before started to feel shaky.

On Christmas Day I rang Richard but he wasn't there; I remembered he had gone to Spain for the holidays. I tried Bess, but she didn't answer either; she and Frank often went at this time of year to the Isle of Wight, where one of their daughters lived and hosted the whole family. I couldn't think of anyone else to ring. What a life, I thought; what an aftermath.

I sat in the front room for a long time doing nothing, then fetched the score of the Rachmaninoff. It was as if I were in a sequence of thought and action and silence from which I couldn't fathom an escape.

I started to think about the relationship between the solo part and orchestra, which Emily and I had not yet discussed. It was time she started practising the work with another pianist who would play the orchestra part (as transcribed for keyboard) on the piano, while she played her solo part; this is a normal element of the preparation for the performance of a piano concerto.

I imagined myself in this role; a little fantasy. I'd play the orchestra part on my piano while she played hers next door. People in the street would stop short and listen, transfixed by the music, a crowd would gather at the window. I set the score on the stand and pretended to play the accompaniment, moving my hands back and forth above the keys. Why could I not do this?

I got up, put some music on the gramophone – Beethoven, Brahms, Debussy, Strauss – disc after disc, and sat listening impatiently. How they bored me, those recordings. All that music by old dead men, great hoary relics shuffled around concert programs, put up again and again in front of a willing audience. I flicked on the radio: Lionel Richie, 'Dancing on the Ceiling'. I turned it off then sat in the silent house thinking about the music I would like to hear; for a moment I could not think of any.

As the date of Emily's return approached I felt relief. I went into a hairdresser on Walton Street and had my wispy hair trimmed to just beneath my ears. On the way home I bought a cream sweater I had been eyeing in the window of a second-hand shop for some weeks. That night Richard rang me.

'I rang last night,' he said. 'Were you out?'

'Yes, I think I was . . .' (I had started to walk again in the evenings.)

'You don't remember?'

'Yes, I remember, of course I remember.' I shifted the phone to the other ear. 'How was Spain?'

'Same old, same old. Mum, I've had a call from a collector, a private collector, who wants to buy some of Edward's papers. Stuff from the fifties and sixties. Parts of them were published, but they were heavily edited and he kept the originals. Apparently these are now considered to contain some great missing piece in the global history of economic thinking. I wouldn't give a shit about any of this normally, except for the fact that he wants to pay an extraordinarily large amount for them. So I thought I'd better check we still have the originals before agreeing to sell.'

I didn't say anything.

'Do we still have them? You haven't given them to the library? Mum? Hello? Are you there?'

'I'm here.'

'You don't have some sort of attachment to these papers, do you?'

How could he even think that? I still didn't say anything.

'Mum, do you think you might be able to answer me? Did you understand what I said?'

'I'm not attached to them.'

'Good. So they're in the study then.'

'Er, well, I suppose I would have to look . . .'

'Mum, are you all right? Are you eating?'

'Yes. Are you all right?'

'Yes. Why wouldn't I be?'

'What about Martha?'

'*Martha?* Christ, I haven't thought about her for months. I seem to go through women like water these days. Look, the reason I'm pressing is because he needs to know now whether he can have them or not. There are some other economist's papers in Boston he's also interested in; it's probably just some spiel to get us to sell, but shall I tell him yes?'

'I'm not entirely sure what's in the study, actually . . .'

And it went on like that for a while, me stalling, him insisting, until he finally said, exasperated, 'Could you please look for them and ring me tomorrow morning?' He added quickly, 'I'm afraid I can't walk away from this sort of money, so could you just do this for me, please? I haven't asked for much,' and he hung up.

I haven't asked for much. But my boy, my boy, you will never know how much I gave. When will I tell you? And if I did, would you hear it?

I went into the study, opened a desk drawer, miming actions with no purpose. I had burnt those papers already, of course. I hadn't thought about the money. I went to the kitchen, made myself some dinner, took a pot of tea to the study and sat in front of the fire.

I heard a car in the street, watched from the window as Emily heaved her suitcase out of a taxi, pulled a black coat over her white shirt wheeled the case across the street and over the kerb. I raised my hand and tapped on the glass but she had disappeared down the easement.

73.

Oxford, January, 2006

Richard rang in the morning. The collector had already telephoned him. When Richard mentioned his ageing and sentimental mother the man had upped the price. Richard wanted to collect the papers straight away.

'I'm busy today,' I said, 'seeing people.' (It was true; it was Monday, I was expecting Emily.)

'All day?'

I didn't say anything.

'Mum, please, could we have a conversation about this? Are you able to do that?'

I didn't say anything.

'Could I come up this afternoon?'

'This afternoon would be tricky.'

He expelled a sigh.

'Richard, I've been doing a bit of cleaning lately.'

'Riiiight ...'

'There was such a mess in your father's study, it was clogged full of junk. It should have been cleaned out years ago, frankly ...'

'What are you saying, Mum? You haven't thrown them out, have you?'

'Not thrown them out, no ...'

'Well, what then?'

But I was too frightened to tell him. Even though it was just Richard, my son, he had picked up some of Edward's verbal style, and the similarity now unnerved me. He got more frustrated with my obfuscation and insisted I tell him what had happened, or else he would assume I was not competent to answer, which enraged me. I hung up, he rang back, and so it went on, until I pulled the phone socket from the wall.

A few hours later I heard a knock on the door and hurried to it, thinking it was Emily, then something about the timbre of it made me pause.

'Mum, it's me. Open up.'

I stood still.

'I know you're in there. I can hear you.'

I still didn't move.

'Oh, for God's sake, just open the bloody door, will you? It's freezing out here.'

He started to knock in the rhythm of 'Land of Hope and Glory', then he started to sing. It was no use. I opened the door, and there he was. Face flushed, hair longer than I remembered it, tall, broad-shouldered. My child.

Quentin Kidd was standing on the pavement looking up at us. I nudged the door closed, headed towards the kitchen. But Richard had gone straight into the study and was examining the bookshelves. He turned when I followed him in.

'Jesus, Mum, you're skin and bone. Are you all right?'

'I'm fine.'

He frowned, looked around the room, frowned again.

'Where has it all gone? These shelves were full.'

When I didn't say anything he went over to the desk, which looked small in front of him, and started opening drawers.

'What are you working on at the moment?' I said.

'Mum, where are the manuscripts?' pointing into the drawer. 'There was a whole stack of them in here.'

I couldn't speak.

'Have you done something with them?' he said impatiently, and when I still didn't answer his voice softened slightly. 'Do you not remember, is that it? Are you having trouble remembering? Do you even know the papers I'm talking about?'

I tried not to take offence, but I knew what he was getting at, what he thought.

He turned away, started rubbing his face. There was dark stubble on his cheeks, his chin, I watched his hands work over it. I knew I would have to tell him.

'What's this all about, Mum? Grief? Or are you embarrassed about not remembering things? Is that it?' and when I still didn't answer he muttered something to himself which sounded like 'sheer fucking lunacy'.

'You know,' I started, 'your father wasn't a kind person.'

'Jesus, Mum. Do you think I don't know that? He was an arsehole.'

'He was very clever. He could be charming.'

'Charming, you think? Look, Mum, I have no compunction whatsoever about flogging his stuff to the highest bidder. And nor should you. If you've lost them, where should I start looking?'

I noticed then that the hem had fallen down at the back of one of the legs of his pants, and I was about to say, why don't we have a cup of tea, but by then he was standing right over me.

'Mum, if things are this bad, don't you think we ought to go to your doctor? Edward did tell me that you have these periods when —'

That did it.

'Richard, I haven't known how to say this to you, but I destroyed those papers. I burnt them all, plus a number of other things —'

'You burnt them?'

'Don't . . . please —'

266

'You didn't. Please say this isn't true! I can't believe —'

'Now, Richard, you —'

'Jesus Christ! I can't believe it!' He was a voluble person, Richard, when he got going, and then I started to make some noise too, what with being in that room and being shouted at — I might have screamed. And then we heard footsteps in the hall and there she was, Emily, standing in the door of the study with bare feet, wearing a dressing gown. We stopped immediately and both looked at her.

III

74.

Currabin, December 19th, 2006

I wish I could describe the stillness of this place, the silence. I
wish I could name the birds I hear, and the old gum trees that
sway over there, by the fence. But I don't know them; I am
a stranger here now. At times the silence feels immense and
I turn on the radio to a station that plays pop songs, mostly from
the eighties. The Eurythmics, 'The Miracle of Love'. Fleetwood
Mac, 'Little Lies', Icehouse 'Crazy'. But after about four or five
songs this music starts to grate and I switch it off; the silence
is restored. Silence? It's the wrong word. The place is full of
sounds, actually, different sounds, ones I'm still learning. I like
it in the early mornings when I come out with my coffee to
sit on the veranda and think about what I shall write. And last
thing at night, I like that time too, when the darkness around
me is everything except for the sky lit up above, that soaring
dome of dark speckled with light, with stars, shooting ones and
falling ones.

For a while now, sitting here, I have been thinking about the
idea of love. I used to think love was akin to being fully heard by
another, so much so that we are almost of that other, and they of
us. But I do not think that anymore. I think it is the not-hearing
part of love, and our response to it, that makes it what it is. The
work of love, the concentration on the other beyond anything
that is reasonable, the retreat, the weary return, the attempts at
reconnection, the beginning again, and then again. The failure
of love, the acceptance of this, the second chance, and the one

after. The attention on what to others would be nothing – a smile, a gesture – so that nothing becomes something to delight in. But I did not see any of this a year ago in Oxford, because I was still thinking so much about what love was not.

75.

Oxford, January, 2006

'What's going on? Alice! Are you all right?'

Richard stepped forward. 'She's fine.'

'You get back!' She shouted this.

'Jesus, all right,' and he stepped back, palms up.

'Who are you?' she said.

'Who the hell are you?'

'I'm calling the police,' and she grabbed at the pocket of her gown for her mobile.

'Great idea.' He got his phone out too. They stood, phones at the ready, neither of them moving.

'Do you know this man, Alice?' eyes flicking to me, flicking back to him.

'How did you even get in?'

'The door was wide open. Alice, can you speak? Are you okay? Please, let me know if you can hear me.'

'I wouldn't worry too much, she often gets like this.'

'She could have had a stroke! Alice, shall I call an ambulance?'

'Who *are* you? I'm Richard, her son.'

'Her son? She doesn't have a son.'

'Ha! Excellent. Come on, Mum, buck up.'

I smiled at Emily.

'Thank goodness, here, let me . . .' and she took my elbow.

'You got yourself a bit worked up, didn't you, Mum? Frightened yourself.'

I didn't look at him. I walked out of the room, down the hall, the two of them following.

'You were shouting at her.'

'There was some noise coming back.'

'I've still half a mind to ring the police. Alice, is this really your son?'

I was in the kitchen by this time. I picked up the kettle, held it under the tap. I was so weary all of a sudden.

'Emily,' turning, 'this is Richard, my son; Richard, this is my neighbour, Emily.'

'Right,' she said, 'okay,' then no one said anything.

I turned off the tap, replaced the lid of the kettle.

'Well, if that's the case and you're all right now, Alice, I'll go back next door. But I'll be right there if —'

'Hang on, you still haven't said who you are.'

'Alice said; I'm her neighbour.'

'But you can't just walk in here like that; I mean, what were you thinking? Do you do this often?'

'As I said,' and I glanced at Emily then because of the tone of her voice, and she was looking right at Richard, 'I heard a man shouting, which was you, abusing your mother, and then I heard screaming. I was very concerned. Thank goodness I was able to get in. I would have hammered the door down.'

I put the kettle on the stove, pressed the knob, the ignition ticked over, failing to catch. I leant over, looked at the element, the stove boomed alight, I stood back. I looked at Richard then, he must have been embarrassed. He was good at hiding it.

'Do you always just walk in here?' he asked again, leaning back against the bench.

'Obviously I usually knock.'

'You visit my mother?'

'Yes.'

'Why?'

She laughed, shook her head, then she said, 'We talk about music.'

'Music?'

'Yes.'

'Are you some sort of social worker?'

'Social worker? No.'

I got the milk out of the fridge.

'Sorry, I'm still not quite following. You know my mother how?'

'Look, I've told you. We're neighbours, we have some mutual interests, we've become friends. Is this concept unfamiliar to you?'

'Mutual interests?' he snorted. 'Sounds like you're joint fucking hedge-fund investors.'

Language, Richard, I would have once said, you're not to speak like that. It was as if I were struck mute, in another dimension entirely, or they were. I couldn't believe they were talking to one another. I got the cups and saucers down, spooned tea into the pot.

'Do you live far away?' she said.

'I live in London.'

'London? Wow. I was thinking you must live overseas, given I've never seen you visiting your mother before.'

He looked to one side, the long fringe of his hair hanging down in front of his face. 'You've got to be fucking kidding me,' he muttered, then, louder, 'What sort of music?'

'Sorry?'

'What sort of music do you discuss together?'

'What a strange question,' she said. 'Well, what do we talk about, Alice?'

'Eighties pop,' I said.

Emily laughed then; Richard's eyes were agog.

'Rachmaninoff,' she said, shrugging.

'Ah,' he said.

'You know,' she said, 'you look very familiar.'

'Me?'

He was wearing a shirt with several buttons undone, tight pants, pointy shoes.

'You look very much like the composer Richard Haywood.'

The whistle started on the kettle.

'You're him, aren't you?'

'Mother, going to get that?'

'I thought I knew your face.'

'Mother?'

I was too busy watching the expressions on Emily's face. He lunged for the kettle, lifted it up.

I made the tea, handed it to them, the cups rattling against the saucers.

They left together, not long after, walking down the hall in silence. I watched them from the front window talking in the street, on the pavement between the two houses. Emily was making what looked like a fervent point. She was moving her hands about, talking intently; Richard was nodding, and then he started up, equally passionately. What were they talking about? She turned suddenly and went back next door; he got into his car slowly and after a few minutes he drove away.

76.
Oxford, January, 2006

The next day Richard arrived at the front door in the late afternoon.

'Hello,' he shouted, shouldering his way down the hall, carrying several bulging shopping bags. He dumped them on the kitchen bench, started unpacking food. 'I thought I might cook some dinner,' he said, very loudly.

This was such a shock that it took me a few minutes to realise what must have happened. Emily must have told him off, I thought, not only for shouting at his mother but for not caring for her either. Something had pricked him. At any other time it would have been wonderful to see him, but I didn't want him so near Emily now, although I didn't know exactly why.

He started to prepare the food; his movements were rapid, he was humming to himself. He almost seemed nervous. We didn't talk much, didn't look each other in the eye. He busied himself with peeling potatoes, chopping herbs, slicing tomatoes, mashing anchovies, pitting olives, pausing every now and then to brush his hair back from his face. I realised, looking at him, that he liked cooking and that he was probably good at it. I remembered making biscuits with him when he was very young, showing him how to press his little thumb into the rounds of dough, then put half a teaspoon of jam into the hollow. I remembered the concentrated way he did this, and the accuracy; he was only two at the time. And now there he was, a man in my kitchen, years of a life behind him that I could hardly conceive. I tried to see that little boy in his features; the two now seemed completely different people.

As he was testing the potatoes in the saucepan with the tip of a knife, a rapid piano scale, a perfect arc of notes, tipped itself into the house.

'Is that her?' looking at me.

I didn't say anything; he put the knife down and walked into the hall.

'That's really loud out there,' he said, coming back, pointing his thumb over his shoulder. When I still didn't reply he went back to the bench and starting making a salad.

Next came a Mussorgsky study, thrown off effortlessly. Richard looked at me, raised his eyebrows. Then she started playing the concerto.

'That's the Rach Two,' he said straight away. 'Mum? That's the Rach Two.'

'It is.'

He stood listening with his hands flat on the bench, entirely still, looking only at the wall in front of him. When she finished the movement he said, 'She's a concert pianist.'

'No, she's not.'

'Of course she is, that was extraordinarily good. Even I could listen to that,' and he went straight up the hall as if homing in on a scent.

I stayed in the kitchen, not moving. As if by not moving I could make things stop. When she started to play the Rachmaninoff again I heard him play a crude version of the orchestral accompaniment on the piano. I rushed up the hall.

'Stop that. You're going to disturb her.' But she had stopped already.

He leapt up, went over to the wall and started feeling it with his hands, palms flat, tapping it, pressing it, his ear to the plaster. There was a knock at the door; he rushed to it.

'Hello there,' he said, scraping his hair back from his face with both his hands.

'Hi,' looking at him, then past him, her eyes reaching me. She was wearing jeans and a dark sweater with a high neck.

'How are you, Alice?'

'Fine,' I said.

'Come in,' he said.

I looked at him, sharply. Come in?

'No thanks,' she said quickly, 'I just wanted to see who was playing.'

'That was me.'

'Indeed. And back so soon.'

'Actually, I'm making Mum dinner.'

A pause, then: 'That's nice, that's good.'

'I've completely over-catered,' he said. 'Why don't you join us?'

I stared at him.

'No, I won't interrupt,' she said.

'You're not interrupting anything, I can assure you. Isn't that right, Mum? You know, I have to say, the way you played that Rach Two was stunning.'

She looked at him quizzically. 'Thank you.'

'I usually hate Rachmaninoff, turns my stomach – over-wrought bloody nonsense – but that was really something. There are some weird acoustics going on here with this wall, which seems quite permeable; I can't understand why it hasn't been noticed before,' his eyes moved to me, then away. 'Maybe things changed in the structure of the place over the winter, all that wet, the flooding and so forth. Your tone,' he went on, 'your touch, they're so beautiful, so clear, and something else I can't quite put my finger on . . .'

'Thank you,' she said again, after a small pause.

'What are you playing on over there?'

'A second-hand upright.'

'No!'

'Well, yes, actually.'

'Truly? I mean, I can't stand Rachmaninoff ordinarily —'

'You mentioned that.'

'But that was very different . . . what's the right way of putting it . . .' and we both watched him. 'None of the overdone Russian angst,' he said, making a comical motion with his arms, pulling a face. 'Lighter, but bringing out all sorts of things I haven't heard in it before, or even thought of. Without the usual pathos, but played so naturally it somehow made it sadder, and also grander. It reminds me of how Imogen Cooper plays Mozart. Or how Glenn Gould plays Bach. Yes, you are the Imogen and Glenn love-child of Rachmaninoff.'

She laughed a little then, or was it more of a snort?

I felt I needed to say something, make a noise, at least, but what? It was as if I were watching something in slow motion, a crash, an accident. My mouth was open, my heart nearly stopping.

'Please come in and have dinner with us. I'd love to hear more about your playing.'

'I've just started to practise for the first time since I got off an international flight.'

'Well, you should eat then. I'm serious, it's the best thing for jet-lag, eat a huge meal as soon as you arrive.'

'I arrived two nights ago.'

'So you must be starving. Come on. It will only take, what, twenty minutes. The food's ready, waiting, just down there.' He pointed to the kitchen.

She laughed again, didn't move. She looked at me.

'What do you think, Alice? You might like to have dinner with your son by yourself since he's come up especially.'

'Oh,' I said, waving an arm about.

280

'Not a cogent answer, Mum. Try words.'

What could I say?

'Come in,' I said, of course.

We sat at the table and Richard served us plates of food – fish with the fancy sauce, the potatoes artfully arranged – wiping the edges of the plates with a tea-towel before he set them down. Emily asked him about his work and he spoke volubly – flinging his arms about, nearly knocking over a glass – about a work commissioned jointly by an orchestra in Scotland and the Scottish parliament, although I couldn't work out if he'd been commissioned to compose it himself or someone else was involved. In any case it had to include some Scottish folk music known as mouth music, or lilting – music created to dance to in times when instruments were scarce, or unaffordable, or banned, so the emphasis was on the rhythm, he explained, and the melody, rather than the lyrics, which were often just nonsense words. He demonstrated in a whiny voice, hi-higgledy-dee-dee-dee, tilting his head from side to side and rolling his eyes. Emily didn't laugh at this, I noticed, she just watched him. I'd never seen him like this; I was still stunned.

'Sounds like an interesting project,' she said. 'How's it going?'

It was as if he were a sail and the wind had suddenly dropped. Poof! 'Oh,' he said, 'don't ask.'

'I've been playing lately,' she said, looking down, fiddling with her fork, 'your "Song for Midwinter".'

'Really? Where did you find that? I thought it was out of print.'

'In a shop in Canada, quite a while ago. A lot of people play you there, you know.'

'International sales have been weirdly good, especially since the album that . . .'

But he didn't finish. She had started to sing, quietly, but very clearly, and I realised it was the modern piece that she had played on the other side of the wall soon after we met.

'You composed it at music school, I think?'

He nodded, watching her, wary.

'It's always bathed me in sunshine, that piece. It's always felt to me like a spot of loveliness in an otherwise frigid, freezing world, yet at the same time it has this taint of melancholy, as if the sunshine is about to leave, which I suppose it always must.'

He asked her then about Canada, and her own musical history, and we heard about her research at the University of Toronto, and her studies at the Royal Conservatory. Then they got up and went into the front room, with me following. Richard started tinkering on the piano, Emily said that what he was playing reminded her of something (a piece I hadn't heard of) then she played another modern piece, which they discussed, and on it went.

After a while, Richard said, 'We should play the Rachmaninoff, me on the orchestra part in here, you doing the solo over there – test out this wall,' and he slapped it with his hand.

I was appalled by this suggestion. I almost shouted, *No!*

'It wouldn't work,' she said at once. 'We couldn't see each other or hear each other properly.'

'All the more reason to try. It would all be done through listening, but a different sort of listening, almost an anticipation of sound. I mean, these acoustics are fascinating.'

'I suppose . . .' she said.

'Come on, Mother, where's the score?'

I didn't move, I didn't speak.

'Is it in the study?' And then he spied it, fallen beneath the piano. 'Here we go. Great!'

As quickly as that she was heading next door, he was smoothing out the score on the stand of the Steinway, and they were playing the concerto together on either side of the wall.

It was appalling. Just as Emily had predicted, it did not work. In fact, I would say it was the worst rendition of any concerto on two pianos I had ever heard. Richard could hardly play it, he made mistake after mistake. The only thing that kept him going was the way he thumped the rhythm out in the bass. At first I could hardly hear Emily's playing with him bashing away there beside me, but then it pirouetted through the wall, or over it, and Richard quietened down. But they clearly couldn't hear each other properly over their own playing. Whenever they started to play together something ruined it: her tempo changed, or Richard would make another mistake, or she'd drop back as if waiting for him, and he would lower his volume, trying to hear her, but then she wouldn't be able to hear him. I don't think they played even one phrase together that night. Eventually she came back over.

'Sorry!' he said. 'I thought I knew it, I did it for a mate once in college, but it turns out I don't remember it at all. I was terrible, beyond appalling.'

She was smiling. 'It wasn't that bad.'

'No, it was. But you were brilliant.'

'Oh, come on.'

'I hear a lot of pianists, and like I said, you play with absolute beauty; it's exceptional.'

For a second she did nothing, then she tilted back her head and laughed, and the only word I can think of to convey what she felt is delight. Then she turned to me and said, 'What did you think, Alice?'

I said I thought it sounded absolutely terrible, the worst thing I had heard in my life, and that it was a ridiculous thing to even attempt in the first place. They both laughed as if I had made a great joke, and that was it, it was over, they both left.

∼

That night I couldn't sleep. Richard's fish dish had been salty; I was drinking water, visiting the lavatory, walking around the house touching things: the banister, the lid of the piano, a bowl of oranges in the kitchen. I started to think someone else was walking around the house too; I could almost hear the footsteps behind me, and I jerked around once or twice, but no one was there. Frightened, I turned on all the lights. Even lit up, so unnaturally bright against the black of the night, the place frightened me. Who's there? I called into the silent night, but no one answered.

77.

Currabin, December 20th, 2006

Joe Cocker, 'You Can Leave Your Hat On'. I turned it off, the
sound of the tractor came back again, *rrr-rrr, rrr-rrr*.

'I think he hates me, Alice.'

'Really?'

'He never even looks at me anymore. I could stand in front of
him starkers, jiggle myself up and down and he wouldn't even
notice.'

Shirley's entire face crumpled. It was the everyday agony of it,
the casual disregard.

'But you're beautiful,' I said.

'Oh no,' she wailed, 'I'm not, not at all. I'm horrible!'

'You are,' I said. 'Look at your face, the structure of it. The
bones.'

'Beneath all the blubber, you mean.'

Pause.

'It doesn't matter anyway,' I said.

'What?'

'Beauty. I don't know why we all go on so much about it. It's
such a distraction.'

We sat quietly for a bit.

'Is he angry about something, but not saying it, is that it?'
I said.

'I don't know. Maybe. But what?'

'Does he hurt you?'

'*Hurt me?* Harold? God, no! Nothing like that. He's just . . . oh, I don't know.'

'Is he distracted by something? His work, something about the block?'

'No, I don't know, maybe . . .' she looked away.

'Well, what would you like from him, I mean really like?'

'Just . . .' and she looked over towards the tractor. 'Just to sit and have a conversation, for him to hear me, you know, see me, look at me when I speak, try to understand what I mean, be interested in that, really interested, and then tell me what he thinks, what he feels. Maybe over dinner, maybe with a candle or something,' and her voice had become a whisper.

Eventually we got talking of other things: Shirley's favourite television show, the people I visit in the nursing home, although I haven't done it this week – I've been too busy writing this and preparing for my visitors.

I dusted their room again when I got up, running a soft cloth along the surfaces, then I made shortbread in the cool of the early morning, using cutters in the shapes of stars and hearts and angels which I'd found at a charity shop in Mildura.

After Shirley left, a bit wobbly, it has to be said, I became preoccupied with my own concerns again – specifically the prospect of my visitors; will they come? – and I got up and walked around the block.

It still hasn't rained. The earth down by the oranges is pulled as tight as dry skin. Where it splits the cracks are as thick as my finger, and the dust around them is a fine powder, which will be lifted by the north wind and deposited in small clots on wind-screens and the sills of city windows.

78.

Oxford, January, 2006

The Monday after Emily returned I was waiting in the front room with the score in my hand. But instead of Emily walking up the path, it was Richard. There he was again at the door, a brown leather satchel in his hand.

'She's not here yet?' he said, after he'd come in.

'Who?'

'Emily.' He put the satchel on top of the piano. 'She didn't tell you?'

'Tell me what?'

'We're going to do another run-through of the concerto through the wall.' He looked at me and added, 'If that's all right with you.'

'How do you know she wants to do another run-through?' I said at last.

'What? She told me.'

'What?'

'She told me. Mum, I think you've got deafer. Have you thought about that visit to the doctor?'

'How did she tell you?'

'How? The phone.' He gave me an odd look and peered out the window, looked at his watch. 'I think I've got the time right.'

We stood in silence for a bit, then he flopped onto the couch.

'You're going to do that thing again,' I said, looking down at him; it was all I could think of to say. 'That horrible thing you did the other night? You're going to repeat that?'

'That's the idea.'

They did play it again that day and, again, they were unable to play it together. I got up and stood behind Richard (by this point I had started to shake with the effort of suppressing my agitation) and when he stopped playing he turned around – and the expression on his face! I was expecting a look of displeasure, if not a great knot of frustration, but he was beaming, he was practically beatific.

'This is pointless,' I said.

'Sorry?' beaming, beaming.

'This is a long process,' I said.

'Yes, and so interesting. These acoustics are fascinating.'

'The acoustics?'

'Yes, Mum. Acoustics, sound in time and space. It's absolutely brilliant here. You're forced to listen so much more carefully, you hear so many different things in the composition, it makes you appreciate it anew.'

'This music here,' I said, pointing at the score, 'you're appreciating this anew?'

'Yes. And, you know, music in general. I'm seeing the compositional detail with much greater attention, but it's also a different sort of attention: how the parts fit together, how they don't, when they fall apart, the reasons for that. It's so interesting.'

'There's a wall!' I spluttered. 'That's the bloody reason.'

'Maybe,' he said, still smiling.

'You can hardly hear the music anyway, with what you're doing.'

'In some ways,' nodding sagely, 'that's the most interesting part of all.'

They ended up crashing on for another hour before easing to a halt (how this was agreed upon I could not detect), then Richard packed away his books, kissed me on the cheek, and I watched him walk past his car and disappear.

288

I listened carefully after that, but didn't hear anything. I pressed myself right up against the wall. Maybe a dull murmur of voices, but I couldn't be sure.

He left Oxford hours later, his car's engine roaring to life in the street. Then she started playing again. The music wound itself around the keyboard then seemed to climb right over it and out the window. I didn't recognise the piece; it didn't matter. What mattered was that her tone was unfettered once more, restored. As her playing rang into the night, I watched the moon rise above the houses, suspend itself above the meadow as if swinging on a string, then soar up and become smaller.

~

A few days later he arrived again.

'She has a job, you know,' I said, watching him unpack his satchel at the piano. 'She's an academic at the university, Oxford University, not that one on the hill. She's got a senior lectureship in the department as well as a fellowship at Jesus.'

'I do know that actually, Mum.' He unbuttoned his cuffs, rolled up his sleeves. His shirt was wildly patterned with distressed edges. His hair was sticking up this time, not flopping over his face.

'Her concert is very soon.'

'I know, and in the Sheldonian with Mary Shergold conducting. It's going to be great.'

He sat down at the piano, put a notebook and pencil at the end of the keyboard, opened the Rachmaninoff score, and started following the music along the stave with his finger, his lips moving soundlessly.

'My point is that her time is very precious and should not be wasted. Cannot be wasted.'

He looked up at me. 'Thank you, Mum.'

'And what about that thing, that Scottish thing – have you finished that yet?'

He didn't answer. Instead he got up, went to the wall and felt it with the tips of his fingers, caressing it, almost, as he had that first night. He pressed his hands flat against it, then his ear. He moved away, looked up to the ceiling, down to the floor, and pressed it again, as if testing its sturdiness.

'What on earth are you doing? Stop that.'

He ignored me, then went back to the piano and picked up the score again.

'You're not helping her, you know,' I said. 'You're doing the opposite.'

'What do you mean?'

'This thing that you're doing, it's not a run-through; it's chaotic and entirely unhelpful. It's anti-music.'

'Anti-music,' he said, looking at me thoughtfully for a moment, 'now, that's very interesting.' Then, as if something had been finalised: 'I think it's going quite well, all things considered, but, you're right, we certainly need to do a lot more practice,' and he dropped his hands onto the keys and played a few chords. 'When did you last get this thing tuned? Bit overdue, isn't it? Like me to arrange someone?'

Their playing that day was even worse, if that was possible. The way Richard played reminded me of a man I once saw trying to catch a butterfly mid-flight with his bare hands, chasing after it in vain, hands like great metallic claws opening and clasping. Emily's playing, when I could hear it, was flat, smooth; it had no suggestion of her usual tone, or of all the work she had done on interpretation. It sounded like half of a duo, an accompaniment; they were both playing like that.

I got up and paced about, I was so worked up. I started to find it difficult to breathe; I leant over the banister, sucked the air back in.

I can see in retrospect that this may look like an over-reaction to what was simply a series of unsuccessful rehearsals, but it was more than this to me, it was a replay of things past and a herald of future disaster. Also, I missed hearing Emily's playing and talking with her properly. We had not met on a Monday in the old way since she had returned. And that evening I didn't see her afterwards either; Richard went over to her place as soon as they finished.

I heard music coming through the wall. Ditties played on the piano first, phrases, chords, like that first night after dinner. Then recorded music: classical (part of a Mozart piano concerto, some Vaughan Williams, more Samuel Barber), pop (or a cousin of pop; I recognised none of it; it was much less melodic than the pop Emily had played me), then more on the piano. It was very late when it stopped.

79.

Oxford, January, 2006

He started coming to Oxford from London almost every day. Something about the anticipation of it paralysed me. I would sit in the house, waiting for the afternoon to arrive like a thunderstorm, anticipating its doom. When I opened the door I would look conspicuously over his shoulder for her, he would peck me on the cheek and head straight for the piano, saying something like, Now, where's that lovely Russian? Whenever he started playing she would come over, but never for long; she'd have a quick chat about nothing, flash me a smile, then go back next door and they would start to play.

And their playing, there was no rhythm to it, no sense of a pulse; how could there be when they could barely play the thing together? So intent were they on achieving basic coordination between the two parts that all feeling, nuance and spirit were lost. Her playing was bland, blurred; it could have been anyone playing.

I said nothing, partly because Richard never sought my opinion; he never turned around and said, What do you think, Mother? as Emily would have. If he wasn't playing he was making notes, or staring at the wall, or at the score, or out the window. (I don't think he even realised I was there listening; one day I jerked up suddenly, sitting behind him, and he turned around quickly and with a slow, growing smile said, Didn't see you there, Mother, how nice.) But most of all I didn't say anything because I was sure it would soon stop, and I decided that the best thing to do would be to ignore it.

So the next time he arrived I went straight into the study. I didn't even wait to say hello to Emily. I would file scores, I thought, I would finish the job. But instead I sat there, a score in each hand, listening to Emily's playing disintegrate next door.

I went up to the bedroom, into the bathroom, then out into the garden, trying to get away from it. I even went into the little shed set against the back fence and stood there fingering the tools (hammer, chisel, axe, saw). Out there I could still hear it, two pianos playing together; that music seemed to penetrate everything – doors, floors, yards, walls.

I would outwalk it, I thought, and I went out the front door and stomped around the block, but even out of earshot it remained with me, it was like a wounded, needy animal, limping and swaying after me. I walked deliberately out of step with it, did ever longer circuits of the streets.

When I got back the house was empty, dark. For a minute I almost wanted to see Richard sitting at the piano with his back to me. Make up your mind, I jeered at myself: silence or disharmony? Is that the only choice? a little voice whispered back. Oh, go away, I thought.

The next day, as soon as he arrived, I walked out. Bye, Mother! he said brightly to my retreating back, and in his voice I heard not hurt but laughter.

80.

Monday again, a week had passed. I sat waiting for her in the front room. Should I just go over there? I thought. Should I just ask?

I watched bicycles glide by. I watched Caroline ride home laden with shopping bags, her front door opening from the inside as if by an invisible hand. I watched Henry bend to look in his letterbox, pull out a postcard from the stack of mail; it was probably from his granddaughter, she was travelling in China. How long was it since I had spoken to these people, or to anyone properly? I watched a large woman walk past with a tiny dog, pushing herself through the air as if she were battling against it, the dog prancing. A gust of wind would have it up in the air, surely, held back only by that lead it was attached to.

She had forgotten. She was busy. I wouldn't bother her. She would come another day. And then he arrived.

~

Their daily sessions lengthened into the evening, then into the night. Her own practice, which she started as soon as Richard left for London, grew shorter and shorter until it did not happen at all.

It was at this point that I became distressed.

I tried to reason with myself. I had wanted her to think about the relationship between the soloist and the orchestra, had I not? Indeed, to play it with another? And was she not doing that? But

I had envisaged this process as a couple of sessions in a room with two pianos. A process complementary to her preparation, one that augmented it, not replaced it.

I walked around Oxford that week while they played in the two houses, thinking these sorts of thoughts, sweating my cold sweat, breathing my fetid breath, my useless, shaking hands out in front of me.

I went into one of those new cafes, ordered a cup of coffee and sat in the warmth. I decided that I was not this sort of woman anymore, this woman who said nothing, did nothing and avoided everything; there was no reason to be like that now. I would talk with them about what was happening. I would ask them how much longer they intended to play through the wall, what the plan was to ensure Emily's concert preparation was not affected, to ensure that she was properly prepared. Richard had mentioned a few days before that he had a meeting with his agent in London on Monday, tomorrow, so he wouldn't be coming to Oxford; perhaps Emily would come to the house and I could speak with her. Or I could go to her. In the meantime I would talk with Richard – in fact, that very night; it would be better to talk with them separately. This cheered me. I bought an iced cupcake as I was leaving, ate it walking back to the house.

The house seemed to be empty, but then I heard a noise in the kitchen.

'Mum. You're back.'

He was standing in the kitchen doorway.

'Coffee? I'll reheat it,' talking as if he had something in his mouth. I looked around. Pastries on the bench, half-eaten, crumbs all over the table.

'Emily had to go and do a lecture.'

'She was here?'

'You just missed her. She waited as long as she could. She really wanted to see you.'

I moved stiffly to the sink, twisted the tap, filled a glass with water.

'She has different commitments this term?' I said.

'This was just some special thing she couldn't get out of.'

I looked at the mess on the table. I didn't know how to begin to talk to him.

'Have something,' he said. 'This amazing patisserie's just opened around the corner from me. Here.'

He was holding out a pastry but I didn't take it. He picked up another one.

'Or this?'

I took it, fingered it.

'Don't worry about the mess,' he said, 'I'll clean it up,' and he brushed his hand rapidly across the table, gathering crumbs, which he threw into the bin.

'Richard . . .' I put down the pastry and glass, and to begin with I did not look at him, and it was as if I were talking to myself or the shed, the back fence – not the person beside me, not my only child. 'I'm concerned about this thing you're doing with Emily, these run-throughs. It's wasting your time, as well as hers, and it's ruining her playing.'

'Ruining it? Mother, come on,' and he was almost laughing.

'She loses her tone when she plays with you. All the interpretation she has spent months perfecting has disappeared. And when you come here day and night she has no time to practise. What's more, when you play together she's shaping her playing around yours. She's losing the sense of the solo part entirely.'

'Oh, Mum,' he said, as if I was cracking a joke, 'she is not.' Still smiling.

I felt a rush of anger then.

'You know she's only doing this to be nice.'

He moved suddenly and I swung around, but he was only folding the empty cardboard tray the pastries had come in.

'I don't think that's true, actually.' He put the tray in the bin. 'If you're worried about the solo part being overtaken by the orchestra part you needn't be; I let her lead.'

'That's not what I hear.'

'Look,' he said, 'it might be a matter of how you see the concerto as a form, whether you see it as a soloist playing with an accompanying orchestra, or as two sources of sound working together.'

'Obviously it's about a soloist with an orchestra.'

'I happen to disagree with you on that, but, practically speaking, it does depend a bit on the work in question. Now, take the second movement of this concerto, there's a constant swapping between who is accompanying and who is playing the melody. The roles are constantly being reversed. Sometimes it's the piano with the principal theme, sometimes it's the orchestra – it's the balance that matters.'

'But there is no balance here, there is no swapping, your playing is nothing like that.'

He laughed. 'Yeah,' he said, 'you're right. We have a lot more work to do.'

I didn't say anything.

'Well, I'll be off then.'

No! I wanted to shout, but he was already stooping over me, kissing my forehead, then he stopped at the door.

'Mum, you do know this isn't just my idea, don't you?' and he was loping off down the hall, stretching up an arm to brush the ceiling with the tips of his fingers.

∼

I sat at the window the next day, but she didn't come; of course she didn't come, I don't even know why I had expected it.

The morning after, I waited until I heard the gate bang, then I rushed out.

'Emily!' I called, 'Emily!'

She stopped, turned.

'Alice,' and something was different, I couldn't place it. Was it her hair, her skin, her eyes?

'How are you?' she said. 'I came around yesterday, I waited for you.'

'I'm well,' I said, although for some reason I was almost crying.

'I'll come around again soon. I'm so sorry, I feel we've hardly spoken lately. I've been so busy with work, and everything else, and, oh God, I'm late again.' She kissed me on the cheek. 'I'll see you soon.'

'Next Monday?'

She paused.

'Sure,' she said. 'Yes, sounds good, Monday,' but after a few hurried paces she turned again and said, 'I think Richard's coming next on Wednesday; shall we make it then?' And off she ran.

81.

Oxford, February 16th, 2006

When he knocked I stayed in the front room for a while, listening to him shuffle his feet on the porch. Then I climbed the air to standing. When had I last eaten, I thought, moving towards the door in slow motion; was it that cake from the cafe? Or had there been some toast after that?

I opened the door and placed my body in front of it to block the view of the kitchen. I had brought the axe in from the shed, it was propped against the kitchen bench; Richard was beaming at me in technicolour, alive beyond measure.

'You can't come in today,' I said, and now I was out in the street looking at myself, a scarecrow of a woman, her whole body prised into a crack in the door.

'Why not?'

'Something has happened to the piano.'

'What?' frowning.

'It's broken. It has given up. It cannot stand this thing you are doing, these hideous sounds you persist in making.'

He laughed, head back, as if this was really funny.

'Let's see if we can make it better then, shall we?' and he made as if to come in. I didn't move.

'I mean it, Richard. It's over. That's enough.'

He looked at me, surprised, then he shrugged a shoulder, scratched his face. Reassessing.

'Do you know,' he said, 'I've just realised I haven't even thanked you for letting me use the piano and the front room

299

for all this time. I'm very sorry. I can see now that it's been an imposition. I should have checked. You've been very generous to allow us to do this; it's been very kind of you.'

I didn't say anything for a moment, then I managed, 'All right. But that time has come to an end.'

'Do you think,' he said, 'that you could bear just, say, three more sessions?'

'No.'

'Please, Mum. I would be very grateful. I can't tell you how significant this all is, what it means to me.'

Means to him? He must have mistaken my puzzlement for wavering.

'Please let me in,' and that voice, that voice, even if I avoided the face.

'Two,' I said at last. 'Two more sessions. And that's it. I'm serious, Richard. You don't realise how serious I am.'

'I do.'

He stepped in, an entirely different shape from how he had arrived, shoulders hunched, everything about him dimmed, and he sat at the piano and quietly unpacked his things. I went down to the kitchen, put the axe back in the shed, and walked out of the house.

When I got back that night a strange thing happened. I heard them play a passage, and they were actually playing it together. More than this, it seemed they had finally learnt how to anticipate the other's rubato, the ritardandos, crescendos and descrescendos. It was a big curve of a phrase that went up in the air like a bridge then tumbled down to a terrible suggestion of hell, and to hear them play like that shocked me, it was extraordinary. Then they started playing badly again, out of step, and there was Richard at the piano, throwing up his hands and laughing.

82.

Oxford, February 17th, 2006

The next day, the last day of their sessions together, I waited for
a rainstorm to pass before walking on wet pavements into town.
I was tired. Something had been drained, as if a tap had been left
on too long.

I passed the delivery door of the Ashmolean and stopped to
watch as two men unloaded a large model ship from a van. It
was an old-fashioned ship like the explorers used to use, Captain
Cook and the like – white sails, complicated rigging – and they
carried it with their arms held like slings, one walking forwards,
the other backwards; when they got it inside, the door shut with
a click.

He was waiting for me when I got back. I let him in then
turned to walk on, away from the house, but suddenly I felt I
couldn't, that I had no energy left; but I had to keep going,
I thought. I couldn't remain.

I can't remember seeing much at all on that walk – gardens,
houses, trees, garage doors rolling up, then down; they had disappeared. All that was left were the patches of uneven pavement
in front of me and the line between the pavement and the gutter,
which is what I ended up following all over North Oxford.

I reached a fence with a train line behind it and didn't know
where I was, panic rose inside me. A train roared past, carriages
flashing, clacking, clacking; the train disappeared. I continued
to stand by the fence looking at the empty track, unable to move,
hardly breathing. After a while a young woman walked towards

me on the pavement and I reached out to her, meaning to ask where I was, but she jumped away from me and hurried off.

I backed out of that terrible place, came to the end of the mysterious road. I kept walking until I found a main road, unfamiliar to me, but scanning the horizon I spotted the university science building and worked out which way I needed to go.

When I got back to the house I could hear, from the front gate, that they were still playing, but I could not keep walking. I lowered myself onto the front steps.

Perhaps it was simply a coincidence, perhaps they had played together long enough by then, perhaps they were making a special effort because it was their last day. Whatever the reason, they had discovered how to play that music together. Emily's playing was beautiful again, in fact it was better than before; that song-like timbre had deepened and become more concentrated, stronger and more directed. At times it was as if she had worked out how to achieve the surge of a crescendo within a single note, defying the very mechanism of a piano. As her notes sang between the two houses and Richard's moved below them I got up and went inside. He was huddled over the keyboard, back bent with the effort of playing the accompaniment, his hands like cupped structures, bridges, rising and falling. Striding out to play the principal part when it was his turn, mimicking her tone as best he could, then becoming quiet again beneath her part as it surged once more. I still don't know how they did it, with no nodding or glancing, no visual cues. It was all in the listening, and the music, and the boldness to play loud when one part held the tune, and the ability to hold the rhythm of the other while playing their own part. On it went, they were stepping into the air with each note, they were two blind people walking into a strange room, arms out, hands searching, stretching, pressing, reaching further and further into the music.

83.

Currabin, December 21st, 2006

The piano was delivered this morning. I rented it six weeks ago
from a shop in Mildura. The men rolled it down the ramp of the
truck, then up to the house, pausing under the low branch of
the old elm. What a sight it was. A great black piano amid fields
of white-painted stumps. I showed them where to put it inside.
Then I sat on the veranda listening to the man tune it. In two
days perhaps I will have to ask them to take it back.

   After they left I sat in the quiet, looking out across the
block, trying to ignore the instrument behind me in the house.
I decided that the stumps did not look like a graveyard, as
I'd originally thought, but like something more compelling:
a monument to an atrocity.

84.
Oxford, February 19th, 2006

I never heard them play the Rachmaninoff together again. True to his word, Richard stopped visiting in the afternoons. But Emily did not resume her practice next door; she stopped playing entirely.

I assumed at first she had gone away, but then I heard the clatter of her gate in the mornings, and the yank and shudder of the pipes. I wondered if the concert had been cancelled (but there were still posters up in town), or if something had happened to her (but the gate banged at the usual times), or if something had happened to the wall (had all the wet weather made it sodden, impermeable?). Maybe my hearing had disintegrated dramatically, or was I deaf only to the Rachmaninoff and Emily's playing? I put on a recording of the concerto, the opening chords filled the room. I turned it off, sat looking at the street.

The silence of that house had been a comfort to me once; no, more than that, it had been a sign of safety. Now it was simply the silence of lack. Why did she not play the concerto? Why did she not practise now that she could? Play the thing! I wanted to yell, thumping the wall. What are you waiting for? Your concert approaches!

~

Into this silence, two days later, the music came. It came from her house and was played on her piano, but this was different music, and it was strange. It had no distinct melody or shape, it

304

stopped mid-air and continued somewhere else. Disparate lines ran parallel to one another. The harmony made little sense to me, the intervals, in particular; these were notes with no recognisable relationship to one another. That would not necessarily have been odd, but the rhythm was also uncertain, variable, sometimes non-existent; there was no particular form or structure I could grasp.

Occasionally I thought I heard something I recognised within it, but then it would step away and became opaque again. It went on and on, this strange music, it seemed to have no sense of climax, cadence or resolution.

When it finally stopped, with no warning, and the familiar noises of the evening trickled back into the house – someone moving their bin, people on bicycles calling out to one another – its presence stayed with me, the uneasiness of it, the discordant quality.

I walked into the study and lifted books from shelf to hearth, but I did not burn them; I walked upstairs, fingered clothing, but did not pack it; I looked at food, but did not eat. The silence of the place gradually rose around me from a hum to a singing to a siren.

85.
Oxford, February 22nd, 2006

The strange music started again the next day, in the afternoon. I pulled on scarf and gloves, went out the door and looked at Emily's house. I could see nothing, of course, just the brick wall of the basement below the porch. The street was cold and there was a scent in the air I didn't recognise.

I placed my hand on the gate of the easement and pictured myself walking down to her door. What is this strange music? I would ask, smiling. And what has happened to your practice? as if bemused. And she would say something reassuring, provide an excellent explanation, and that night (prompted, in part, by my enquiry) her practice would resume. I kept my hand on the gate for a while, then went back into the house.

~

The music developed quickly, arcs of weird intonation clashing with one another, strands that were deliberately unconnected moving slowly towards the idea of a rhythm that came together then fell apart.

I was not doing particularly well at this point. I wasn't eating much, I was paying scant attention to the cleanliness of the house, my clothing and my person (all this I realise in retrospect). I was listening for music I could not hear, but thought I should be able to hear, and its absence concerned me greatly. Why could I not hear it? Where had it gone?

The next day, listening to that strange music, I started to

hear my own performance of the concerto, with all its horrify-
ing faults, and all the shame that had been stuffed away rolled
up and over me. And the day after that, when it began again,
I crashed my arms onto the piano and the strange music stopped
for a minute, but then it arose somewhere else.

I turned on the radio, which made it disappear. It was a
program where people ring up and request a love song. I heard
Cyndi Lauper, 'True Colors', one of Emily's many favourites.
The synthesiser playing an Alberti bass, the sentimental melody,
the babyish voice telling me she sees my true colours and that
they are beautiful, like a rainbow. I felt wetness on my face
and looked up, thinking, this house, this damn house, now the
ceiling didn't work, let alone the walls. I turned off the radio,
raged up the hall into the study and started pulling things onto
the floor – books, papers, scores.

I heard a knock at the door; I lunged for it. A man stood in
the shadow of the porch: thin hair, a mousy moustache.

'Yes?'

I am here to enquire about the disappearance of a type of music from
the house next door. I am here to enquire about the disappearance of
a woman ——

'I've got your groceries,' holding up the crate. 'Shall I bring
them in?'

'No.'

'Uh, okay,' and then he looked closely at me. 'Everything all
right in there, love?'

And this was when they asked? I thought. Now?

'Just leave them there,' I said. 'Please.'

I dragged them down the hall. After that I left the house,
every bit of me pulling every other bit. It was rubbish day
the next day, bins were out already, more were still to come,
tomorrow morning they would all be gone and the street
would be strewn with litter. How many crescendos are there

in this world, I thought, how many diminuendos, accelerandos, ritardandos?

The strange music had stopped when I returned and I felt a good deal better; perhaps it was the exertion, or the fresh air. I decided I would eat something, would cook myself dinner, then go around to Emily's and ask her what had happened to her practice, and what this new music was. Of course I would do this, I thought, and why had I not done so already?

I went into the front room, pulling off my coat and gloves, thinking about what I was going to cook, but I only got one glove off because now I was listening to something else.

Breathing, I thought, moving closer. Yes, breathing, but with a note in it. Then a shh!, a titter, soft laughter.

I should have moved away from the wall, but I stayed; I was plastered to the plaster.

Several random notes were pressed on the piano – clusters, bunches, sudden bangs, like things dropped – then a tapping began, wood against wall. And then a puffing sounded, a sudden blowing out of breath, and over this a cooing drifted in treble clef, lightly at first, meandering, until it funnelled into a crescendo, full-throated. It dropped, then rose, then dropped, then rose, and so it went on for some time until it finally dropped and stopped.

I stepped backwards, tripped, felt pain, and then the carpet beneath my hands. I sat in the dark, blood beating.

I woke in the middle of the night, still in the clothes I had walked in – the purple scarf, the one red glove. I went into the bathroom, drank water from the tap. Rising, I caught myself in the mirror, leant forward, touched a finger to glass, moved back.

Downstairs, I turned on the light in the study and started gathering up all the papers, scores and books I had pulled onto the floor. I pulled them into piles then pushed the piles across the floor into the front room and stacked them against the wall, making sure they would not fall. I stacked them higher and higher until a new wall began to form, and when I could reach no further I got a chair from the kitchen and reached some more.

86.

Oxford, February 23rd, 2006

I was lying on my side with the new wall behind me and the old wall behind it. I lay listening. No strange music. No notes, scales or arpeggios. No Bach, Beethoven, Liszt, Brahms, Rachmaninoff or even Cyndi Lauper. I heard a car backfire somewhere far off, then the hysterical yap of a small dog. I got up, looked out. Morning light glinting off the wet road. Leaves lay in dark, fecund clumps on the tiles of the porch next door. A wind was bothering the bare limbs of the trees, a car approached on the other side of the road, wheels dipping in the gutter, throwing up water in slow motion. I will wash, I thought, I will dress, I will brush my hair; I did none of these things. I sat on the lid of the lavatory for a long time then got into bed.

When I woke late in the day there was a strange taste in my mouth. Blood, I thought, but wasn't sure. I went downstairs, made a cup of tea, sat holding it at the kitchen table. I switched on the radio. Hey folks! a DJ said. All you lovers out there! Do you want ——. I snapped it off, then wrenched the plug from the wall and carried it, cord trailing, out the back door and left it on the cement. I washed the mug, got dressed, got the axe from the shed, put it in the pantry and left the house.

It was the beat that I remember most, the way it thudded so suddenly in my veins, just a tap at first, a lone tambou-rine, then a snare drum, soon the snap of a cymbal, now the punch of the bass. Before I knew it there was a whole marching band of them, huge drums hit on both sides, rotating wrists, flicking sticks, marching knees, marching feet, and nothing to hear but the beat, nothing to see but those sticks hitting the skins, the boom of it shuddering every bit of you, shaking my bones, quaking my veins, gathering itself after so many years, and the speed of it, like a barrel down a hill, faster and faster, a mind of its own, boom-boom! BOOM-BOOM!

Out the door, down the footpath, through the gate, down the easement, into the yard. There was a wall of glass, a wood-framed door. I knocked, waited, then leant, hands cupped, against the glass and looked through it. A black couch, a white rug, a table, bookshelves, an upright piano, pieces of paper strewn around it. I waited for a while but she wasn't there.

Into the city, the streets were busy, Hilary term in full swing. Past the museum, past the library, the bookshop, the pub, college walls soaring beside me, a dark valley between them. The building reared before me: Geography. I stepped in.

The porter was standing behind a desk with his back to me. I walked past him into a hall with a shiny wooden floor, antlers and old framed maps on the walls and a curved, carved staircase in front of me. I started up it, went through the door at the top into a narrow corridor.

'Can I help you?'

High heels, tucked in blouse; a secretary.

'I am looking for Dr Emily Green,' with a posh accent.

'I haven't seen her in today,' voice artificially loud.

'Do you know where I might find her?'

'You could try the college,' turning away.

'Jesus?'

'I think so,' voice sing-song, back inside her room.

Natives in the maps, I saw, on my way back down, their bare backs turned. Across the shiny floor again, polished nightly, surely, all those feet. The porter didn't look up as I left; no reason to, I suppose.

311

Over to the college. Two men in uniforms in the lodge. I strode past them into a quadrangle lined with rows of swaying daffodils (strange that, no daffodils up anywhere else; a micro-climate in there, perhaps). A young woman walked towards me, short hair, glasses, androgynous; I asked her where the room was, she gestured to a building.

'It's locked though,' pushing her glasses up, 'you need a code. You might ask the porters,' and she peered at me, not suspicious, I didn't think, just curious, making her point.

I waited until someone came down the stairs, a boy, taking two at a time, caught the door. Her office had a notice on the door listing consultation times. I waited outside, but the minutes slid by and I knew she wasn't there either.

Back on the streets, looking above collars, scarves, below hats, bicycle helmets, looking at faces, looking at hands, peering at sleeves, x-raying gloves, then thinking, thinking of more places. Was she at a film? She sometimes mentioned those. I walked to the cinema, scrutinised a milling, waiting crowd, but she wasn't there. Had she gone to a yoga class? I went over to the hall she'd talked about, but the door was locked, the place was empty. Out to dinner with friends? She did that a bit. I walked in and out of restaurants along Walton Street, then some in the city, and at times I thought I saw a woman who looked like her sitting at a table eating, but it was never her.

It was getting too dark to see anything clearly; I walked back to Chardwell Road and checked her place again, then went back to the house, but when I opened the door and saw the stairs in front of me they had become insurmountable. One of my legs hurt, I seemed to have injured it – all that marching. But also the stairs took me too far into the house, the thought of which I suddenly couldn't bear. I sat in the front room instead, by the window, kept watch from there, the hurt leg propped up on a chair.

Night extended, the silent time approached, descended; I kept looking out of the window, peering into the dark. My leg started to throb; it was where the beat now resided.

~

Morning. I was still at the window, looking at that scene, the gate, the footpath, the identical houses, the street, the gutter. But I didn't see him coming, just heard the knock on the door, no, the flick. It took me a long time to reach it, as if there were numerous doors and gates I needed to unlock before getting to it. There he stood, beaming like a full moon, holding up a paper bag of food.

'Mum, how are you? I just need to check something out with the wall in the front room, if you don't mind.'

I didn't move.

'Hel-lo. Mum? Would it be possible to come in?'

I stepped back slowly. He was smiling widely.

'I won't do this now,' he said, 'because I know you wouldn't like it, but sometimes I do just want to give you a great big hug.'

My hand was still twisted on the door-knob; I was staring at it, trying to work out how to untwist it.

'Mum? Are you okay? You seem a bit . . . out of it. Shall I cook you some breakfast? I was thinking the other day that I could cook a big stack of meals and —' But he had stopped. He was standing in the doorway to the front room, looking at the new wall I had made of papers and books, which I'd forgotten about.

'What's this?' voice low.

'Filing,' I said, and I started down the hall, thinking he would follow me, and that I would get to the kitchen first, where the axe was still in the pantry, but he didn't follow me, he kept standing there looking at the wall.

'Filing? What do you mean, filing? Jesus Christ,' and he moved his arms about, 'look at this!' And then he looked at me and said, 'Oh my God.'

What did he see, I thought, what did he see that I had missed?

'Mum? What's happened? Are you limping? What's going on?'

I walked into the kitchen and went to go to the pantry, but he came in behind me and started looking in the cupboards. I sat down at the table; he walked straight out of the back door. I got up again to reach the pantry but as quick as that he was back in the room, tall, very loud.

'There are bags of food out there. The food I've had delivered you've just tipped out there. My God!'

I looked at his shaking arm, the pointing finger.

'Have you not been eating again? Is that it? Are you not feeding yourself?'

I had started to shake too. I was holding the edge of the table. He grabbed the bag of food he'd brought from London, pulled a plate from the cupboard, crashed it down, piled food onto it.

'You have to eat. You're making yourself sick.'

I glanced at the mounds of shiny pallid dough, festooned with fruit, chocolate, nuts, icing.

'Go on,' pushing it closer to me. 'Eat something.'

I looked away, started to get up again from the table. He yanked open a cupboard and then the fridge, crashed a skillet onto the stove, opened a carton of eggs. 'Mum, do you know what day it is?' he cracked some eggs, threw the shells into the sink.

'Who's the prime minister?' he said, pouring the eggs into the hot spluttering pan.

Now I was moving towards the pantry, putting the kettle on the stove on my way, thinking about how, exactly, I would place my body.

'Who am I?' he said.

I hadn't put any water in the kettle. I went back to the stove, picked it up, took it to the sink. He lunged forward and wrenched the gas off.

'I knew it was on!' I said, more loudly than I had meant to.

'All right, all right,' flapping his arms.

'Where is she?' I said then; I couldn't help it.

'What? Who?'

'*Where is she?*'

'Jesus, what are you talking about? Calm down.'

'Where is she? I can't find her. I've looked and looked!'

'Mum, I think you might have finally flipped.'

'Since you started coming she's stopped practising properly.'

'Ahhh.'

'What have you done?'

'What have I *done*?'

'I need to know what —'

'*What do you think I've done?*'

'I won't allow it, Richard, I —'

'I love her! Can't you see? I love her.' And his voice was anguished, but it was more than this, or other than this; it was as if he had been waiting to proclaim it.

'Love?' I said. 'Love?' But like an echo.

'Yes, Mum, at last.'

He turned and walked back down the hall.

87.

Oxford, February 25th, 2006

The phone was ringing.

'Mum? I've rung the doctor, she can —'

I hung up, pulled the socket from the wall.

I felt wetness again, looked up. This house, this damn house, it was collapsing entirely, it was time to go.

Hands sliding along the walls. Through the gate. Down the path. Across the yard. To the glass.

'Emily!' I shouted, thumping on the glass wall. 'Emily!' But she wasn't there.

I walked into town again. The beat was uneven now (boom-BOOM! Boom-BOOM!). I stopped, listened; nothing. I kept walking. Boom-BOOM! Stopped again. It was my leg, I thought, I was still limping.

I reached Geography and walked in, but something was wrong with me that day: walking wrong, looking wrong, sounding wrong.

'Excuse me.'

I pretended not to hear, kept walking.

'Excuse me! Can I help you?'

'I am looking,' accent haughty, 'for one of your staff.'

'Who?'

'Emily Green.'

'Not in.'

He was taller, this one, and thinner. He had a lunchbox open on the desk behind him that had been packed carefully;

I glimpsed a neatly cut sandwich, a square of yellow cake in plastic, a shiny apple. I limped around him, went into the hall, but before I could cross that shiny floor he stopped me.

'She's not in,' louder, and that floor, like glass; we were just balancing, teetering.

'You need to leave.'

'I need to find her. I have been looking for her for a very long time.'

'Off we go now,' cupping his hand under my elbow.

I sat on the kerb, resting, remembering.

One of the nights after Edward died I went to Evensong in the college chapel. It was dark, lit only by candles, and everyone looked at me when I walked in, so I sat in the first pew I came to and sat very still.

I heard a growl behind me, an old man clearing his throat, readying it for speech, for outrage. You can't sit there, he said, and I froze, my bowels liquefied. It's Fellows only. Then, swooping towards us out of the dark, a woman in a black robe, white collar, spectacles, her hair in a neat bob. Everyone is welcome in this chapel, she hissed. It's Fellows only! he rasped. She's sitting in the wrong place! Everyone is welcome in this chapel, she repeated, more loudly. I groped for my handbag under the pew and fled.

I got up from the kerb and went over to Emily's college. I made to stride through the gate but one of the guards got in front of me.

'No tours today, ma'am.'

After some remonstration he showed me out.

I sat down on the pavement again, leant against the wall to wait; I had those consultation hours in mind. After a while the guard came out, looked at me, came over.

'Is there someone we can call, love? What's your name?' and he leant down, reached for my handbag. I snatched it to me and with a shot of pure pain down my injured leg I rose and scuttled off.

I looked for her in restaurants, cafes, bookshops, libraries. I looked for a young woman whose hands could stretch a thirteenth and turn a thin steel string into a bell, a mouth, a lung, a soul.

My breath was ragged and I was tiring. The bells of the city started to chime their slow, unsynchronised cascade, reminding me of a conversation with Edward when we were courting: Did you know, he said, that the bell in the tower at Christ Church College still follows a time five minutes behind Greenwich Mean Time? Oxford Time, it's called. Why? I said. Because, he answered, it is their history and they think it is right.

I came to a bike path; cycles were swooping out of the bleak light towards me, curving, tipping, bells ringing, people shouting. I huddled to one side, but kept inching forward. The path was lined by a hedge, recently trimmed, the rough ends sticking out, sticking into me, and those bicycles kept swooping, weaving. I came to the end of the path. There was a hill before me; a group of young men and women dressed in shorts and singlets were running up and down it. They started up the hill together, but it wasn't long before they parted. When they got to the top, the fastest waited, but as soon as the slow ones arrived they ran back down. After a while the slowest couldn't keep up at all, they looked exhausted. One stopped, bent at the waist and vomited, another walked for a minute in jagged circles, but the others kept going as fast as they could, up and down, up and down.

I stopped watching them; I looked around. Where was I? I had no idea how to get home. There was a bus stop nearby; I waited, sitting on the bench. When a bus pulled up I got on. It must have been some sort of special service because it did a long loop around the entire city then set me down in the centre. I walked back to Chardwell Road.

I checked her place again, but it was dark, no one was there. Outside my house I stopped; I could not go in. I could not bear even the thought of going in.

I walked back into the city. I went into a department store that was open late. Bright lights, racks of clothing, flute music. I found the bathroom, sat on a lavatory seat in a locked cubicle and dozed. A voice woke me, saying that the store was closing. I walked back past the racks of clothes, the lights, the flute music, back into the street.

~

That night I looked for her all around that ancient city. I looked everywhere I could reach: in the windows of the college and university buildings (startling many a person from various pursuits); down through those mesh-covered windows that indicate rooms below street level. I looked in the cobbled lanes and ancient streets he had once shown me, but there was not a trace of her in any of those places. (Did she ever even exist? I started to wonder at one point.) When people on the streets were getting scarce (except for those late-night revellers by the kebab vans, whom I avoided), I stopped looking with my eyes and used my ears instead. I listened for her. I heard an entire room throbbing with washing machines, a man bawling on a phone, a door banging repeatedly. Soon I was able to blot out all that and listen only for her music. I heard someone practising the trumpet, the crash of a dance beat, the warbling of a carol.

I kept walking outwards through suburban streets to empty roads so long they were landscapes in themselves and lined by fences and fields. Out there it was only the wind I could hear after a while, and my own footfall, and then the silence itself, which soon became beautiful to me; it was conducive to thought.

Eventually I found myself back at the house, I let myself in and headed straight for the kitchen. I got the axe from the pantry, took it up to the front room, lifted it as high as I could and let it fall. A note rang out, a B, a key flew past me, the axe bit the carpet. I went for a leg next, a sideways chop, and then some indiscriminate hacking. The wood was dry and over-varnished but gradually the cut became deeper. Finally, with a hum so sonorous it was really a sigh (and not an unhappy one, I found, to my surprise), the thing knelt before me. I left the axe on the floor.

Now the sun was a widening slit on the horizon and I walked straight towards it. It led me to the meadow, which stretched before me like a great body of water, and I swam into it. I soon realised I was moving up and down more than I was moving forward, and then I felt compelled to lie down, but in all that water I would drown, surely. As a compromise I started to crawl, but that didn't last long either, the ground was too muddy. I turned onto my back and lay looking up at the stars. We moved in tandem for a while until they started to fade and that slit on the horizon widened and widened to become a great hole torn in the side of the world. With great relief, indeed enchantment, I turned my head towards it.

88.
Oxford, February 26th, 2006

'Drink this.'

I lifted an arm, it made a crackling sound. I sipped.

I saw that I was wrapped in silver; I was wrapped in the sky. Turning my head I could see a box filled with flashing lines and numbers and I seemed to be tethered to it. It was not unlike one of Edward's graphs, that box, except for the lights and movement.

Richard was walking to me, the soles of his shoes squeaking on the hard, shiny floor.

'Mum,' sitting down heavily, 'you're with us.'

I looked around, but it was only Richard and me in that white room.

'Someone found you lying in the meadow. You were coated in ice.'

'A frosty climate.'

'What?'

A gurney squeaked by in the corridor.

'Hypothermia ... dehydration ... malnourishment ... exhaustion ... untreated tear in the leg ... Third World complaints, or those of a mountain climber ... You could have died.' I only heard bits of what he was saying.

I closed my eyes and when I opened them again, Richard had gone.

I sipped the drink, heard that crackle again when I lifted my arm.

Someone washed me, a warm sponge smelling of disinfectant searched my skin.

I was propped up, a shelf was wheeled in front of me, a meal presented. I ate slowly, thoroughly. It was night again.

I tried to get out of the bed but my legs wouldn't let me, and tubes were still attached to my wrist. I listened to the box beside me, which seemed to be set to F sharp, although I couldn't be sure. I had perfect pitch as a child; not anymore. I made up chords and harmonies around the note, then a melody augmented by the squeak and pitch of wheeling trolleys, the beat of feet and sudden voices. I invented a clef to take account of these things; it looped around an outsized stave then shot off the page like an exploding star.

In the morning Richard was there again, standing at the door with a group of people who all looked the same. They watched him move his hands as he talked, as if he were conducting. I glided my hands over the doorframe, floated up to the cornices, drifted through the window, danced on the lawn.

He came over. 'How are you, Mum?' There was a different air to him that day, which alerted me. 'I have some great news. They've got a place for you in one of the best nursing homes in the area. It's like a miracle, they're so hard to come by.'

I was waiting, I was listening.

'You usually have to wait months.'

I started pushing myself up. My leg was heavy; they had done something to it. I knew this would happen, I thought.

'It has a music room,' he said, 'and a beautiful garden.'

I didn't blame him; it was understandable. But none of this made the prospect attractive. A nursing home! A long-stay hospice, more like it, and in that respect no different from the house I had lived in. And a hospice was not what I was after, not anymore.

'Hypothermia,' he was saying again, then another verse: 'You weren't eating . . . You hadn't washed . . . The house was in a state . . . You burnt valuable papers and books that a lot of people wanted . . . You went wandering . . . You got lost . . . You had an incident with an axe.'

'Oh that,' I said, waving a hand. 'A minor matter. Poetic flourish. Don't read too much into it. A little piece of history.'

'What?' Silence, then he resumed. 'I can't just sit by and watch you destroy yourself, Mum . . .' His voice broke and I had to look away.

'Where is Emily?' I said.

'She had to go to a meeting. She visited before.'

'No, she didn't.'

'She was here last night. She sat by your bed. You were asleep.'

He spoke again of the nursing home, how it was an outstanding model of its sort, how I would be transitioned there straight from the hospital, and he started to discuss some of the logistics – what things would I want brought in from home? As he was talking a woman in a wheelchair slowly inched herself past the open door, down the corridor: an elderly woman, her head tipped to one side, her eyes unblinking, her tongue lolling. And amid all this she just walked in, Emily. She had on a white jumper, her hair was glossy and fanned out over her shoulders.

'Alice,' she said, 'you're awake. How are you?'

'Excellent,' I said.

'Great. I'm so glad to hear it. It doesn't surprise me. Richard, could we have a word?' and he got up and they both left the room.

I heard voices in the corridor, their voices, which soon rose and grew heated.

'So passive,' I heard him say, 'just sits there,' and then her voice, angry. 'Passivity is the strongest indication of . . .' but then the voices suddenly dropped and went away.

Another meal was wheeled in front of me; someone took my blood pressure.

Emily came back in by herself, and she looked different. Her face was red, she was frowning. I stared at her, willing.

'Alice, I need to apologise,' she said.

I frowned. 'What for?'

'For not coming around to visit.'

'Don't worry about that. You were busy. Besides,' an after-thought, 'Richard says you were here last night.'

'I mean back at the house. I told you I was busy with work, but that wasn't quite right. In any case, I'm very sorry to have stopped coming without really saying anything.'

'It was good in the end, a good thing to happen. A gift.'

She rearranged herself in the chair.

'I got swept away.' And her face started to crumple. 'With Richard, and ... and all of it. It's been an amazing time, life-changing.' I watched her face, such misery, watched her struggle to take a breath. 'I've got my feet back now,' she whispered.

'It's all right,' I said.

'They're saying you could have died. I feel partly responsible.'

'What? No,' very annoyed. 'Those stupid doctors.'

'They're saying you're to go into a nursing home. I was talking with the staff.'

'Richard's been telling me about it.'

'Yes. We disagree on this, fundamentally.'

'Do you?'

'We do. I'm very angry with him about it.'

'That's no good,' I said. 'A disagreement.'

She looked at me for a minute, then got up.

'Alice, do you think you could stand another visitor? Do you think you could bear with me for a bit while I look someone up?'

'Of course,' I said.

324

I put the television on, switched it to mute, watched people's actions, their mouths, hands, bodies moving with no sound.

A few hours later Emily came back, accompanied by a man in a bow-tie with a fastidious air about him. She introduced him as a professor of medicine at the university with a special interest in hands and wrists. He had a dedicated treatment program in London, she said, where he also conducted research. He stood patiently while she said all this, his own small, pale hands crossed in his lap, the short cuffs of his pink shirt exposing narrow wrists. When she finished speaking he said, May I? And he took my hands in his.

He looked at them, he turned them over, he pressed and prodded parts. He asked me questions about the paralysis I had experienced, how it had started and progressed, whether it had manifested since. He told us that focal dystonia was a neurological condition that causes involuntary bodily contractions. Research in primates had shown that over-training particular fingers can result in focal hand dystonia, so some musicians' dystonia may be related to only certain movements of the hands, or even certain pieces of music.

Emily said something about the contribution of anxiety and perfectionism to the condition, and they discussed the relative contribution of emotional and physical components to causation.

'Well,' he said finally, and for the first time he smiled, a small, close-lipped movement, 'with the right treatment – hand exercises at the piano, injections of Botox, and possibly some cognitive therapy – I believe that you would be able to play the piano again. I would be happy to treat you myself at my centre in London. There would be no charge as we are particularly short of elderly research subjects at the moment. I do hope that assists.'

Emily smiled at him broadly, and escorted him from the room.

I sat looking at the wall in front of me. Richard came back in.

'What's going on?' he said.

'I got Butterworth in,' Emily said coming back in behind him. 'You just missed him.'

Richard frowned, rubbed his head. 'What did he say?'

'He said that Alice's hand condition is treatable, that he will be happy to look after her himself for free, and that focal dystonia can cause enormous emotional distress in musicians, which would explain any uncharacteristic behaviour, rendering her removal to a nursing home entirely inappropriate.'

He stared at her.

'I don't think this really changes matters,' he said eventually. 'How is treatment of her hands going to make her eat again and look after herself properly?'

'As I've explained, treating her hands will reduce her emotional distress. You need to —'

'Think this through? I've lived and breathed this my whole —'

'And here is the solution! Why would you not want to at least *try* letting her stay in her own home and taking her for treatment? I will take her!'

Their argument got worse.

'Please leave,' she said at one point, but he didn't leave. He stood there with his arms crossed.

'What do you think, Alice?' and by this point her face was pale, her voice strained. 'Have any of us even asked you what you think?'

I looked from one to the other.

'Oh for fuck's sake,' Richard said, 'this is fucking ridiculous. She is not competent enough to —'

'Alice, I can guarantee that I will look in on you a few times a day —'

'You can't,' he broke in. 'You don't have the time; don't do this to yourself. And what about that job in London – so that's all off now, is it?'

'I will arrange a meal service and a cleaner for you, Alice.'

'And you're paying for this? And will stand over her pleading, begging her to eat?'

'I'll do whatever is required to assure all the relevant people that you are capable of living independently, as you have done for many years.'

At this point Richard looked up at the ceiling, snorted.

She turned to him. 'The reason why I'd like you to leave,' she said, 'is not only because I'm so unimpressed by your treatment of your mother, but also because I don't think she feels able to speak freely in front of you.'

All the blood left his face; he turned and left.

She sat motionless, as if something enormous had just been dropped in front of her.

I looked around the room for a bit, patted the sheet.

'Emily,' I said, 'how is the concerto going?'

She roused herself.

'Fine. Great. I had a rehearsal with the orchestra the other day, which went well. We have another one next week. You can come along if you like. I mean if it wouldn't —'

'So you're still doing the concert?'

'Yes,' frowning, looking at me. 'Why wouldn't I be?'

'You don't practise. I never hear you practise it.'

She stared at me, she gaped.

'Alice,' she said. 'Oh Alice, I should have said. I just assumed Richard had told you. I practise in the Sheldonian now; they let me use the piano there that I'll be performing on. If I can't use that I play on a similar one in the music department. There's also a suite there with two pianos side by side that Richard and I use – did you really think I wasn't practising at all?'

I tried to sit up. The room had become brighter, I was noticing the colour of the walls, the texture of the bedclothes, the smell of the air.

'I was mistaken,' I said.

More tears welled in her eyes. She looked so sad it was almost unbearable. Then I saw something by the door, just a flash, I couldn't be sure.

'Why do you play his music?' I said.

'Whose?'

'Richard's.'

'I love it,' she said, and then she smiled. 'It falls so easily beneath my hands,' the tears were falling again. 'I've had such —' and she could hardly get it out, 'such pleasure at the piano playing it. It just feels right. Something I am part of, or was ...'

I couldn't bear it now, how sad she was.

'It's not Billy Joel,' I said.

'No,' trying to smile, 'it's not.'

'Or Cyndi Lauper.'

'No,' but now the tears were sliding again. It was as if the wave of grief, of realisation, had now hit her.

'I suppose the problem is,' I said, looking away, 'that such music will inevitably stop. I mean it has to, doesn't it? No music can go on forever; we all have to stop playing at some point, and what then?'

'And then the good part begins.'

'What do you mean?' turning back to look at her.

'Oh, I don't know,' she said, as if tired now, tired of it all. 'Real life, I suppose. Living.' She wiped her cheeks with the back of her hand, sat up a bit. 'Anyway, Alice,' voice back to normal, 'what do you think of this plan to keep you out of a nursing home and to help you play the piano again? We can make this happen, we really can – you heard the professor. I'd really like to help you do this. I feel I owe you this.'

'Owe me? Not at all. It's quite the other way round, I can assure you.'

'Alice, you completely changed my approach to the piano, and to music – to life. You don't realise it, but you helped me

328

so much. And it's because of you that I met Richard —' She stopped, took a breath. 'Also, someone ought to have told you about treatment for dystonia years ago; it's not right. Just think of it, Alice. Think of it. You playing the piano again after so many years,' and now she was staring at me, no tears anymore.

And I did think about it then, playing the piano again, playing scales, arpeggios, Bach, Beethoven, Liszt and Brahms (if not Rachmaninoff) and other pieces that I did not yet even know. And Emily would be next door, and she would come around at least once every day. And when I finished playing she would put her head around the door and say, That was very good, play it again, and I probably would.

There was a flash by the door again, I was sure I had seen it. 'It's a very kind offer,' I said. 'The kindest of offers.'

'I think this is the right thing to do, Alice.'

I looked at her carefully, at her eyes, which had been all-seeing, and didn't look away. At her mouth that spoke such wise words, at her hands that could catch and hold so many things, at her broad shoulders, which carried so much and so easily, and I thought then of all she had said and done, of the time we had spent together, and how I'd felt in October and November and December, and I concluded that this was enough. Yes, this was enough, and so I said: 'No thank you, Emily.'

She blinked.

'No to what?'

'No to the treatment to fix my hands. No to playing the piano again. No to staying in Chardwell Road. No to it all.'

'Right,' and she took a deep breath, let it out. 'I mean, it's your choice, of course.' She sat there for a few moments. Then she said, 'Can I ask why?'

Richard walked back into the room.

I could have said it then, it all flashed before me – my disastrous performance of the Rachmaninoff concerto, everything that had happened before it, all that had happened since. But there was so much, and I found I still couldn't start. Maybe I was out of practice. Maybe it had something to do with that place, Oxford. Or maybe it was simply that there were more immediate priorities.

They were standing a few feet apart, not looking at each other; both of them had their arms crossed.

'I think it's practice time,' I said, 'isn't it?'

89.

Currabin, December 22nd, 2006

It is dusk. The land cools. Three galahs sit on the top wire of the fence with their beaks open, fat grey tongues poking out. Time for a drink.

When did I last do anything except write? I wondered this morning. I took the car out for a break – and because I couldn't bear yet to finish this. The car came with the house; I found it parked in one of the big sheds with a notice under a windscreen wiper, the letters hand-scrawled: Looks like shit/Runs like a dream/Keys R inside. Frank taught me to drive one summer when Edward was away. We bowled down Oxford side streets as he yelped, in his mild way, Left! Right! No!

About ten minutes after I left the block I saw an extraordinary sight in the distance. It was the colour pink and a great mass of it was billowing in the space where the land meets the sky. With the lack of rain the top surface of the land had lifted itself, shuddered and dispersed. It came closer and closer to me, or I to it, red dust landed in clots on the windscreen and slid down the glass, then whole clods of earth careened out of the sky and landed, thumping, on the bonnet and roof. Branches skittered across the road, the white grass at the verges was bent flat. I saw a piece of fencing wire tremble and lash free, a big lone gum tree swept into the shape of an arrow, and finally the storm was upon me, slamming hard into the side of the car. I held the wheel tight and drove straight into it.

All of a sudden everything was dark, still, quiet. I flicked the headlights up to high beam, lifted a sticky hand from the wheel, stretched it out. I was driving very slowly; I could hardly see a thing in front of me, the dust was so thick. Small trees beside the road swayed in a slow waltz. I felt the bitumen of the road beneath the rolling tyres. As quickly as it had descended the darkness lifted, the dust dissipated, and I was out of it, and the car sped forward.

When I got back I was overcome with a feeling of doubt so huge that I got all the food I have made these past few days (soups, stews, quiches) out of the freezer, wrapped the sultana cake in plastic, packed it all in the boot, reversed down the drive, fast, and gave it all to Shirley. She said she wouldn't accept it but I made her.

And now I sit here to write the end of this. Every day, it is like throwing myself off a cliff; it is the only way I can do it. If I am going to do this, I can only do it with my life in my hands and the knowledge that it could all be blown away on the wind, any day now, any day.

90.
Oxford, March, 2006

My room at the nursing home was on the second floor and had a view of the car park, which was almost empty on the night I chose, a Saturday two weeks after I had arrived. In the middle of the car park stood a golden ash and a solitary squirrel was scampering up and down it, intent on mysterious industry I could not fathom, despite watching it for several hours. I had the window open as far as it went, about the width of two fists; a breeze was pushing the brown curtain out and sucking it back in. I could hear cars on nearby Banbury Road, but mostly it was the television next door I heard, which was turned up loud, as usual, on a foreign language news channel. An elderly man lived there and every time I walked past I saw him sitting hunched up next to it, shoulder touching the screen. Once I'd seen him jabbing at the controls with a finger, muttering.

The night before, I'd watched the woman across the corridor from me die. I was still thinking about it. Her door had been left ajar as people walked in and out, to sit by her bed and to hold her hand, or to simply look at her. When it got late her door was propped open all the way, and I could see her lying on her back in the bed with her eyes closed and her mouth open, a dark well in her face. I think they had removed her false teeth, which would account for the sinking chasm of it. After she died (there had been no sound or movement from her to mark this) the staff came in, covered her body with a sheet and wheeled the bed swiftly out. Then two women, relatives, perhaps a daughter and a granddaughter, started putting her things into two black garbage bags, backs bent, not talking, just stuffing the things in.

I glanced at the clock on the wall; it was time. I picked up my bag, the stick they had given me from behind the door. I walked out of the room, down the corridor, got into the lift, got out at the ground floor, then walked over to the front door. I punched the code into the pad at the side (I'd watched visitors do it, noted the way their fingers moved over the buttons), the doors slid open soundlessly and I walked out. Just like that. I walked out.

I could have asked permission or told someone of my intentions; I didn't have the time, I couldn't risk it. I had waited far too long. On Banbury Road I flagged a cab and it skimmed along the wide road into the city centre.

I got out at the Sheldonian Theatre and started up the long flight of steps, but something was not right; there was no one around. I got to the top; a sign at the entry said Sold Out. And then I heard it, that sound of a theatre full of people waiting for a performance. And I did not have a ticket. I had not bought one, I had assumed I could buy one at the box office. I had not accepted one from Emily or Richard; I'd thought it best to keep out of their way entirely after wrecking things between them so badly.

There was an usher standing at the door of the auditorium. I went over to him quickly and asked him if there was one more ticket, if he would let me in. No tickets left, he said, shaking his head. I looked past him, saw the orchestra walking into the performance space.

'Please,' I said, 'I'll stand at the back and no one will notice me.'

The violin played the concert A, the strings took it, the woodwind, the brass, the whole orchestra was tuning up.

'I can't,' he was young, with acne on his cheeks. 'It's regulations, see.'

'But regulations,' I said, 'they don't mean much, do they? I mean not to you, not to me.'

The A was surging, rising, splitting, the flutes were throwing scales into the air.

'Lady, tickets for this concert have been selling on eBay for hundreds of pounds.'

The tuning stopped; the conductor was making her way to the podium, high heels tapping on the hard floor then muffling as she stepped up onto the carpeted podium.

'If you turn your head away,' I said, 'you won't see me. You won't hear me, either, I can guarantee it. I'll just slip past you and no one will ever know. Please. I'll give you all the money I have,' and I fumbled for my purse.

'Sit there,' he said, pointing abruptly to his own seat, right at the back near the door. I clasped his hand in both of mine.

Emily walked in not long after, and instantly everyone was still. How relaxed she was, the way she walked, the way she sat, and how content, how at home. She looked at the conductor, she looked down at her hands, lifted them and began to play, and out they came, those opening chords. And that night she emphasised the top note in them, which I hadn't heard her do before, she intoned them like a bell, and as she played it was as if the whole neighbourhood, the whole town, was walking towards her, walking towards that music, and as the music got louder their footsteps got louder too, and soon there was a great converging, the people and the music, and I knew it would be a brilliant performance (not perfect, better than that) and the strings took the theme, the music swelled, the melody soared, and I rested my head on the back of the chair and listened well.

At the interval another piano was rolled onto the stage and positioned facing Emily's, then a screen was placed between the two pianos. The audience returned, the lights were dimmed. Emily came out again and then Richard; they took their seats at the pianos on either side of the screen. Then they began to play. And I knew this music, of course I knew this music, this strange music, except, listening to it now, I could hear that it contained references to the concerto, which had not been in it before, surely, and they tossed these references back and forth between them, and soon they were transformed, onwards, beyond it, transcending the concerto, creating something else. There was a stopping and starting to their playing, a falling apart, but then a drawing closer together, and then another falling apart, which created a mood that had us all sitting forward, eager, salivating, almost, as the music slowly built then dropped, built then dropped. And when the various climaxes arrived it was as if they were poured over us, warm and glorious, until the music built all over again. It was a beautiful thing, that music; it was like a conversation, I suppose, but more than that, because it went somewhere entirely different, yet still existed between them. I wondered why I had found it so strange at first, because it suddenly seemed to make such sense to me; perhaps it was just that it hadn't sounded like that at the beginning, it had taken a while to form, or perhaps I was simply listening differently.

When it finished, after a slow, calm dwindling, like hands being held then slipping out from one another, just fingertips touching, then nothing at all, the applause started, and it was loud, and soon people were standing up and shouting. Emily and Richard got up on their respective sides of the screen and they smiled and bowed, still standing by their pianos, and the audience kept clapping and roaring, and they kept standing there and bowing. I expected them to step beyond the screens and join hands, embrace, bow like that, but they remained where they were. I started willing them to do this, and I was sure others around me were expecting this, too. I found I wanted them so badly to do this, it was as if my life depended on it. But they didn't, they turned and walked off in separate directions. The audience kept clapping, and eventually they came back on, and someone gave them both large bouquets of flowers, and they bowed again, and then again, and Emily waved and Richard placed two hands briefly on his chest and pointed to her, or where he imagined she stood, and that was it, they both walked off.

The theatre emptied around me. I sat looking at the empty stage. Still waiting, still hoping. I sat there for a long time.

'You have to go now.'

'What did you say?'

'The concert is over, everyone has gone. You have to leave.'

I looked up. It was that boy again. I thanked him for the seat and looked back at the stage, picked up the stick.

'So,' I said, standing up, 'no encore.'

'They didn't need an encore after that,' he said, puffing out his cheeks.

'What did you think then?' I asked, partly because I still couldn't bear to leave the theatre.

'Oh, well. This was a very important concert.'

'Was it now?'

'We had reviewers from all the London papers; a few even came from New York.'

'For the Rachmaninoff?'

'No, no, that was just to start,' he sniffed. 'For Haywood's new work. It's been years since he's composed a thing, you see, been quite a fuss, written about everywhere, Facebook pages, the lot. "Wall Music",' he said. 'Brilliant, hey?' and he handed me a program.

Wall Music, it said, *A Concerto for Two Pianos*. Composed by Richard Haywood with Emily Green.

'It says here,' I said, pointing, 'that she wrote it too.'

He looked at the paper, frowning.

'Oh yeah,' he said. 'Still, you know . . .'

337

I stood at the top of the stairs looking down at the White Horse pub. A lot of people were standing at the bar that night, concert-goers perhaps, or perhaps not. Nothing much changed in this town, I thought, not really. A taxi was parked outside the pub; I asked the driver to take me to Heathrow.

91.

Currabin, December 23rd, 2006

The sun is falling, the cicadas have started up, the birds are swooping in the gum trees by the fence, and they are happy now, because there was rain this afternoon after that whirl of dust, but no great storm in the end, no thunder or lightning, just an opening up of the sky, a great, tumbling birth of water onto the soil and roof. Afterwards, when I came back out here, everything looked and smelt different. I sat on the veranda among the birds and insects drinking coffee. Under the apricot tree three white corellas are eating something out of the ground, pulling at it with their beaks.

I came here because I did not come before, and now that I have seen the place (and watched the oranges die) I won't stay anymore. I was told this morning that the place has finally sold. Someone local has bought it and intends to replant it with indigenous species. Acacia, dodonaea, feathery cassia, eumong wattle, heath and grasses, and mallee, which pleases me. The birds will be pleased too. I am told such planting will bring sulphur-crested cockatoos, mallee ringnecks, red-rumped parrots, fairy wrens, red-capped robins, eagles and even more galahs. And if the mallee grows old some rare bird species – the mallee fowl, the mallee emu-wren, the regent parrot, the black-eared miner, the red-lored whistler – may return to this little patch.

Shirley told me about the birds. She came around at lunchtime to discuss the sale, and also to tell me that she and Harold are reconciled. I asked her what had happened, what had made the difference, and she wasn't precise about it, she just said that last night she asked him to sit and listen to her, which he did, and then she listened to him, indeed for quite some time, and that tonight they will be having a candle-lit dinner.

I will be leaving anyway. My visitors have called from the airport, asking for directions. They are coming, and the happiness this brings me; I am full to the brim.

I wrote to them as soon as I arrived to tell them where I was, and to invite them to visit, when they were ready. Six weeks ago I heard about the arrival of the baby and their plans to travel to Australia, but I didn't dare believe it would actually happen. Perhaps it means I have been forgiven, for all that I thought, and all that I did.

What does it matter? Here is a car on the drive, three passengers in it, Emily and Richard, back together, and their baby daughter, Grace, six weeks old. How she has made the journey I do not know, it is like a miracle – but it doesn't matter, none of it matters, just show me the child, show me the girl.

I rise on wobbly legs to greet them.

92.

Currabin, December 24th, 2006

It is night, three people sleep in a temperature-controlled room down the hall. I can hear the low hum of the enormous air-conditioner, the occasional whoosh as it powers up again to meet the heat of this night. The sight of them together yesterday, walking towards me up the drive, such happiness, such bliss. Then holding my granddaughter in my arms, the feeling of it, like a perfect aria, the note that hits a perfect pitch and hovers, hovers.

After I leave here I am going to find a place in London that is small and modern and has good heating and is near a park, where I will walk and look at the trees and the birds, and write all day, and see that child. And I will write, because that is what I do now instead of playing the piano, it is what I like. One voice exchanged for another: it may appear a loss, or an act of sacrificial love, but I don't see it like that, for writing suits me better. Besides, it is not only a voice, is it? It's a different way of thinking, of being, a different way of life.

I think resurrection is a process rather than an event. I think it is a to-ing and fro-ing between a certain sort of life, and a certain sort of death. I think I have written this to ask you to put your hand inside all sorts of strange-shaped wounds, to ask you to believe. And to finally tell them, of course.

How long will it last, this happiness, this peace, which I see in my son and his new family? The odds are stacked against them, surely. Family is such an ideal, a romance. How differently most of us relate and live. Living in hope for those times of grace, of music, making up all sorts of stories.

~

Before we had dinner tonight, I was bringing a load of washing in from the line, and it was growing dark (I perform such tasks slowly, partly because I am old, partly because I am thinking about what I will write next; the words are piling high) and when I turned with the basket in my arms I saw that the old house was all lit up, and through the kitchen window I could see Richard stirring something on the stove, frowning with concentration. They had brought the bassinet into the kitchen and Grace must have woken up and started to cry, although I could not hear her from where I stood. I watched Emily bend and slip her hands into the bassinet, every muscle of her body moving with care, and she lifted Grace, put her over her shoulder, and Emily started bobbing in a circle, her mouth moving, perhaps she was talking to Grace, or singing, then Richard's mouth started moving too, his face now relaxed. He put the whisk down and went to them and they all circled together, Emily holding the child, Richard holding Emily, the three of them moving to the music I could not hear.

The sun had almost set behind me, I was casting a great shadow across the lawn, and I walked through the darkening garden, past the shapes of trees and shrubs, where the birds were already nesting. When I got to the back steps I put the basket of washing down to open the door, but by then the singing had stopped, and the baby was calm. I walked into the kitchen, got out these pages. I turned to face my family. I am an old woman, a happy old woman, and I am alive, I am alive, I am alive.

London, June 1st, 2016

Excerpt from BBC News, Radio 4, 8 a.m.

'The writer Alice Murray died last night at the age of 85. Murray's unique and controversial novels and essays were all written in the last ten years of her life. Her work dealt with life's largest and most basic issues: morality, love, faith, happiness, and the role of culture and the economy in shaping human thought and behaviour. Murray is survived by her son, the composer Richard Haywood, her daughter-in-law, Professor Emily Green, and her beloved grand-daughter, Grace Green.'

Acknowledgements

While I was working as a researcher in the field of intimate violence, I interviewed people who had experienced sexual and/or domestic violence, almost all of them women. Their accounts stayed with me; in the end they changed me. I am very grateful for the opportunities I had to speak with them, and for their trust and courage.

I have also drawn on others' research in this book, including Debra Parkinson, Kerry Burns and Claire Zara's evocative work *A Powerful Journey*. Domestic and sexual violence is common, of course, and when talking about my work in this area I ended up speaking to many people about what had happened to them. But all the people in this book are fictional characters and any resemblance to real people is entirely coincidental.

I was lucky to find *The Incorporated Wife*, co-edited by Hilary Callan and Shirley Ardener. Ardener and Lidia Sciama's chapters were of particular assistance in understanding the life of a college wife in its historical context. Thanks, also, to the many people I interviewed for my own research on social exclusion in Oxford and Britain; and to all those with whom I have worked in this and related fields. (I should note here the liberties I have taken with aspects of the physical and social architecture of Oxford — glorious allowances of a writer of fiction.)

I would like to acknowledge my wonderful piano teachers: Janet Potter, Clemens Leske Snr at the Elder Conservatorium of Music, and Jan Lappin.

There are others who have helped and encouraged me: Tom Carrig, Sophie Cunningham, Anna Funder, Kira Georgakopoulous, Joan Grant, Clare Harding, Matt Hooper, Derek and Sue James, May Lam, Anne Manne, Alice Pung, Lauren Rickards.

Thanks to Nikki Christer at Penguin Random House for her belief, and her brilliance; to Catherine Hill, an editor of outstanding skill and sensitivity (what a pleasure it has been). My agent Clare Forster took this book to a place it would not have gone without her. Thanks also to Amanda O'Connell, Sandy Cull, Linda Funnell and Anyez Lindop.

Great thanks are due to my parents, Cherrie and Bill, whose love of music, books, nature, social justice, each other, and us, is such wonderful germination for a writer. My siblings Catie, Nia and Peter, always in my head and heart, are to be thanked, too. My husband Josh's support has been bold and unequivocal, and his belief in this essential; I thank him with all my heart. Most of all I would like to acknowledge my daughters, Beatrix and Helena, because I have learnt so much from them about life, and feelings, and what love is.

Zoë Morrison was a research fellow and college lecturer in human geography at Oxford University, where she completed her DPhil as a Rhodes Scholar. Her work in research and advocacy has addressed social exclusion and violence against women. Zoë has an LMusA in piano performance. She lives in Melbourne.